To Kevi[n]
To Teri

my life is between these pages
Hope you enjoy
Jack Sullivan

# *Shields of Honor*
## *The Exciting Life of a Naval Reservist*

### *by*

# *CDR. Jack Sullivan USNR*

1663 LIBERTY DRIVE, SUITE 200
BLOOMINGTON, INDIANA 47403
(800) 839-8640
WWW.AUTHORHOUSE.COM

© 2005 CDR. Jack Sullivan USNR. All Rights Reserved.

*No part of this book may be reproduced, stored in a retrieval system, or transmitted by any means without the written permission of the author.*

*First published by AuthorHouse 06/14/05*

*ISBN: 1-4208-3332-4 (e)*
*ISBN: 1-4208-3331-6 (sc)*

*Library of Congress Control Number: 2005901665*

*Printed in the United States of America*
*Bloomington, Indiana*

*This book is printed on acid-free paper.*

# Dedication

To all of my family, both living and deceased, to all of my friends who entered my life, even momentarily, and enriched it I dedicate this book.

To my deceased wife Joan who made my every accomplishment possible.

# Contents

Dedication .................................... v

Forward.................................... xi

Preface ..................................... xiii

Acknowledgements ............................. xv

Chapter 1 My early life........................... 1

Chapter 2 I begin my Novitiate ................. 25

Chapter 3 My life as a Naval Aviation Cadet ..... 38

Chapter 4 I get my Wings and Commission .....53

Chapter 5 Marriage and Career ................. 66

Chapter 6 I'm recalled to the Navy for Korea...... 94

Chapter 7 Back to the Police Department ...129

Chapter 8 My Reserve Squadron ...............139

Chapter 9 Jet Fighters are eased
out of Floyd Bennett ..........................150

Chapter 10 Police Cases .......................155

Chapter 11 I'm recalled to Naval
Service a third time ..........................172

Chapter 12 The Navy Assignes me
to Training Squadron 1 .........................185

Chapter 13 My tour in Iceland at Naval Station Keflavik..................207

Chapter 14 My tour at the Naval Air Test Center Patuxent River Maryland...............236

Chapter 15 My Tour at NAS Cubi Point in the Philippines ...............................248

Chapter 16 My last Tour in the Navy, Naval Air Test Center, Pax River ................. 275

Chapter 17 Life After the Navy .................280

Chapter 18 I go to work for Grumman Aerospace at Bethpage New York .............287

Chapter 19 I go to Iran with the F14 Tomcat ...........................................291

Chapter 20 The C2 Cod Program...............338

Chapter 21 Back Home in Maryland...........363

Chapter 22 Retirement in Maryland...........371

# Forward

My life as a Naval Reservist has taken me around the world and provided me with an education and background that has served me well. I have met and become friends with people of all different social strata who, like me, have served this Country in wartime environment. My prayer is that this Country will always be able to count on her young men to serve in time of need. As my Marine buddies would say "SEMPER FI"

# Preface

What made me write this book? My children were always amazed, when I would meet an old friend and talk about events they had never heard of, that much of my life was shrouded in secrecy from them. " Dad you led an interesting life will you please write a book and tell us about it", was their plea. Many of my friends joined them in this request so here is my story, my life, told in simple terms and simple language. The recurring theme is that I am an American, a Naval Reservist and I responded to the call of my Country to the best of my ability each time. How successful I was will be left to the readers to decide. I was proud to be a naval officer and pilot and serve with some of the finest Americans this Country has ever produced. As I was a Reservist there are other sections of my life that the reader may find interesting. They, too, help make this story complete.

# Acknowledgements

To my son John and my daughter Maura who asked me to write this book. To my daughter in law Suzanne for her love, hospitality and encouragement. To Wayne and Bev Putnam and Jeanne Davis who made my life bearable after the death of my wife by providing me with love and companionship. To my friend, Ed Forsman, who taught me to use the computer. To George Bailey and Patricia Sullivan who took time to read this book, made suggestions, and encouraged me to finish it. To Lydia Banome who persuaded me to publish this book and lastly all of my new friends at Heritage Springs who immediately welcomed me in my new community and made me feel at home. I will forever be in your debt.

# Chapter 1
# My early life

In a small section of Queens, New York, is a peninsula of land that extends into New York harbor. In the year 1923 this peninsula, called Rockaway Beach, was mostly a tourist attraction frequented by folks from the City in the summer months, which enjoyed the ocean and the pleasures it provided. Perhaps I thought I was a tourist for it was here that I was born on August l6 1923. The Good Lord was kind because He provided me with parents, Cornelius and Catherine Sullivan of whom I would later state, "If God were to let me choose my parents I would have picked these two." My mother was the most ethical person I've ever known and I can't recall a single incident where she equivocated, even slightly, with the truth. She was frugal and could do more with a dollar than most but was generous with her family. Her brothers were all tradesmen and had taught her the rudiments of their skills. She could do almost anything and as a youngster

I was always amazed to see her change washers in the faucets or replace worn sockets in lamps that other women would have to call trades people to accomplish. Even my father was in awe of her skills and would often ask her "isn't there anything you can't do honey? "She was also the disciplinarian and would spank me for serious infractions. One day she became frustrated with me and after spanking me for a repeat offense burst out in tears, stating, "I'm so ashamed of you Jackie". That did it and I burst out in tears as well begging her not to be ashamed of me and promising her to be good. From that moment in my early youth all she had to do was tell me she was ashamed of me and she regained complete control of me. In later years I realized it was the love and respect that I felt for my mother and my fear of losing it that motivated my actions. I had my first example of true leadership. My Dad was different. I didn't see him that much as he was working hard at his job and attempting to start his own business. It was always a delight to see him as he was kind with a wonderful sense of humor and always had a small present for me each day. In later years I would seek his counsel on any problems that might arise knowing that he had my best interest at heart and would give me solid advise. In my early years it was my mother's love that sustained me but as I grew older my Dad's influence grew stronger and I thanked the good Lord for them both.

As an aside let me brag a bit and state that at 9lbs 12 oz I was the largest baby born in Rockaway Beach Hospital at the time and it was fitting that I should be named John L Sullivan. That I was named after the famous heavyweight champion was soon dispelled as my mother told me I was named after my grandfather in Ireland and the Lawrence was chosen because she always liked that name. Accident or not I bore that name and would soon have to prove it to my contemporaries. My mother and father had a small apartment in an area called Bayside Place and that is where I spent the first few months after my birth. My mother's brother, Fred was a master carpenter and had built a three story eighteen room house at 311 Beach 90$^{th}$ street. It was here the family moved shortly after my birth. Again the Good Lord was kind because my Grandmother, Barbara Hetzel lived on the second floor with my Uncles Ed and Fred all of whom would play an important role in my early life. The third floor was ours and the view was spectacular. None of the few houses on the block were three stories so our view of the bay was unobstructed and some of my early memories are of watching the boats moving around on the water. When I was two and a half years old my sister Marian was born in St. Joseph's Hospital in Far Rockaway. Marian was to become one of the outstanding human beings I ever knew. She became a lawyer, a chemist, a math major and an engineer. While she became an icon in the business world it was her charitable nature that would win her the hearts and minds of her friends. By deeds and example she greatly influenced my life.

My cousin Jack Hetzel came into my life early on as he was one week less than a year older than me. We always kidded one another about this because I would call and congratulate him as each milestone was reached, first our teens, then our twenties and so forth and next year I would receive a call from him on the same subject. As I had no brothers, 'Hetz' (as I called him) was the one that assumed this role. Hetz's older brother Fred was our mentor as well as tormenter. Helpful when he thought we needed it and our enemy when he thought our plan of action was wrong. In retrospect Fred was right most of the time but to two young willful lads he was a force to be avoided and circumvented whenever possible. Hetz's older sister Mildred could be counted on as an ally but I suspect only because she was not as aware of our mischievous nature as was Fred. While I can't think of anything that was felonious I can sure think of plenty of pranks that would have resulted in spankings and groundings if our parents had ever learned about them. Many a time we would go to the Bay with paddles we had crafted from orange crates and lumber uncle Fred had in the cellar and borrow, sometimes without permission, someone's rowboat for a trip around the bay. We always returned the boat to its proper place, because if it had been known we had borrowed it we might have had a problem with the owner. We were even known to invite friends to accompany us. This was done before we started school so we weren't aware of the exploits of Tom Sawyer. For certain, this was our own idea to be improved on in later years after we read about the exploits of others.

While I have been talking about the Bay, we were fortunate to have the Atlantic Ocean a few blocks away in the other direction. Hetz's mother, my Aunt Frieda, was a swimmer and we would accompany her to the ocean where she taught both of us to swim. The waves presented a real problem for me but Hetz mastered them the first summer. I was envious but not a fool. It took me two years at the beach to join Hetz in diving under the waves and making it out to the last rope where all the big guys hung out. The second year we mastered the Australian crawl and swam past the last rope into the open sea. The first few times we did this the lifeguards responded by swimming out and ordering us back to the last rope but they eventually discovered we could swim and finally we were allowed out in the open sea with the really big guys. Diving under the waves was my first right of passage but being allowed out past the last rope by the lifeguards was an acknowledgment of my second right of passage and was observed by my contemporaries which made it all the more enjoyable

My uncle Fred made wine. In the basement there was a room he called his wine cellar. This room was kept locked and the only time I was able to view it was when I was with him. It was filled with wine casks (barrels) that contained the wine he would make in his wine press. He was very proud of his wine and his friends were eager to receive samples. I would watch him siphon wine from one barrel to another. He would insert one end of a small hose in his mouth and suck on it until the wine would flow, he would then insert the hose into the barrel he wished to transfer the wine. Naturally all of this held a fascination for me and I would intensely watch his every move. One day the wine cellar was left unlocked. I had access to it and was anxious to follow his example and transfer the wine from one barrel to another. I used his small mallet to remove the bungs on two barrels. I then inserted the hose in the upper barrel, sucked on the hose until I got the desired flow of wine then quickly placed the hose into the lower barrel. After a bit of wine was transferred I shut off the flow by squeezing the hose replaced the bungs and repeated the action in two different barrels. Each time I would get a mouthful of wine. When I was satisfied with my handiwork I left, after carefully locking the wine cellar. A few days later I accompanied my uncle and one of his friends to the wine cellar. My uncle was to have him sample a new wine he had just made. He gave him a taste of an older wine first then the new wine. The friend thought they tasted the same. My uncle tasted them both and blamed it on the wine cask. I never said a word and that is probably the only reason why I am here and able to write this book.

School was next. PS44 was about four blocks away. There we many ways of getting there but walking the tracks of the Long Island Railroad were the most dangerous hence the way we chose. The Long Island RR was ground level then and the tracks provided us with a short cut as well as a means of avoiding the school monitors who guarded all the street crossings and were eager to prove their worth to the teachers by putting a couple of rebels like Hetz and me on report for some minor infraction. The track meant that we only had to pass one guard station and we soon made friends with this fellow thus making the passage to school fun. School was easy for me because Hetz would tell me what to expect. His being a year older sure helped. I still managed to get into mischief though and one story is worth telling. I was in Kindergarten and the teacher took us for a walk on the boardwalk to show the children the rides at Playland (an amusement park). Hetz and I had explored every inch of Playland when it was closed for the winter and gated up hence this "walk" was boring so I convinced a classmate to join me on the beach where we could collect some shells. We slipped away undetected and began our adventure. When the teacher returned to the classroom a head count detected our absence. The principal was notified and a search was being prepared when we returned. My first trip to the principal's office! The interrogation began with our names, John L Sullivan and my companion Jack Johnson. I remember telling my mother the principal was crying when he talked to us and we both felt real bad. Only later did I learn from my mother that the principal was a fight fan and was amused by the names of two heavyweight champions that caused all this trouble. His crying was really his supreme effort to avoid laughing. We were not punished and soon blended into the class with little further disruption. Unless you can call falling in love a disruption. Mildred Ryan was a pretty girl who frequently sang to the class. This bothered one of my classmates and we fought it out after school down on the beach. I upheld her honor, the problem was solved and Mildred sang on for the rest of the term. Mildred and I remained friends until we moved to Flatbush in 1934.

Hetz moved away when I was in my fourth year of school and I missed him. Even though we would stay in touch and our parents would visit each other frequently I didn't have his constant companionship.

My father's brother Mike lived in Broad Channel in the summer months and we were always happy to visit he and my aunt Kitty. My cousins Tom and Ed were there and we always had a great time with them. Tom was the older and Ed was closer to my age. He was my buddy and would take me around Broad Channel and I soon met all his friends. My father would sit on my Uncle Mike's porch and the two brothers would talk and it wasn't long before others would join them and a poker game would break out. Mr. Powers, uncle Mike's neighbor would join them and so would others in the neighborhood. My Mom and Aunt Kitty were great friends and they always had things to talk about so the poker game meant nothing to them. Ed and I would take the beer can to the saloon on the corner and get beer for the poker players and there was always money for some soda for us. When my uncle Tom would come we knew it would be a lively evening. My Aunt Francis would join the women and my sister Marian would have the companionship of my cousin Marie. My cousin Tom, Marie's brother was a year younger than me and would pal around with Ed and me. As the evening wore on my Uncle Tom would recite the old Irish poem "they're hanging Danny Devers in the morning." This poem had a profound effect on me because it talked about the young brother of two IRA agents the British were searching for and couldn't locate. The Commanding Officer thought if he arrested the young brother and threatened to hang him the older brothers would surrender. The mother pleaded with Commanding Officer but he wouldn't relent and the hanging took place. After hearing that poem I developed a burning hatred for the Brits and the next school day I searched out Fordice Thorn, a classmate of mine, who happened to be British, and we had a fight in the schoolyard. Naturally this information was relayed to my father and he sat me down and demanded to know why I had started a fight. When I told him about the Poem Uncle Tom had recited I saw a look on his face I had never seen before and he told me something that I never forgot." Son you are an American, you were born here. I am an American because I became a citizen of this wonderful Country and this is now my Country. I fought for this Country in WW1 and if necessary you will fight for this Country. Ireland is not your Country, The United States is your Country". He said it with pride and I will always remember his words and the look on his face as he uttered them. I apologized to Fordice the next day and we became good friends. Dad lit a spark in me that day that nothing has been able to extinguish and I hope my love for this Country has shown brightly enough for my children to have seen and want to emulate.

    I became friends with Tim Snyder who lived down next to the Courthouse on 90th and Beach Channel Drive. Tim was older and playing baseball in high school. He was a good ballplayer and he and his friends practiced all year round and my useful purpose was to shag balls while they were taking batting practice. A task I willingly performed because it made me part of the gang. They gradually taught me to catch and throw properly and even allowed me to take batting practice. It was hard work for me but later on I realized that I was light years ahead of my contemporaries as I could throw and catch better than any of my classmates. They also taught me to understand the game and I could always be counted on to throw to the right base. In later years I played varsity baseball in Prep school. I also played for my church team and this team was made up of men who had played college and semi-pro baseball. As a fifteen year old to play with men and be sought after was heady stuff and <u>then</u> to hear such things as college scholarship for baseball at that age made all the sweat and tears of chasing balls for Tim worthwhile. I guess it shows what practice will do and I learned at an early age if you want to do anything well, work hard and make it happen. I don't know if that was Tim's plan but in any case it worked

We moved to Brooklyn in 1934. My Dad had started his own business and had to be to work at 3:30 a.m. He had a wholesale meat market in New York and was doing well but there was no way he could get to work from Rockaway as the earliest train to New York was at 6 AM and by that time half of his day was over. It was exciting for both Marian and myself because we each had our own room, new friends and a neighborhood full of kids our age. I met Johnny Kennelly who became my best friend. My sister became friends with Joan Fay, a beautiful girl who would later become my wife. That being said there is a lot of history between that period of my life and where we are now. Flatbush was a kid's paradise in those days. We lived on Avenue M the second house from Nostrand Avenue. My next-door neighbors were the Tashjians. The mother and father were Armenians from the old country. The father was a printer and a good one because he was immediately employed upon arrival and stayed with the same company for the rest of his life. Mr. and Mrs. Tashjian was what I called them and I don't know if I ever knew their first names, even if I had I probably would have had a tough time pronouncing them. They were also the first eastern Europeans I had met and because of the wonderful impression they made on me I have always felt a kinship for all the Armenians I have met since. Their son Rod was the oldest and Harry and his younger sister Elmus rounded out the family. To spell Rod's and Harry's name in Armenian would be beyond my capability so they will always be known in my speech, memory and this narrative as Rod and Harry. They were two good guys and real friends to this day.

On the other side of my house were the Allegrettis. Gus was the older and Joey was the younger. They were both younger than me but two nice youngsters. Gus would grow up and star in the television show Captain Kangaroo and would marry Carol Lawrence (the singer) Across the street were Jackie Teehan and Jimmy Larkin. They were classmates as well as good friends. Russell Wessell lived two doors down, a blonde Swede who was always up for a little excitement. The last house was occupied by the Ramos brothers, Dave, the older was my age but a half year behind me in school, his brother Paul was my sisters age and really wasn't in the gang, except when we needed someone to round out a team

Around the corner on 29th Street were the Kennellys. Peg was the oldest and a terrific athlete. John was next and he soon became my best friend. He was a year older and probably shaped my life more than any friend I ever had. Kathleen, Joe and Donald were the rest of the clan. Mr. Kennelly was the Dock Boss of the two Grace Line Piers in New York. Johnny and I would work for him in the war years prior to our enlisting in the service. Mrs. Kennelly would laugh at my stories so she naturally became one of my favorite people. John was left-handed and we started out as partners on the handball court and by the seventh grade we could handle any two players at the school.

We were building a Catholic School in my Parish, "Our Lady Help of Christians". At the far end of the construction we had a tennis court that was for the use of the Priests. It was fenced in and the top section was made of chicken wire. Naturally it was off limits to us kids and a formidable lock was installed to make certain we could not gain access. When you have a friend named Cosmo Uqueza no lock is going to stop him. We enjoyed the court until the custodian found us out. He installed a locking device that even baffled Cosmo so we had to enter the old fashioned way. We had to climb the fence. I bring up the tennis court because we had fashioned racket from apple crates and would play tennis scoring points as we did in handball. Johnny excelled and his father bought him a tennis racket. He made the varsity at Bishop Loughlin High School in his freshman year.

Baseball and football were my sports and the time I spent with Tim Snyder paid off. We had a softball team in grade school and if it wasn't my turn to pitch I played center field. Regardless of which position I played I batted fourth. This isn't ego this is just the jump I had on the rest by playing with the big guys in Rockaway Beach. In grade school I could throw a football a 'sewer'. A New York kid would know exactly what I mean. A sewer was a manhole cover that was placed in the middle of all our streets and was 44 yards apart. If you could throw a sewer it meant you could throw a football at least 44 yards. In grade school that was a feat. I wish I could brag about my grades. While they were not bad they certainly didn't rival my sisters. Sports were my focus. We had a touch football team that could play with the best of them. Later on in my life when I was an aviation cadet in the Navy we had a team comprised of young men that had played touch football in the streets of New York and we went through the whole season undefeated.

In Brooklyn the spring meant street hockey played on roller skates. The puck was a three-inch square of hard wood and the goals were apple crates placed over the sewer hole covers and held in place by a round peg of wood fitted into the sewer hole cover. The streets would turn white from the skate marks and we were forever improving on the hockey sticks to make them last longer. When one of the gang discovered that a skate manufacturer offered a guarantee on the life of the skates we all bought them and probably caused them to have second thoughts as we were turning in our worn wheels every two or three weeks for new ones. City life was great, so many opportunities for fun and games. None of my friends suffered from obesity, we were all hard and lean from the various sports we played after school. Mr. Kennelly played soccer and to get us ready for this new sport he had us run dashes, one sewer or two. These races soon attracted youngsters from other neighborhoods. Mr. Kennelly would time us and we soon discovered which of us was the fastest in each of the events. We also became aware of our neighbors and this led to challenges in the various sports we all participated in. These rivalries continued through our school years and friendships were made that lasted through our life times. When I played football and baseball at Brooklyn Prep later on it was amazing how many of them would show up on opposing teams. Mr. Kennelly probably developed more athletes than he ever imagined. He also had us run distances, around the block was just over a quarter of a mile and he would have us run around the block several times and time us. Holding the record for around the block was a status symbol and I held it only to break it, as I grew older.

Those were the days when physical strength and athletic powers was the test of a young man, sometimes getting them in trouble as well. I remember coming home from school one day, it had snowed and the fresh snow was ideal for snowballs. We were out of the range of school monitors. Throwing snowballs was a capital offence and it was a sure trip to the principal's office. We approached our Church, Our Lady Help Of Christians, on the corner of Avenue M and East 29$^{th}$ St. and one of the Baldo brothers challenged me to throw a snowball over the roof. This was easy but I never calculated my leather jacket would bind me. The snowball arched gracefully and plunged through one of the stain glass windows with the sound of an exploding rocket. My jacket had betrayed me, my arm hung up and the full force of my throw was restrained. Nothing to do but run and my companions fled at the speed of sound. Why? Because our Pastor, Father Churchill was a bear, tough as nails, and even having served as altar boys would not mitigate a transgression such as this. When I arrived home the weight of my problem was evident because my mother asked me, "What have you done?" When I told her she gasped, as these windows were very expensive. She explained that I must tell Father Churchill what I had done and that my family would pay for the window, if only on the installment plan. I walked the one block to the rectory wondering if suicide was an option. When I rang the bell I expected the housekeeper to answer the door but the good Lord was going to make me pay and Father Churchill answered the door himself. I often tell the story that I have received Air Medals for exploits as a Navy Fighter Pilot that took less courage then to stand there and tell the good Father what I had just done. He told me to come in using his usual stern voice and when we were inside made me explain how it happened, as he already knew all about the window being broken from the sexton who was inside the church at the time. Our identity was not known because all the sexton had seen were the blurs of fleeing young men. He asked me if it took courage to admit that I had broken the window. He would never know how much. Father Churchill listened to my account and the proposal my mother had made and then the miracle occurred. He forgave me and told me that because I came and admitted it, it would cost my family nothing. He had a spare in the basement of the church and the Sexton would install it. If I live to be 90 let it be known to all my family and friends that I should have made it to 100, ten years of my life were given up in that day in the rectory.

There are more stories that come to mind. Playing for the Championship of the elementary school softball league. I pitched that game and my usual catcher, Julius Migden, was home with a cold. Welton (wimpy) Hewitt was on first base and knew I was flustered without the other half of the battery. We had won every game thus far and PS 100 was our final game. I couldn't find the plate and walked in two runs before my good friend Jack Bowne came in to relieve me. Mr. Hall, our coach, put me in the outfield because he wanted my power at bat. Even though I drove in our only run we lost by one run. My fault and it seemed that the whole school must have been there to see it because I never heard the end of it. Wimpy and Jack Bowne tried their best to console me and even Julius Migden tried to take some of the blame but I was devastated. Even winning the handball championship wasn't enough to make me forget that I had lost the Softball Championship for my school.

The softball team stayed together, after we graduated, and we played on Sunday afternoon in a locked school playground. It was illegal but not destructive and we played other teams for a dollar a man. Heady stuff since my allowance was only fifty cents. We didn't lose often and never to the same team so we came out ahead. Once we found ourselves surrounded by the police. The neighbors thought we were making too much noise and since the playground was locked for the weekend we had no business being there. We were asked to climb the fence and were carded and asked which school we attended. Most of my old classmates attended either James Madison HS of Erasmus Hall HS, Jack Bowne and I told this Irish Cop, Brooklyn Prep (A Jesuit School).

*Shields of Honor*

He looked at us and asked us" what the hell are you doing here"? "Get out of here!" Our names never appeared on the list but nothing came of it anyway as all the police were doing was satisfying some irate citizen,

Another story has to be told as I remember it. Remember me mentioning Cosmo Uqueza, my friend who had mastered the lock on the tennis court? Well this particular Saturday we had a baseball game scheduled with another team from our grade school. They came from another block. We were wagering money on the game but found ourselves a man short. Cosmo had been grounded by his mother for some infraction and was locked in his room on the second floor of the house. We pleaded with his mother for his release, if only for the duration of the ball game. Not having the nine men needed was a forfeit with all of us having to pay the money to the other team so we pleaded real hard. We were standing in the driveway talking to Cosmo through his window when he decided he would join us anyway. Mr. Pratt's car was parked in the driveway. Now readers remember this was 1935 and Mr. Pratt's car was vintage 1929. Cosmo was going to jump from his second floor window to the top of the car. We all waited and Cosmo jumped...right through the cloth roof and hung up halfway through. He wiggled his way through the hanging roof, opened the driver's side door and stepped out with the stuffing hanging from Mr. Pratt's car roof. We played the game with nine men and won. When we returned, Mrs. Uqueza was arguing with Mr. Pratt. The damage had been detected! She argued that it couldn't have been Cosmo as the door to his bedroom was still locked. None of us stayed around to see how this turned out. My sister Marian was a good friend of Jannis Pratt, Mr. Pratt's daughter, and later that week told me of Cosmo trying to sneak back into the house and Mr. Pratt seeing him so I guess Mrs. Uqeza lost the argument. Cosmo had the innocent look of an angel, nobody meeting him for the first time would ever take him the imp he was. He was our true friend, we liked him and nobody could criticize him to us.

I mentioned that I lived two houses from Nostrand Avenue; well Nostrand Avenue had a trolley that at the time ran from Avenue U to the Junction (Nostrand Ave & Flatbush Ave) where the IRT Subway started. When Cosmo would be up that way he would hitch a ride home on the Trolley or the Nostrand Avenue " Rocket" as we called it. On one occasion the motorman saw Cosmo, stopped the trolley in the middle of the block and chased Cosmo for about forty yards. We could have told him nobody catches Cosmo in that distance. He walked back and Cosmo, unbeknown to the motorman, caught the same trolley but hid from view. When the trolley was in the middle of the block where Cosmo lived he pulled the pole from the overhead wires turning off the power and dashed through the alley leaving the frustrated motorman to walk around behind the trolley and reset the pole on the overhead wire. When we later asked him why he had done that to the poor man he replied with a straight face "because he was mean!" Cosmo's parents had come to this country when he was a baby and I can't recall whether they were from Brazil or Argentina. They were nice people, kind and refined and Cosmo would for the most part give you the same impression. His folks were strict with him and I never heard him answer back to either of them but there was a wild streak in Cosmo. How he turned out in later years I can't answer as I lost track after my second year in Prep School when I went upstate NY to school. I would like to think he connected with some company that could use his energy, resourcefulness and ingenuity.

I graduated from PS193 in June of 1937. I took exams for all the Catholic High Schools in Brooklyn and was resigned on going to James Madison HS with the majority of my classmates, When I took the test for Brooklyn Prep I was notified that while I hadn't won a scholarship I passed the entrance test and if I could afford the tuition I would be accepted. Prep was expensive, two hundred and fifty dollars a year was what Fordham University was charging in those days. I learned that my father had asked Vinny Lombardi which Catholic School I should attend. Vinny had told him to send me to Brooklyn Prep. Vinny had graduated from Fordham University and his father and my father had businesses side by side in the West Washington Meat Market in New York City. Without name-dropping let me tell you that Vinny Lombardy was one of the "seven blocks of granite" at Fordham and later on become famous as the coach of the Green Bay Packers. While at Fordham he stopped by to see my father and my Dad had him go around the corner to where I was playing sand lot football. He watched me pass and called me over to give me some tips. He was recognized and my stock was on the rise among my friends. When he graduated his father invited my family to the party he threw for Vinny. Vinny spent a few minutes with me that day too asking me how my team was progressing and how I was throwing the ball.

But now back to the story. My folks sacrificed and I went to the Prep. I wish I could say that I was a great student but I was not. I failed Latin and Algebra my first year and had to attend summer school to be tutored. This cost my folks additional money and is, to this day, one of the things I still regret when called to mind. Sports filled my day and I can't tell you how many nights I fell asleep while doing my homework. Prep was tough. It was a school for scholars with emphasis on grades and I was an athlete. To make matters worse, Johnny Kennelly, my best friend went away to become a Christian Brother at this time. I visited Johnny several times at the Junior Novitiate for the Christian Brothers at Barrytown, New York. The Junior Novitiate as it was called was a high school, but more than a

High school in that it was preparing these young men to become Teachers of the Catholic Faith as well the usual curriculum. They woke up at 5AM, prayers at 5:30 Mass at 6 AM, breakfast at 7 AM work detail from7: 30 AM to 8 AM. School was from 8 AM to noon, lunch then School to 3 PM. Free time after school from 3PM to 4:30 for sports. Prayer at 5 PM followed by supper at 6PM. Work detail till 7 PM. Our time to study was from 7 PM till 9PM.Chappell then Bed Johnny taught me the whole program during my visits and the seed was planted. My mother and father were both faithful Catholics, my father was the usher at three masses on Sunday and both he and my mother were daily communicants. While I was not their equal I took my faith seriously and I considered joining Johnny if the Christian Brothers would have me. My second year at the Prep was a little better grade wise but I still didn't take it as seriously as I should have. It was a great school, the classmates I had were real pals but sports were still my focus.

When I saw Johnny the next time I asked about signing up. He wrote to me and gave me the address of the Brother in charge of recruiting at Manhattan College. A letter, a phone call or two and I went to Manhattan College to visit Brother Felix. A two-hour interview with Brother Felix and a written letter explaining why I wanted to become a Brother followed. At the end of my sophomore year I received a letter telling me I was accepted and would start my Junior

*CDR. Jack Sullivan USNR*

year at Barry-town.. My parents, naturally, were informed of all my preparation and were pleased that I had been accepted. Being good Catholics they placed Service to God above me having a family and perpetuating the name. Johnny was also following my efforts and he was pleased when the results were announced.

# Chapter 2
# I begin my Novitiate

That summer Johnny was allowed home for July and August and filled me in on all the rules and regulations that would soon fill my day. I went to daily Mass and Communion with my mother. Dad was still working. When it came time for Johnny to go back he obtained permission for me to accompany him, as the new recruits normally were to arrive the following day. Strange as it might seem this proved to be a real advantage as I was the only unfamiliar face everyone introduced himself to me and I had a chance to meet the old hands without the distraction of all the new faces that arrived the next day. I hoped I would be able to do justice to the new friends I met. I have never been in the company of more dedicated young men in my life. Even those who did not persevere and for one reason or another dropped out before taking their vows were splendid examples of young Catholic men. Arguments were unheard of and the only disagreements were over sports teams

We had a monthly advertisement of faults. Shots " as we called them. Each student, or junior novice, would stand in the front of the common room, face the Brother Director, and his peers would tell him what they perceived his faults to be. This was taken very seriously and as Brother Director would explain before each session that even perceptions were to be considered by the accused and acted on to eliminate even these perceptions. I have often thought that this type of action taken in other quarters, with different type people would lead to grudges, fights and hard feelings. In this environment and with these people it worked and worked well.. Later as we were taught mental prayer we would do this through introspection and self-examination. Being able to search your soul for what motivates any action you take and identifying it as self aggrandizing, or for the common good can make you comfortable in your own skin. I think those nights in both the junior and senior Novitiates have served me well throughout my life.

The first week set the pace because it was constant action. Up at 5 AM, wash, shave, make your bed and be in Chapel at 5:45. Morning prayers, Mass then to the refectory to eat by 7AM. Community chores after eating in total silence. A series of hand signs would request the different platters of food. After eating we would be dismissed to begin our chores. My job was to

*Shields of Honor*

sweep the refectory, pull out the chairs and make sure the space under the tables were cleaned. Others washed the dishes using a complicated washing machine. Seniors with knowledge of the machine usually performed this job; others would be assigned to the Dormitory or the Chapel or perhaps to the common room. The classes began at 8'o'Clock and continued to l2 noon. We had lunch at l2 Noon. During lunch a series of readers were called on by Brother Director to read from lives of the Saints or other spiritual books. If you did not read and pronounce your words distinctly you were reprimanded and called on frequently thereafter until you mastered the art. Everything had a purpose. As a Brother and Teacher you would be called upon to read to the class later on in your career and your training began here. In some cases it was perfected here. After meals the chores began again and by 1 PM we were back in classroom. We completed our studies at 3 PM.

Now here I should tell you a little more about St Josephs Normal Institute as known to the State Regency. It was located on the Hudson River in a little town called Barry -town. It was obtained from the Rockefellers in exchanged for a small parcel of land owned by the Christian Brothers that the Rockefellers wanted. The grounds were 245 Acres and contained small farms that grew corn, potatoes and sundry other small crops. Chickens, hogs and a small head of cows provided us with meats and milk. Most of the work on the farms was done by hired hands, as was the cooking in the refectory. After school and on Saturdays we would work on the farms when the crops were to be harvested. Since I could drive, I would drive the truck. I was never allowed to drive the truck off the property, as I had no license. I still remember the corn harvest. After it was completed we would put corn in a big, 55 gal. can and cook it. Butter and salt were added with a paintbrush and a big shaker. I have never tasted corn that was better and to this day I remember those afternoons with the same joy and excitement I experienced back then.

It wasn't all work in the afternoon after school. There was time for play as well. In the fall it was football, both touch and tackle, we had leagues formed by age and we all participated. On occasion we would play a team from another school. These were great days and the faculty and the student body would be there. It was always on our field so we had a bit of advantage. We played a team from the Christian Brothers Academy in Albany NY. Theirs was a 150 lb team and Mal O'Sullivan and I both weighed about l60 lbs but since most of our team weighed much less Brother Augustine, our coach, decided to play Mal and me. Both of us caught touchdown passes and we won. I think the opposing Coach knew we were a bit heavier but took it in stride and both teams enjoyed a meal together later that day.

When the winter set in we had a pond some seventy-five yards long and fifty yards wide that froze. We would constantly keep shoveling snow off it to keep it clear for ice hockey. I didn't ice skate when I arrived but boy did I learn in a hurry. Once I could skate my roller-skating and street hockey skills took over and I soon was elected one of the Captains. The fellows from New England and upstate NY were the stars. No roller skate hockey for them. They were raised on ice skates and it wasn't till my second year on the ice that I considered my self in their league. I was bigger than most and learned to block in football so I was good as a defensive man the first year and worked on offence my second year. Brother Augustine, our coach was raised in Detroit and played for his varsity team in high school. He was, without peer and when he played for one of the teams they won.

You are not supposed to have favorites but Brother Augustine was mine. Later on when I had finished the indoctrination period of my senior novitiate I asked Brother Augustine to present me with my Robe. Brothers would come from all parts of the country to present the Robes to their former students as they began their formal Novitiate training and it was considered an honor.

Ice hockey, skiing and tobogganing were the sports we enjoyed. I mentioned that we were on the Hudson River. The railroad passed through the front of our property and formed a cove that was three miles long and a half-mile wide. This froze in the winter but we were not allowed on it until it had frozen at least a foot thick. The wind was mostly from the north and varied in speed but when it was right we would skate to the far end and race the freight trains the length of the cove. With the right wind we could just about keep up. I remember hitting a rough piece of ice and sliding on my leather jacket for over a hundred yards. I must have been racing at 45 miles an hour at the time. This was heady stuff for a lad of my background .The winter sports were exciting and invigorating and while I loved my family I never felt homesick, to be perfectly honest I don't think I had the time.

The School had less than 100 students. My class had twelve; the academics were what set this school apart. While we had only about two hours in the evening to study and do homework this was the number one school in the state in academics. It led all others in the state Regis exams, both in passing grades and in marks. One of the reasons was the work of the brothers. If you found yourself in a bind while studying, rather than waste time you could ask for assistance from a classmate or the event of a real problem you could go to the Brothers quarters and get help from your instructor. This might amaze people but it worked and helped me become a much better student. My marks improved dramatically and I began to believe I could handle any studies in the future. More importantly it made me realize that if time was of the essence group study was the answer and I would use it in future endeavors.

I had no worries that I did not fit in nor did I have any question as to my vocation. As to prove it we had a visit from a Brother Superior who was in charge of foreign missions. He viewed all the records and interviewed four of us in person as to our willingness to serve in foreign lands. My duty would be in the Philippines. This will strike a cord with anyone reading this who is acquainted with my Naval Service .I can't remember sharing this with my parents but it could have been the Superior wanted it kept secret.

Mal O'Sullivan's folks lived just a few short blocks from mine in Brooklyn and our parents became friends. When we were on summer leave Mal, Bill Betz, another neighborhood lad, and I would pal around together. Bill Betz was to later leave from the Junior Novitiate and like me would become a Naval Aviator. I would become his best man at his wedding and he would be in my wedding party when I got married however that was to be in the future and this is now. Summer vacation at home was great but I was anxious to get back for my senior year. The summer went by quickly and although I was happy to spend the time with my family I wanted to finish High School and begin my Senior Novitiate. Mal and Bill felt the same way and when the time came we went back.

My folks drove me up and spent part of the first day with me. I met some of the new arrivals and of course I was and felt like one of the old-timers. Seniority always counts no matter where you are. My senior year was exciting. The fall was football season and the big game was New York against New England, To make things even Mal O'Sullivan and I had to be on opposing teams, We were both from Brooklyn and that would ordinarily make you a New Englander but since the Brothers decided we had to be on opposing teams he was assigned to New York and I to New England. Two of the Brothers coached, one to each team. Brother Augustine coached New England, Brother Morris New York. We had three weeks of practice and the entire student body took it very seriously. We used the same field, the only one we had, so there wasn't much secrecy, but heck, who cared? The entire student body and the whole of the faculty watched the game. Uniforms were provided by the Christian Brothers Academy in Albany. They also provided uniformed Referees. The game was exciting but ended in a scoreless tie. Athletics was a trademark for the Brothers and they worked hard at keeping fit, I can understand why and imagine my classmates who persevered are still in good physical shape. We took an extra subject each day as I have previously stated and we now began to study teaching methods. Phonics, standard arithmetic and reading skills were basic. We were encouraged to read as much as time would permit. Classics and Religious works were the staples but our library was pretty extensive and since we had to submit a book report each quarter we read as much as time would permit.

Johnny Kennelly's class was in the Senior Novitiate . To my chagrin Johnny left before taking the Robe. When the senior class from the Junior Novitiate graduates they go immediately to the Senior Novitiate. There is a period of time when they still wear their civilian clothes. They perform all the functions of a Senior Novice but they are on probation. When they receive the robe they have been accepted as full-fledged Novices. Johnny never received the Robe. He dropped out early and went home. My best friend dropped out and this hit me like a ton of bricks but I was going to persevere and immerged myself in my studies. You spend so much time in Chapel that your thoughts are on God and what He wants you to do. The three years I spent at St Joseph's Junior and Senior Novitiates formed a framework upon which my entire life would be judged. When I was wrong, and there would be plenty of times when I was, I knew it. I mentioned introspection as a form of prayer. Judging yourself and determining your motivation was what it was all about. Some people might think of this as a conscience but its more than a conscience, it's an active, sincere way of actually understanding yourself. Making yourself detect the false reasons your mind might provide for taking or not taking an action. The Saints were classic examples of people who knew themselves and the difference between the Saints and me is that I didn't always take the path I knew I should have. Well at that time I did take the right path and I stayed where I thought I belonged. Johnny left and I stayed. I did not consider myself superior as I recognized each of us must understand their calling and recognize whether they have a true vocation. My heart told me I was going to be a Christian Brother and I was going to teach in the Philippines. Case closed. I would obey what I considered God's Will.

One day you are a senior in the junior novitiate and the next day you are in the Senior Novitiate and on probation. For three months you will learn what is expected of a senior novice. What had seemed a disciplined life as a junior novice now became almost hectic. Your every mistake was disciplined and you were reminded what was expected of a Novice. Gradually these mistakes are less frequent and the discipline becomes less harsh. The Novice Master becomes mellower and you settle in to a role you will live for the rest of the year. You anticipate taking the robe

When it came time for me to take the Robe I remember the overwhelming emotion that went with it. While in the Junior Novitiate we would watch this and seeing our friends take the Robe made us aware of the reason we were here. It was a day of joy for all of us and we could only imagine how it must of felt to the New Brothers. New Brothers in every way but the vows, they took their new names and because we were from New York area. Our first name had to begin with lettered A, B, or C. Mine was Brother Celsus Lawrence. I would be called Brother Lawrence. Our Robes were not new. Others had worn them but that was never a consideration. They were ours!! The routine didn't change much but even the hired hands looked on us as different now. No more trying to get us to talk, we were accepted for what we were Novices, Brothers in training.. When our Novitiate was over we would depart for Washington DC where we would begin College and receive a degree from Catholic University. This was to be my path.

In December we were attacked by Japan. Even as Novices we had to register for the draft but as religious we would be exempt .In March while we were outside walking a plane passed overhead. I now recognize it as having been an SNJ or AT6 as the air force designated it. We had a BENIDECARMUS, which meant we could speak to one another. A college graduate who had come to our Novitiate told me both services had severe shortages of pilots and were taking selected high school graduates into pilot training. This sat on my mind. I had trouble thinking my Country had been attack and here I was a healthy specimen and I wasn't helping. The end of March I asked to see the Novice Master and told him how I felt. He listened, told me to pray and we would talk about it again tomorrow. The next day when I stated I still felt the same way I received a train ticket home. No questions asked. Walking down

*CDR. Jack Sullivan USNR*

Brother John L. Sullivan
Know to the order as Brother Celsius Laurence.
Nov. 1941 - March 1942
Junior. Te
1939-1941

to the train station in civilian clothes and looking back on the buildings I had spent three years of my life in is something I will always remember. I was within three months of taking my vows and going to Catholic University. Was I doing the right thing, would I be sorry? Am I placing my Country before my God or does my God expect me to serve my Country in its need? Thus began a new chapter in my life.

# Chapter 3
# My life as a Naval Aviation Cadet

My parents were surprised to see me but I was welcomed with open arms. When I told them I wanted to enlist in the Navy and become a pilot my mother recalled when we moved to Flatbush one of my early adventures was to ride my bike down Flatbush Avenue to Floyd Bennett Field and there I would watch the Navy Pilots flying their aircraft. I would sit outside the fence and watch them man their aircraft and taxi out to the runway for take off. I did this so often that I became a recognizable figure and one day one of the pilots came over to the fence and asked me if I would like to see his aircraft and sit in the cockpit. He arranged for me to meet him at the main gate and escorted me through and allowed me to sit in the aircraft and gave me a cockpit check out. When I returned home later that day I told my mother of my experience in exciting terms remarking that the airspeed indicator went up to 400 knots. Now it was my turn to see if I could qualify as a pilot.

My father had flown as an observer in World War #1 but he was not that excited to have me enlist right away. He felt that going into the service from the Novitiate might be too big a step and wanted me to get used to civilian life first. He was pleased that I felt the need to fight for this Country and recounted some of his experiences in flying. I heeded his advise and it was a few months before I enlisted. Mal O'Sullivan's dad set me up to work for The American Machine and Foundry and I worked there for several months before my father thought I was ready to enlist. I passed both the written exam and the flight physical for the Naval Aviation Cadets and was put on the list to be called for active duty.

Finally, the notice came, a final physical at 120 Broadway in NYC and I was on a train to Colgate University to begin my Cadet training. Because we were without a college degree we were sent to colleges to work on our math, take engineering, navigation, aircraft and ship identification courses and work out physically more intensely than I ever had before. How it happened I can't tell you but I was made platoon commander, it didn't mean much but if anyone made a mistake it was my fault, at least partially. By the end of our four-month stay at Colgate we were in superb physical shape. A four mile run meant nothing to most of us and I remember sprinting the last two hundred yards to finish first in my Platoon, (thanks Mr. Kennelly),

We went our different ways after Colgate and I was sent to Arkansas State Teachers to begin my flying. We flew piper cubs but it was flying. I still remember when my instructor got out of the airplane and told me to fly it around the field and return to pick him up. I soloed and felt like a king. I got thrown into the pool and my classmates bought me beers that night. I was the first but it wasn't more that a day or two when I could return the favor. Now that I had soloed I would fly around our designated areas and practice turns, spins and stalls. I was fascinated with flying and felt elated that I had control of this machine and could make it do what I desired. At eighty miles an hour you could catch up and pass those slow moving cars on the roads below. I remember catching a truck just before we turned from behind a hill and suddenly feeling the full force of a headwind. The slow moving truck that I had caught slowly pulled ahead of me and I was not able to catch it again. I was humbled but also became very aware of the effect wind can have on an aircraft. My instructor laughed when I told him of my adventure.

I was now the company commander and as all we had was a company that meant I was in charge.. I wore my Cadet anchor on my collar but as company commander I also wore Lieutenants Bars attached to the anchor. This was great fun because our Army W.A.C.S attending Link Trainer Operators School at the same college didn't know the difference and I received salutes from them all the time to the delight of my classmates. Some of these WACS were good looking young women and I dated several of them. The young Coeds at the school looked at us Cadets as something special. We were going to be Officers. The fact there were only eight male students left on the campus and most of them had physical deferments didn't deflate our egos as the young Southerners were Patriots and the rest of the student body, instead of looking for deferments enlisted in one of the Services. We were undergoing training and since we were at a college with all these lovely young ladies made the war seem distant somehow. We were really spoiled by the attention we received from the WACS and the female students. While this was the upside there was a downside as well. Some of my friends became airsick, some became very nervous in the air and couldn't follow instructions and washed out. These events took some of the joy away but the program went on. We received forty hours in the Piper Cub and then went on to preflight.

My Preflight School was the University of Georgia at Athens. All the Preflight Schools had bad reputations.. No flying, all ground School and Phys Ed. Again upon arrival I was made the Platoon Leader and this time I only knew a few of my platoon mates. You were to pick a primary sport and you would spend a majority of you time in that sport. My Company Commander, A Navy Lieutenant was a former professional football player. He picked me to play football. This was great and fit into my plans until our Battalion Commander; a Navy Commander, found out my name was John L Sullivan and made me prove it. Thank God a number of people before him thought the same way so I proved I could fight.. I still got to play football and since the Professionals were allowed to revert to amateur status it was the first chance to see how the game was played at that level. The pros didn't just tackle they want to see how much of you they can shove up in your helmet. I could run and I knew it but I found that I was only a half a step faster than a 6 ft 3 and 250 lb former professional linebacker and since I didn't have the angle I couldn't run away from him. As the game progressed we devised a play where I would loop a pass over his head to an end that would purposely miss a block. It worked and we beat them. He came over after the game and congratulated me. He reminded me that he had hit me as hard as he could and was amazed that I kept getting up with a smile on my face. My Company Commander was pleased but I was sore and beat up. To give you an idea of the teams these Preflight Schools had. the University of Georgia had Trippi, an All American and a top rated team but they would not consider scrimmaging against us. Before graduation I was made the company commander. It made up for some of the physical torture.

Next came Primary Flight Training at NAS Memphis in Tennessee. The primary trainer was an N2S Stearman. A biplane that could cruise at 80 MPH and had a top speed of 100 MPH, it was more plane than the Cub and about 20 MPH faster. We flew from the rear seat and our instructor sat in front and communicated his desires through a gosport. A gosport is unheard of in this day but it was a tube with a mouthpiece on the instructor's side and two tubes that were connected to the earpieces in the student's helmet. Crude but it worked. When the instructor became irritated it became a weapon and the decibels it was able to generate would cause your ears to ring. Take offs and landings were the first taught. Later you would have to shoot landings to a circle and he would cut the power at various times, places and altitudes and ask you where you were going to land. You made the approach and he would critique your choice, your approach and your headwork if it weren't the best choice. We all became proficient enough so these landing stopped and we were taught to slip tom a circle. Here you cross controlled the aircraft and burned off speed and altitude before leveling the aircraft and landing within the confines of the big (not so big) circle. If you overshot you had your ears cleaned out, We flew formation after completing check rides in all the other phases and receiving the crowd pleasing ( UP' S )( an up on a check ride indicating a passing grade)

Formation flying was done in my day in a monoplane called an N2T (TIM). It had flaps and they were lowered manually. Now the TIM was ten MPH faster than the N2S so upon entering the pattern you had to lower the flaps to keep from overrunning the slower N2S. I enjoyed this and we teased the students who were behind us in training flying the slower aircraft. When we finished formation flying I was through with Primary Training. As an aside I should tell you that formation flying was the next to the last phase in Primary as a rule. Because I didn't have any hops cancelled for mechanical, instructor, or scheduling problems I was three weeks ahead of my class and had no one to fly formation with so they called me in and told me they were going to experiment with me and have me fly the final phase first and formation flying last. This meant I would move to the front seat and fly the same series I had flown from the back seat. Sounds easy but it wasn't. The view from the front, your familiar guides has been changed dramatically. My instructor noted this immediately and told me most students find the formation phase from the front seat gives them more time to acclimatize to the different view from front. Since formation flying is easier than slips to a circle and the other maneuvers we had to accomplish in earlier phases of training this additional time in the front seat was important. . No doubt the reason the training syllabus was so constructed. I was an experiment and it almost spelled disaster for me. My instructor saved me. He recognized the problem and aborted several flights giving me more time to familiarize my self with the front seat before I had to take my check. This phase of your training was important and was used to help weed out the weaker pilots. It didn't slow down our fun in Memphis though. The girls in town loved the Cadets and our weekend liberty was enjoyable despite the looming check rides that awaited us at the Base The Navy was getting harder on the aviation cadets as they realized the pipeline was sufficient for the needs of the service. I gained three weeks by consenting to the experiment but wrote a paper suggesting it not be considered as the norm

Hope the powers to be agreed because I was transferred as a class of one to Pensacola for basic training in the SNV. No more biplanes, no more fabric wings, we are now to fly metal monoplanes. The new aircraft were more powerful, heavier and a lot faster than the previous aircraft. We attended ground-training classes to learn all the systems of this more complicated aircraft. When we completed this training we were ready for our first flight. No more backseat flying, everything from here on would be from the front seat. I learned an important lesson early on. We had a student lose an engine and make an emergency landing in a farmers field. A second student called the accident in on his radio and circled to keep the victims plane in sight. While providing the Base with details he became distracted. He pulled back on the stick and that combined with low airspeed put him into a stall from which he never recovered and he was killed.. I was shaken, this was the first fatality among my friends. My instructor called all of in and went over the cause of the accident. Fly your aircraft. Don't become distracted and when you are at low altitudes this is even more important. As I put this on paper now I remember one occasion later on during the Korean War when I was flying a Banshee jet in the landing pattern. I was on my downwind leg and remembered something I wanted to add to the notes on my knee board. The few seconds it took to add to my notes almost put me in the water. Only a frantic radio call from the LSO telling the aircraft at the ninety to pull up saved me from disaster. In private the LSO asked me how it happened and I remembered this accident.

    The SNV had a fixed landing gear. It could not be retracted. It was set wide apart so crosswind landings would not affect it as much. We spent more time doing formation work. Break ups, join ups and changing positions in the formation. Hand signals were used to donate various wing positions. In the beginning it was step up formation in which the wingmen flew above the leader. I remember flying with a British Cadet. We changed positions in the formation and he was the leader, I was a wingman and could look down into his cockpit. I watched a warning light come on in his instrument panel and he just stared at it. When I realized he wasn't aware of the action he should take I gave him instructions on the radio. The instructor was furious and immediately asked me to identify myself. After the flight was over it was the first item mentioned in the debrief. Radio silence was to be observed and if something was to be said it must be directed to the instructor. Discipline was finding its way into my every action in an aircraft. Basic was easy and the SNV was an easy plane to fly. It was over in a hurry and we went to Whiting Field for Instrument flying in the SNJ.

Whiting Field was located in Florida but was the farthest away from Pensacola. When I arrived and looked at the pictures of the instructors one of the Marine Officers was a neighbor of mine from Brooklyn. He lived a block away and I didn't remember him as being a friend or an athlete. While he recognized me I did not receive a warm welcome. He was an Officer and I a Cadet seemed to be his mindset. Even though we had a friendly conversation it was predicated on my remembering who was the officer. Perhaps it was his way of telling me he could not show favoritism. Fair enough because instrument flying is as much mental as it is flying ability. We had patterns we were to fly that required us to change altitudes, direction and airspeed. There were no autopilots, this had to be done by hand. Remembering what you were to do next was as important as being able to execute. You could read the charts for your next move but they happened so frequently you must memorize them. Flying, remembering the next move, adding and reducing throttle to correct your airspeed taxed me to the point that when I returned from an instrument flight I was soaking wet. To this point it was the most difficult thing I had encountered.

We flew the beam in those days. Its unheard of today but it consisted of a beam transmitted from a radio station. If you were on the centerline of the beam you heard a constant buzz. Move off the beam and you heard the buzz and the letter A or N depending on which side of the beam you were on. A heading correction would bring you back onto the beam. Wind would move you off it requiring a second or third correction. As you approached the station the beam became narrower and corrections smaller until you flew over it and there was a null, no sound and you knew where you were. You the took up a magnetic heading for a specified time waggled you wings, the instructor popped the hood and if all had been done correctly you would be looking down at the airfield. It was a great feeling and usually provoked an attaboy from the instructor. We started each flight with an instrument take off. You were under the hood and couldn't see outside of the cockpit. The instructor would line you up give you the heading of the runway and you would insert it in your gyro compass. He would give you 25 Inches of Manifold pressure, waggle the stick which meant you had control of the aircraft. You applied full throttle and holding back pressure on the stick, after checking the trim tabs a dozen times. This accounted for a perfect take off and climb. After passing through 1000 Ft you the established a climb schedule and reduced the throttle accordingly. Repetition if done correctly works miracles and these instructors would settle for nothing less. We came out loving instrument flying, waiting for the day when we would fly the SNJ from the front seat Final Squadron, from here we would go to our Operational Training Squadron and then join the Fleet .

We were sent to Barin Field in Foley Alabama for final Squadron. Barin had the nickname "Bloody Barin" because one day five students were killed in accidents. It was also the largest Squadron in the Navy with some 550 Aircraft. The SNV we had flown at Ellyson Field was easy to land because of the wide, fixed landing gear. The SNJ was not as easy because the gear was closer together and the gear was also retractable. This meant you had another step on the landing checklist, namely lower the gear. On paper this doesn't sound like much but believe me many a pilot was not only embarrassed by this omission but to some it ended their careers either by washing out or by serious injuries. We began our final Squadron by soloing in the SNJ. Before we flew the first flight we had to study the aircraft in ground school. Know the various systems and above all know what you could do in the cockpit to handle any of the emergencies that might occur. This took time but it was necessary. Next you had to understand the traffic pattern. We had two fields at Barin, one for take offs and one for landing. Because we had so many aircraft flying at the same time it was important, for safety sake to know where you were supposed to be in the traffic pattern at any time, who had priority and who had to give way.

While these Cadets had progressed to final Squadron and had shown the aptitude and skill to make it this far the higher horse powered SNJ caught up with some and we had fatalities and washouts. After we soloed in the SNJ we were taken to the acrobatic area where we were to demonstrate our ability to perform slow rolls, snap rolls, barrel rolls, loops and spins entering and exiting on precise magnetic headings. We worked on squadron maneuvers, breakups, join ups, changing positions and changing leads. Instrument flying was not as difficult as earlier at Whiting. It was designed to make you believe your instruments and you were put in unusual attitudes and made to recover quickly. Navigation, both overland and over water was next and tested your ability to recognize drift and wind speed.

The last phase was gunnery and bombing and combat (dog fighting). This was the most enjoyable and here is where my exuberance got me in trouble. I was so excited with watching my tracers rip into the target sleeve that when I finished firing I did a barrel roll on climb out. My Instructor was furious and much of the debrief was devoted to my transgression.. My flight, made up of Smitty, Dad Meldahl, Chuck Watters, Shep, and Scooty were irritated with me as well

*Shields of Honor*

We finish final squadron and prepare for graduation.
Jack Sullivan (author) top right.

Barin Field - My flight of cadets that I trained with, 1944.

because the Instructor insisted we fly the hop over. No more of this nonsense I promised my flight mates and they eventually forgave me. Air to air gunnery, air to ground gunnery and bombing were easy for me. Combat flying, dog fighting was my forte. The only combat fight I lost was my first flight with my Instructor. The second resulted in a draw. This was true for all my later fights in operational fighters as well. The only one I remembering loosing was to a Navy pilot flying an FJ3 when I was flying an F9F6. Later when I checked out in the FJ3 I realized the FJ3 aircraft was far more maneuverable and I felt much better. I learned early on that you must know the aircraft you are flying, its strengths and weaknesses and use this knowledge in combat. Final Squadron ,or the last of it, was easy. There was one hiccup though. We were night flying the night someone buzzed Mobile Alabama. Every one that was flying that night was suspect and grounded until the Navy could complete their investigation. Nobody admitted to the infraction and nobody ever claimed they knew who it might have been. After a week in a grounded status we were back flying our last hops and completed the training. We graduated and got our wings and commission. The folks couldn't make it as travel in wartime was rough but that didn't take away from the thrill of finally getting my wings.

# Chapter 4
# I get my Wings and Commission

I went from there to operational training in SBDs. This dive bomber was the backbone of the fleet but it was to be replaced by the SB2C since the new aircraft was bigger, heavier, faster and had better range. Scuttlebut had it we would transition to this aircraft in the near future but for now the SBD was ours to master. It was a good aircraft but when flying it from runways you could run out of braking. The brakes faded after continuous use and many a pilot found himself with little or no brakes left after ten minutes of taxing. Out side of this problem we found out the SBD was a lot like the SNJ we had flown in training. It wasn't as nimble but it did in Knots what the SNJ did in Miles per Hour. I also found it could wind up in a dive, especially if you didn't use the dive brakes. I climbed to 24 thousand feet and dove it straight down out of a split S and went through 400 MPH before recovering. I watched the wings ripple but the aircraft was solid. I think others had done the same thing, we were all anxious to break the 400 MPH barrier. We were almost through training when they decided to transfer us to SB2Cs. We were packing when the hold order came. The SBD was through, the SB2C was in but the tails of some SB2C aircraft came apart in carrier landings and the aircraft was grounded.

What to do with us? The Navy needed Ferry Pilots and we were available. We were checked out in F6Fs and F4Us (Hellcats and Corsairs) and sent out to deliver aircraft to Squadrons that needed them. This was like dying and going to heaven for me. These were front line fighters, the best we had, and I got to fly them. They were a lot faster than the SBDs and much more maneuverable. As a side benefit we were told by our fellow ferry pilots about Spartanburg. It seem that if you had to RON (remain over night) in Spartanburg the gent that supplied you gas had a number of girls that wanted to meet Navy Pilots. You could review their pictures and if they were available they would come and pick you up at the field. Dinner and dancing sounded great to this young tiger and I availed myself of the opportunity. Another interesting thing happened. I checked out in the hottest aircraft we had, the F8F Bearcat. This aircraft was designed to intercept the Kamikaze suicide pilots. It was powerful, fast and could climb like nothing else we had in the inventory. I picked up a new one at Grumman and was heading down to Jacksonville.

I was close to 10,000 ft when I noticed a glint of sunlight off a wing of an aircraft. A P51 Mustang soon joined me. When he joined up he tried to contact me by radio but as we both had a limited number of channels we could not talk. He then motioned me to add power and we were in a race. At 54 inches of manifold he was maxed out and I had 61 inches if I needed it. I used it and sprinted ahead as though I had been catapulted. I had plenty of speed and pulled up into a loop. He turned to watch me. I came out of my loop, turned inside of his turn and joined up on him after doing a barrel roll around him. He went to Guard Channel and asked me what I had under the hood. I smugly informed him this was an eight not a six and he couldn't stay with this little tiger. I have told that story in every Navy Bar I have ever attended. F8 pilots will tell similar stories.

After three months of this choice duty we learned that the Navy needed instructors in final Squadron. Guess who was available? We received orders to Pensacola and Flight Instructor School. We had two weeks leave before starting School so I decided to go home and show the Wings, I had a new set of whites that I treasured. Carefully packing them in a hang bag I started out on the long train ride. Seat were hard to come by in those days and even when you had one you would give it up to some woman that needed it more than you did. I began to wonder if any woman, not in a family way, traveled by train . I pulled into Penn Station with the whites in impeccable condition and caught the Subway home to Flatbush Ave. I changed in the Subway bathroom and stepped out of the subway looking about as good as A Naval Aviator could.

I would later tell my future mother in law a version of this story that ran like this. When I got out of the Subway I needed a comb so I went to the five and ten on the corner. I bought a comb and the salesgirl insisted it be put into a bag. I shrugged her off telling her I had immediate use for it and proceeded to go outside to the mirror in the scale and comb my hair. A gentleman, looking very official, asked me where I had gotten the comb. Inside I replied. He then told me he was a Detective, hired by the five and ten to combat a series of small thefts. Would I mind going inside and pointing out the saleswoman. We went inside and instead of saying yes she had sold me the comb she said she didn't remember. Didn't remember a young Naval Officer in his whites? She then said if she had sold me the comb it would have been in a bag, as she had been directed. My mother in law was speechless, then volunteered", she must have been afraid of losing her job, Jack." Well then I was asked to accompany the Detective to the managers office, which I did. The manager was not present but I was asked to wait while the Detective sought him out. After almost ten minutes I was ready to walk out when I discovered the door was locked and I could not get out. Now I became mad and determined to get out of here. A window over a roll top desk led to an alley between the two buildings. This I knew because we had run through that same alley when younger. I opened the window and, careful not to soil my whites slipped one leg out over the window sill and was about to lift the other one out when the door opened and the Detective ran in and started to pull my leg.....just like I'm pulling yours now Mom. My mother in law gave me the first of her now famous "God forgive you Jack Sullivan " and the rest of the family roared with laughter.

Anyway I did come home and I did bring one of my buddies with me. George had gone through flight training with me and had the same path SBDs then ferry command and finally would end up as an instructor. Mom and Dad were happy to see me in my uniform. Marian came home later and was surprised to see me as I had warned them it might take some time for me to catch a train. Dad had steaks for us and George couldn't get over it because steak was hard to come by in those days.

The next day was Sunday and after Mass the gang collected. Some of my buddies were home on leave. It was exciting listening to their tales. Mostly the girls were home and the sight of two young Navy Pilots had the desired effect. George was amazed at the attention he received as I introduced him to every girl I knew. He had planned on going home to Boston the following day but decided to stay a few days and get to see New York. Mom and Dad were always gracious hosts to my friends and I found out later Mom kept in touch with friends of mine that I had long since lost track of. I took George out that night and we went to the Pennsylvania Hotel where we met two Barbizon Models who were our companions for that night. We hit several bars and finally wound up in Leon and Eddies on 52$^{nd}$ St, and since it was Sunday night a bunch of the Comedians working New York were in the bar, Milton Berle and Jacky Leonard to name a couple. The floor show was a give and take with these comedians. We thoroughly enjoyed ourselves.

When the show girls came out for their last number the headliner was Sherry Brittan. She appeared almost nude and was a very attractive young lady. When the act finished the girls picked customers to dance the final number with. Most went for the comedians but Sherry came to me and our dates thought it was funny. When I danced with Sherry I found out she had an advanced degree and was very intelligent. She not only recognized the uniform and wings but was aware of the amount of training it took to produce a Naval Aviator. While the dance was short she made a very favorable impression on me and I must say changed my original conception of her. That was the good part. The bad part was that she wore body makeup and my whites picked it up. Our dates thought it was hysterical, and every time it was mentioned the laughter burst out again. We took them to the Pen Station and they took the train home to Long Island after telling us what a great time they had. Names and phone numbers were exchanged, but our time was limited and we never contacted them again.

George wondered what my mother would think of my stained whites. We went to bed and hung our whites up to be cleaned the next day. It was late and we were tired. When we woke up my mother had washed and ironed our uniforms telling me that mine was soiled from the subway ride. Neither George or I contradicted her and the matter was settled without further explanation. George left a few days later but he told me Boston was going to seem tame by comparison.

When I left home to report to Pensacola for Instructors School, I had fond memories of my latest New York visit. Instructors School was really a review of our Cadet Training as far as flying was concerned but the classroom work was designed to teach us the proper way to instruct the students. We had gone through it as students and responded to the instruction, now we had to make certain the students would react to us as we had reacted to our instructors. Another element was added to our instruction. We would be the first class of Instructors to take a flight of Students through the whole syllabus. We had different Instructors for each phase of training. One checked us out in the SNJ and soloed us. Another taught us Instruments, another gunnery, another over water navigation etc. Now we had to become proficient in all these phases to instruct in them as our students progressed. Our period of training was naturally much longer but I must admit, fun. We prepared for our first class and briefed them thoroughly on what to expect. From the questions they asked I realized I had gotten the essentials through to all. Since we had them each day we got to know them as individuals. We could joke with them about their personal lives and this helped us put them at ease. They got to know us and would, respectfully, joke with us as well My first class of Cadets made it all the way through and every one of them graduated and got their wings.

As this method was a test case, we were under the microscope by the Training Department. It soon became evident that it worked and more of the instructors went through advanced training.

Barin Field was known as Bloody Barin because in one day five Cadets were killed in accidents.. The Squadron was the largest in the world with 550 planes and over 100 Instructors. This had taken place before my time but the whole Instructor corp. was aware of it and safety was paramount. The name stuck, however. After instructing for almost a year I wanted to get home and see the folks. Christmas leave was almost impossible for junior Officers so I requested a cross country flight. These were flight where in we tested our navigational skills and in our case could not extend for over a thousand miles from home base.

I'm now a flight instructor.
May 1945, after three months of instructor's school.

Washington DC was as close as I could come to New York City and my home. My plan was to fly to Washington then catch a train to New York City. My cross country was approved and I flew to Washington and landed at Navy Anacostia. I followed taxi instructions and was parked in an outlying section of the parking ramp. A few minutes later a jeep pulled up and the driver said that he had been instructed to bring me to operation as soon as possible. When I arrived in operations I was greeted by an irate operations officer who derided me for taxiing across the VIP parking area with an aircraft that was leaking oil. He would not allow me any explanation and he seemed to get more agitated as he repeated the offence. I was to be put on report to my commanding officer. I was bewildered as all I had done was to follow instruction given to me by the line signal man. When he asked my name I spoke up firmly and said "Ensign John L Sullivan, sir". He looked at me for a minute, then asked if I were any relation? The present secretary of the Navy was John L Sullivan, a fact that was not lost on me. I replied "yes sir" and his tone changed completely and he gave me a lengthy explanation as to why they keep the VIP parking spot immaculately clean. He then asked me if I needed a car and again the Irish in me prompted to tell him" no, as he would be sending a car for me at the BOQ." There was no more talk of the report to my commanding officer and I walked out after closing my flight plan and made my way to the train station. After hearing the story my mother was concerned that I might be in trouble but my father saw the humor in it. In any case nothing ever came of it and I never met the operations officer again.

Barin Field was a busy place and even though the war was almost over the tempo of operations did not decrease. Naval Officers who had been selected for Aviation during the war were now free to begin the training and some of my students were senior in rank to me. It made for an uncomfortable situation but our Commanding Officer reminded us that as instructors we were the pilots in command of that aircraft and our students, regardless of rank, were under our control. It worked and I never heard of an instructor having a problem in this regard. All the instructors were friends but there were four of us were real close and we generally hung out together. Dick Baker, "Mac" McPherson. Bob Grammer and myself. I had an old 35 Ford dubbed "The black Bug". The key could always be found in the ashtray and whenever one of my buddies was late for a flight the car would be pressed into service, I never knew where it would be at the flight line. Until Mac and Dick bought their cars it was our transportation to Mobile, Alabama. I should tell you this was our liberty port of call and we used to kid that we knew every eligible girl in Mobile, worth dating. We even dated some girls that weren't eligible but I'll leave the interpretation of that to the reader. These were my friends. Now I have to tell you a sad story. USO troupes would come to the Pensacola Complex of five bases and have a show for each of the bases on a different night. They were always well attended by the cadets and Navy families. They usually came into Pensacola first and the Officers at Mainside were the first to date the girls. This particular day The USO troupes came into Mobile and Bob Grammer met them. He was a very personable, good looking young man and obtained dates for the four of us. We met the girls and dated them every night. We would meet them after the show, regardless of which Base they were playing. The last night they were to spend in Mobile. We were flying that afternoon and Bob had to fly that night. He would join us after he finished. We arrived

The Black Beetle - 1935 Ford
Car I bought as an instructor at final squad at Barin Field. - May 1945

in Mobile in time to take the girls to dinner and would go to the Officers Club afterwards and Bob was to join us there. Bob was killed that night in an accident near Mobile. His plane crashed into a house and nobody else was injured. We got the word and rushed to the hospital. Bob was still alive but the Doctor didn't give him much of a chance. He was trying to talk but was incoherent. He died an hour after we arrived. We were grief stricken. An aviator lives with death but when it's a close personal friend we are not immune from the deepest feeling of grief. Dick Baker and I escorted Bob's body home. We met Bob's mother Myrtle and all the relatives. Even in the midst of their sadness they found time to treat us like favored guests. We had to explain the accident to a number of the relatives as some of them had to travel great distances to attend the funeral.

I stayed in touch with Bob's mother for quite a while. I am still in touch with a cousin of Bobs who lives on Long Island with her husband. Herb and Nina Demuth kept me aware of Myrtle's health and well being and would also inform his mother of my progress. They are still my friends and Bob is often mentioned in our conversations.

# Chapter 5
# Marriage and Career

Dick and I returned to Barin and were informed the Navy was downsizing and that a number of the Junior Officer would be released in June 1946. We received our orders the beginning of June and were scheduled for release to inactive duty on 30 June. We decided to go to New Orleans to be released there. My car was being worked on and the engine was completely rebuilt. It would not be ready by the end of June so we took Dick's car to New Orleans. When we arrived we were surprised to see there were a number of companies that wanted to hire ex Naval officers. The Officer that helped us complete the paperwork advised us the Mexican Government was looking for flight instructors and gave us a contact. We thought it might be worth considering so we contacted the gentleman. He interviewed us and thought we were well qualified. It seems the Mexican Air force was thinking of establishing a training program. They wanted to train instructors and begin a Program in Mexico City. We were provided funds to go to Mexico City and be interviewed by members of the Mexican Air force. We had a great time in New Orleans and then headed to Mexico,

Crossing the boarder was an experience. Since we had a car we had to sign papers we would not sell the car in Mexico because in Mexico the cars were worth about twice the price they would fetch in the States. That paperwork being completed we crossed the border and decided to get a hotel room. We went to a fine restaurant and had a beer. Because that tasted so good we had a second. What happened to the signs we could read so well when we came into the place? Check the label on the beer. 12% alcohol!! We are used to 3%. Thank God we found it out before we had to drive. Mexican beer is potent and would take some getting used to so be careful Yankees! The second night we remained over night in Monterrey. We were touted on a couple of clubs the hotel manager thought we would enjoy. We even got to see a cock fight! The third day we arrived in Mexico City and reported to the Mexican Air force. We were provided quarters and told to report the following day.

We had a night in Mexico City and managed to see some of the livelier places in town. The Government buildings are in a square and the Catholic Cathedral is on the other side. Prostitutes line up by the fence of the Cathedral and if business is not going well will go in to the

Cathedral and light a candle. I tried to engage a Priest in conversation but his English wasn't up to it and we were taken on a tour of the Cathedral. I'm sure that is what he thought I wanted. I never did get a reading from the Clergy on the practice of the Prostitutes lighting candles. We met the next day with a Colonel who interviewed us. He was very pleased with our experience, background and training. He repeated what we had been told in New Orleans and invited us to tour the facilities. We observed ten, almost new SNJ (AT6) aircraft. They trained their cadets in small numbers. We realized the base was some 6000 ft in altitude. The service ceiling of an SNJ is some 23000ft. We used to conduct our aerobatics at 8000ft. Oxygen is required at 10000ft. When you do the math you recognize there isn't much altitude to play with. We took several of their pilots up and put them through a basic fam hop. While they were good they were not as precise as our students in final Squadron. Bad habits had crept in and there was not a pilot designated to give them check rides. Dick and I agreed Mexico City was not a good training site We asked if they had some field at a lower altitude where they could train their pilots. The Colonel turned to his staff and after a few minutes of Spanish asked if I meant an outlying field that would be flown to from Mexico City? We suggested the outlying field would be the training base and all flights would begin and end there. More Spanish and the answer was this would have to be considered at a higher level. We would meet tomorrow.

Dick and I went out on the town again but this time one of the pilots we had flown with was our guide.

We discovered something of the life of the wealthy in Mexico. The oldest son usually takes over the father's business, the second son usually goes into Government service of some kind, either the military or politics. The third son seems to have more freedom of movement to choose for himself what he would like to do. We were with a second son and his father had a big spread outside of Mexico City and we were invited to visit the ranch next weekend. In the meantime we visited clubs we would never know existed had it not been for our guide. We were fascinated by the music and bands at most of these clubs and the floor shows would never make it in Disney world but Hugh Heffner would love them. When the week- end arrived and we made it out to the ranch and there was a bull roast in progress.

A number of the older son's guests were already there. We met the parents and they were friendly and gracious. If anyone has read the novel "Tom Jones" or seen the movie, remember the "Old Squire" in it? The father was the old squire. He was friendly, always smiling but a letch. During the week- end he must have patted the fannies of every female servant he came in contact with, fat or skinny, old or young it didn't matter. What amazed me was the smile on his face and the giggles from the servants. I honestly believe they enjoyed his attention. The mother, on the other hand, seemingly ignored his overtures to the servants as though she hadn't noticed them. He was so friendly and outgoing that everyone relished his company. I must confess Dick and I enjoyed his company. He took me on a tour of the facilities and tried to sell me on the joys of living in Mexico. The mother was delighted when I asked if I could accompany her to Mass on Sunday. She, her youngest son and I went to Mass. Everyone else had an excuse for not going. The Mexicans decided it would be better to continue sending their cadets to the States to be trained. Our friend told us the blonde Texan girls were a big attraction for the cadets and they would rather go to the States for training. It wasn't said but the thoughts of a training base in some small, lonesome location would not be the choice of the officers who would have to man it. Mexico City with its clubs and nightlife was where they wanted to be. We agreed and bid farewell to our Mexican friends and headed back to the States.

We crossed the boarder, after presenting the proper paper work and took off for New Orleans. We always had a great time in New Orleans, we had phone numbers and would call ahead to make sure we had dates. We spent two days there and headed back to Barin Field. My car was ready when we arrived so we headed out to the Base to say farewell to our friends. Many of them had received their orders to inactive duty and were preparing to leave. One last big group party and we left for home. A short stop in Jacksonville to see some friends and we started home again.

The roads in 1946 were not the roads we have today. Most were two lanes and wandered through small towns and villages. We were in South Carolina, it had just rained and the roads were slick. We were rounding a curve with trees blocking our vision when we suddenly came upon a hay wagon blocking our side of the street and there was a car following the hay wagon at a crawl. We attempted to pass both when a station wagon filled with school kids appeared on the other side of the road. Dick pulled back in and with his hydraulic brakes managed to stop behind the car. My 35 Ford had mechanical brakes. I pulled in but to avoid hitting the station wagon I had to steer off the road. I went down a steep incline and rolled end over end. I could see it happening in almost slow motion and put my hands on the roof of the car and rolled with it. The car ended up upside down and my leg was caught between the door and the steering wheel. I was unhurt but couldn't free myself. Dick's face appeared in my window. He was white. I guess he expected to see me a mangled mess and when I smiled at him and asked him to please open the door he greeted me with a loud "son of a bitch !"When he opened the door and I crawled out I realized we had company. The school kids, their mother the driver, the other cars occupants, the hay wagon driver and other cars that came upon the scene. Everyone was amazed that I had not been injured.

A neighbor called a tow truck and an automobile dealer arrived. He was interested in the wreck and when I told him the engine had just been rebuilt he offered me two hundred dollars for the car. Before we finished Dick had sold his car as well and we proceeded home by train

Dick spent a few days at my house and then left for Bridgeport. I was still on terminal leave for a few days so I went to Floyd Bennett Field to see about joining the Naval Reserves. Little did I dream I would fly more hours in the Reserve than my buddies on active duty. On Sunday I went to Mass. As usual all my buddies went to 12:15 Mass as well and we all met outside the Church. I guess I was the last one back because I was the only one in uniform. A lot of the girls said hello and I told the same story a dozen times to as many people. Yes I was back and I wasn't sure exactly what I was going to do. My friend Johnny Kennelly took me to an ice cream parlor that had become a neighborhood favorite. He met Mr. Fay, George Fays' father. George and I had gone to Brooklyn Prep together but I had not remembered meeting his father. A short time later two young ladies came over to the table where we were seated, said hello to Johnny and joined us. The smaller of the two was evidently fond of Johnny and sat next to him. The tall, beautiful blonde sat next to me. When Johnny introduced them I realized the blonde, Joan Fay, was a friend and classmate of my sister, Marian. I had not seen Joan in ten years and I must say I was amazed at how she had matured. She was one of the most beautiful young women I had ever seen. She was friendly and I was determined to see her again. Johnny and Grace Hockschwender, the young woman that had sat next to Johnny on our first visit to Lobensteins, saw to that. After the first two encounters I asked her out and we began to see one another regularly. My mother and sister were pleased because Joan had always been a favorite of theirs. My folks had known the Fays from Church and Joan had visited our house on many occasions while I had been away.

Because I was not sure what I would do I had no thoughts of getting serious about any girl. However Joan and I grew closer and closer with every date. She and Grace came over to the house one night and opening the door pleaded in unison "Mrs Sullivan can Jackie come out and play!" The folks all thought that was funny and my mother turned to me and told me to go out and play.

Mr Kennelly, Johns' dad was the Dock boss at the Grace line Steamship Company. He told me to come on over and work as Longshoreman while I was waiting to get back in college. This proved to be a great experience. I was signed up with the Union and put to work. I was paired up with another recent hire, and world war 2 vet, Eddie Dunphy. Ed and I hit it off and we not only worked together as partners on the Dock but hung around together as well. Eddie lived in Queens with his family. He also had just returned from the war, having seen action in Europe with the Army. While we both realized the Docks would be temporary they provided us both with the money to prepare for the future. We used to laugh because we enjoyed the physical labor. We took any task we were assigned to be a challenge. Our good nature and willingness to work helped us fit in with the old-timers and we didn't have to endure any of the slights inflicted on some of other new workers. Another thing we enjoyed, the hiring boss always picked us as a team. I should say longshoremen are picked from a shape up each morning and the number chosen depends on the amount of work available on the Dock. When two ships were in most of the men were hired. The real old-timers had what could be considered a steady job. The" new mickys" (recent hires) might not be hired to work each day. We were lucky. Because of our work ethic we were some of the first" new Mickey's" hired. Another bit of luck, because Ed and I were about the same size and weight, 5:11 and 170lbs we were teamed as coffee loaders.

A coffee bag weighed 154lbs and was made of a tightly woven burlap. To lift the bag you had to have two small hooks. These hooks had a handle about three inches long that fitted in the palm of your hand. A hook extended from this handle that fit between your forefinger and the middle finger,. Your forefinger was placed over the back of the hook and between you and you partner you lifted the bag. Old timers talked about stacking the bags eleven high. Naturally all the new mickeys wanted to try it. Believe me it was a feat and only after practice could you do it. You had to be well coordinated as a team and the last bag had to be palmed and tossed to make it happen. When you could do this you were then challenged to lift a coffee bag over you head. Again strength had to be combined with skill. 154lbs is not that heavy but a coffee bag is a dead weight. The secret was to push you hands as deeply into the bag as possible, lift and swing the bag so that it rests on your shoulders than with you palms push it over your head. When you could do this you almost, I repeat almost, lost the New Mickey name.

It was during this time that I was going to the YMCA in Brooklyn. I would run a mile on the indoor track, play handball and swim . On one of these nights I discovered an obstacle course set up and young men lined up to run it. I fell in line and when I completed it the gentleman doing the timing told me I had run it in 4:0 time. He informed me this would be part of the physical exam for the upcoming Police Department test. It turned out he was a Police sergeant assigned to the Police Academy and talked me into signing up to take the test. He later provided me with instructional material to study. While I might not want to be a Policeman it was an ace in the hole, is the way he put it. Little did I think he would be proven correct?

Joan and I became closer and closer as the days went by. My thoughts of finishing college competed with my thoughts of getting married. A number of my friends in the Reserve Squadron were completing college and they all told me you can't get married and go to college at the same time. It will be too much of a struggle. Joan and I decided to get married. I bought her an engagement ring and we set the date. The wedding plans were finalized. The O'Club at Floyd Bennet Field (NAS NY) would host our Wedding Reception. This was great because Joan and our friends loved the club. We spent many Saturday nights at the club with our friends. A band would be playing our favorite songs, the bar was inexpensive and the Club packed with Navy Pilots and their dates. These were wonderful times and great memories now. Joan was a hit with all my friends and fellow pilots. The friendships she made at the club prepared her for the life she would lead later on in the Navy as a Navy wife.

As the day drew closer for our wedding I managed to get an apartment for us. This was rare as most of my married friends started their married life living with their parents. One of the checkers on the docks had an apartment. It was the second story of a single family house and was presently occupied by a widow. She wanted to move in with her daughter but couldn't sell her furniture. I bought it and later sold it to another friend. The apartment was mine and Eddie Dunphy came over and helped me paint it after Joan had picked out the colors. Now let me regress a little. I want to talk about Joan and her family. When I started to take Joan out I got to know her family. Her father was the outside sales manager for Ryerson Steel Corporation. He was a friendly person and well suited to the position he held. He reminded me of the actor, Robert Young, and his mannerisms were much the same. He was impressive, kind, considerate and yet a strict Dad. Joan's mother was attractive and one of the sweetest women I ever met. She was the law and her family recognized it. Judith was her younger sister. She was my friend from the time I first met her and remains so today. Joan's younger brother Paul became my buddy and I would take him to see those action and science fiction movies Joan didn't want to attend. We bonded and to this day are still buddies. George Fay junior had married a French girl, Marcell .and was overseas in Germany. He was a Captain in the US Air force.

 I would be invited to Sunday dinner at the Fays. Mom Fay was a great cook and Sunday dinner was a formal affair. Dad did the carving and everyone was required to be in attendance.

 Later on when Joan and I became serious and I was ready to buy the engagement ring I asked her father if we could talk. Everyone was home and knew what the conversation was about. Dad and I went into the kitchen and sat. I told him I wanted to marry his daughter and asked his permission. We talked finances, where we would live and all the small talk surrounding such an undertaking. He smiled and told me he would be happy to have me as a son in law and gave me a big hug. We joined the family in the living room and dad told them (what they already knew) Joan and I were engaged and had his blessing. I remember telling my mother in law that one of the reasons I wanted to marry her daughter was that in later years she would look as beautiful as her mother. Irish bull, well maybe, but I honestly meant it. The whole family laughed and with the same love and affection we all feel for one another today hugged me.

It was a special moment in my life and even thinking and writing about it now floods my heart with warm feelings.

The wedding day came and our friends surrounded us each. My best man and ushers were at my house changing into our formal attire. Johnny Kennelly was my best man, Dick Baker, my old buddy from the Navy was one of my ushers, another, was Ed Dunphy, Bill Betz another Navy Pilot and a friend from St Josephs' Novitiate was another, Walter Hardt, an Army Pilot (P47s) the last. Joan had her sister Judith as her maid of honor, Grace Hockschwender, my sister Marian, Jean Brooks, and Marie Duff rounded out the wedding party. I mention everyone, as it will be of some consequence to my friends and family. Father McMonigal married us on October 4th 1947 at Our Lady Help of Christians Church located on Avenue M and East 28th Street in Brooklyn NY. Joan was beautiful as a bride and her picture is hanging in the dining room of my house where I see it every day. We planned to go to Bermuda on our honeymoon but the day before I got married the Grace Line Pier burned to the ground or I should say to the waterline. We went to Williams Lake, a resort in upper New York State, instead ,and met some new friends.

When we returned home I received a notice that I had passed the Police exam and would be in the first class so I had a job. Joan was working as a secretary on Wall Street so we weren't penniless but my working as a Police rookie sure did wonders for my self-esteem. I was not unemployed.

Our apartment was on Troy avenue one half block from Church Avenue. Convenient to the streetcar and Subway so transportation was no problem. We had no automobile at that time. Joan was learning to cook and I was her victim. I say that with glee because right from the very beginning she was a good cook and worked her way into the excellent category.

As a Rookie with the Police Department I was assigned to the Police Academy. Classroom work took up half a day and the gym and pistol range took up the other half of the day. Law, criminal procedure, and Police procedure took up much of our time. Only a law student takes more law than a Police recruit and the lawyer doesn't have to know Police procedures. We were reminded we would have to make decisions in a split second that Judges and District Attorneys would review after consulting law books. This fact became apparent later on in my work as a detective. The Police Academy recognized our class as special. We were all veterans of a war. We knew guns and had all gone through vigorous physical training in our respective outfits. We were to have a class leader. The question was asked, "How many of you were officers?" Eight out of thirty two of us were officers. What rank? O'Connell was a lieutenant colonel and became our class leader. His main job was to carry a roster of the names, addresses and phone numbers of the rest of us. He had fought through all of Europe and had received battlefield promotion starting with second lieutenant and working his way up to lieutenant colonel. He became a good friend and while we are on the subject let me fast forward twenty years. One of our numbers is now a Police Captain and he and O"Connell were preparing a twenty year anniversary party for our class. Some had already put in for retirement. O'Connell was given my address by the Police Department Military Service Bureau and contacted me at The Naval Air Test Center asking that I attend. Joan couldn't make it and as it was to be a husband and wife affair she suggested that I invite my sister to attend. I drove to New York, picked up my sister and drove to the hotel where the event was to be held. It was a gala affair and a great chance to renew old friendships. Most of my classmates had read, in Spring 3100 (Police Magazine) my exploits, as a jet pilot in Korea and that was number one on their questions. I met O'Connell's wife, and I didn't get a chance to introduce my sister because these two were already hugging one another. It turns out they were classmates in St Johns Law School. O'Connell and I were amazed and delighted. After the affair we were invited to O'Connell's apartment in Styverson Town. Along with several other couples we drove down town to his apartment and had a great time swapping stories and bringing one another up to date on our lives.

When we left as a group we again said goodbye and Marian and I headed North to where my car was parked. The rest headed south to where they had parked. As I was putting the key to the lock of my car I heard a scream from where my friends had headed. Marian was standing back on the sidewalk and she yelled, "He is trying to strangle her!" A split second later I heard my friends yell, "get him Sully". I stepped out into the street in time to see this big black man running towards me. From his size I judged him to be heavier than my two hundred pounds and prepared to tackle him low. He was looking over his shoulder at my friends who were chasing him. He never saw me. I hit him at knee level and he went over the top of me. I put one hand behind his head and pushed him into the street. He was unconscious when he hit the ground. I untangled myself when this little Puerto Rican threw himself onto the unconscious black. My friends arrived and told me that right across the street from them this fellow had grabbed a Puerto Rican girl, torn her blouse off and was going to rape her in the street. They had come to her aid and the perpetrator had fled in my direction. When they called they knew I was in the perfect spot to intercept him. The Puerto Rican who threw himself on the perp was the girl's brother in law. It seems the girl was at a party in her sister's house and her husband ,who did night work in the Post Office, had just called to tell her he would meet her to take her home. When she crossed the parking street to the main road the perpetrator had grabbed her. The wives and my sister were attempting to fix her clothes and comfort her. A cabbie, with tire iron in hand showed up and when my sister asked him to call the Police on his radio he replied they are already here, pointing to us. I laughed when my buddies told me I hadn't lost my touch. The Police arrived and took custody of the now conscious black man and I later learned that O'Connell was furious when he learned that he had missed out on all the action. Marian summed it up on the ride home when she said "never a dull moment when you're around Jack".

Now back to my time in the Police Academy. We were assigned to various Police Precincts for patrol duty so we would be aware of the problems in various ethnic and geographical boundaries. The Police officers picked to act as our tutors were men with some time on the force. Most of these men had come into the Police Department during the depression and were remarkably well educated. It was amazing to me how much of a grasp they had on the social problems of their area. I learned a lot listening to them and was amazed at how well they functioned. They could see a problem develop and more than once watched them take preventive action before a more serious problem could develop. They would take the time to explain why they had acted and what could have happened if they had not taken the action. Particularly in precincts described to be rough it was interesting to note the friendship they had with business owners and shopkeepers. They would point out that a shopkeeper was a good friend and in time of emergency could be counted on to call for assistance should you find yourself in deep trouble. One even told me he made sure each of them had a phone number they could call to get him assistance. Later on I was in a patrol car when such a call came through from a shopkeeper and it was reassuring to me to see the rapid response policemen gave to a call for help from one of their own, The term "thin blue line" might be true but if the public assists, such as this shopkeeper did, the line becomes firm and strong in a big hurry. I enjoyed the time I spent with these experienced policemen and

I listened to and absorbed all the advice they imparted. When my classmates talked about their experiences on the streets I could see they valued the advice they received as well.

The range officers remarked they had not seen a class shoot as well as we did. They were not aware we were all veterans and in questioning us found that some had been on different pistol teams in the service. Two members of my class were recommended for consideration for the Police Pistol Team. The rest of us passed the firing test on the first attempt. I later fired well enough for a medal and points towards the Sergeants examination. Having confidence to be able to hit what you are aiming at seemed very important to me and the few times I had to fire my gun I did so knowing I could and would hit my target.

As time came to graduate. We had already been measured for our uniforms and most folks will be surprised to hear that the cost of these uniforms was the responsibility of the policeman. Some had to buy them on the installment plan, and the money was deducted each month from their check. The slang term for the uniform is "the Bag" and of course no self-respecting rookie would call it anything else. Graduation day came and the ceremony was held with all the pomp and splendor it deserved. The Mayor of New York City and the Police Commissioner were present and spoke highly of the class of World War 2 veterans that were graduating and O'Connell with his battlefield promotion to lieutenant colonel was singled out as the caliber of men that would soon be patrolling our streets. Most of the local news outlets covered the story and we went to our first assignments feeling special.

It is sometimes hard to explain to people the fascination of Police work. It certainly isn't the pay. It is not the hours, as we work around the clock on different shift each week. It certainly isn't the family separation as most of the time you are working different shifts than your family and friends. It's the feeling that your actions make a difference. If someone needs your assistance, whether it is for protection or in time of an accident, your being there can mean the difference of life or death. That feeling of your true worth cannot be measured in terms of dollars and cents. Some hardened veterans probably would not speak of it in those terms but when you engage them in conversation and they tell you of their exploits it becomes apparent that down deep they feel the same way about it

After the Graduation we split up and went to our various assignments but not before promising to get together on our first anniversary.

I went to the 84$^{th}$ Precinct. Jim Reilly and I reported in together in our brand new uniforms. The lieutenant on the desk dutifully logged us in, assigned us lockers upstairs and then sat us down to tell us about the precinct. The 84$^{th}$ covered from Fulton Street to the Manhattan Bridge and included the Navy Yard and Sands Street. We had the East River and a hotel district. We had Myrtle Avenue and three subways. We had a black district, a public housing district, and a money district of people that had homes overlooking the harbor. In short we had all the problems you could imagine in one Precinct. He reminded us we would be expected to perform in a manner that would be acceptable in each of these areas. I would remember these tips and when I inquired of an old timer how he handled it he gave me some advice that I have used in every position I have ever held in the Police Department, the Navy and all my time in Grumman." Be polite, start slow, and keep your cool. You can always get tough if the facts warrant it but if you start out tough and you have to pull your horns in you have lost it."

Reilly and I were assigned the same shift and we became good friends. He was a very friendly fellow, always smiling and soon became accepted by the old timers. I had the good fortune to have been a fairly good softball pitcher and when this was discovered I was asked to try out for the precinct team. I not only made the team but also became the pitcher. We won the next six games and qualified for the quarterfinals. The Captain was our greatest fan and attended most of the games so I quickly became a known entity in the precinct. When we got to the semi finals we played a team in Staten Island with the best softball pitcher I have ever seen. He had pitched no hitters and we soon discovered why as we had only two hits in the game. One was mine and it wasn't much. It was a fluke off the end of the bat that spun around crazy and they couldn't field it in time to throw me out. I died on first. They could hit me and even though the team fielded well they still got two runs and eliminated us. I talked to the pitcher after the game and he told me he had pitched in the Army during the war and had gotten some expert advice and instruction from a professional. The Captain was disappointed but also recognized the other pitchers ability. They won the title later on.

I was recommended to try out for the Boroughs Base Ball team. I did and was picked up. This meant playing three games a week. It meant being taken off the chart for three days. This did not sit too well with some of the non-athletes and when the season was over I could feel some resentment. In a matter of months this was resolved. I had a lot of friends by this time and Reilly worked on the guys that resented me being gone to play ball. They all came around and at one of our outdoor outings one of them actually shuck my hand and told me he had misjudged me.

My neighbor Eddie Strubey was a Detective in the BCI (Bureau of Criminal Identification) He was teaching me to read and to classify fingerprints. When he thought I was ready he brought me over to meet his Captain. Fingerprint experts were hard to come by and eagerly sought. The Captain gave me a test and I classified ten sets of prints correctly. He then had me compare a set of prints with those in a file and pick out the ones identical. I did that successfully as well. He acted as though he was impressed but warned me my transfer would have to be approved by the Chief of Detectives. This took some time but three months later a Teletype message was received at the 84th Precinct transferring me to the BCI. Every one of my buddies knew this meant a promotion to Detective and they had a little party for me.

I had a year in the job at this time and was the first of my class to make Detective. I found out that even this had a probation period to it. It was three months later before I was called across the street to Police Headquarters and the Chief of Detectives presented me with my Gold Detective Shield. When I returned to the BCI I was asked to show my shield. The shield was thrown around the office, kicked around the floor before a smiling Ed Strubey gave it back to me. Another initiation I wasn't aware of but was happy to go through. I couldn't wait to show my Gold Shield to Joan and called her at her office and told her we would be dinning out this night. She was as happy as I was and couldn't wait to tell the folks. Work at the BCI was a Godsend. First it was day work. As Joan was still working on Wall Street we would go to work together. Different subway stops but at least we boarded the train together. She usually beat me home but that was fine too as she could shop for food on the way home.

*Shields of Honor*

My Reserve Squadron:
Top Row L-R: Skitty, Ray Ketchum, Ran Daniels, Dad Myers, Joe McGuiness, Bob Dipble
Lower: Bob Booth, Jack Sullivan, Don Grey, Tom Crowe

We could spend our evenings together and for a Policeman that was rare.

One problem that I did have was my Reserve Drills. We finger print experts would be required to work one Saturday and Sunday about every two months. You were alone in the office and had to classify and search prints that came in from recent arrests. The Detectives would wait for the results and take a copy of the yellow sheet (arrest record) with him. If a lot of prints came in you tied up Detectives because some of these searches took time. If I had a Reserve Drill that same weekend I would have to switch with a friend. One Lieutenant, in particular, hated to allow switches. I could get a copy of orders from my Squadron and give them to the Military Service Bureau of the Police Department who in turn would order me to report to the Navy. This seemed high handed and I really didn't want to go this route. It all worked out when the Captain took an interest in my flying and I could tell him of my problem. He soon solved it by having me post my Naval Reserve drill schedule well before the Saturday/Sunday roster was made up at the BCI . Post world war 2 we had entered a period referred to as the cold war. Our reserve squadrons were asked to remain combat ready and we were subject to recall to active duty should our relationship with communist Russia take a turn for the worst

I was flying with VF835 at Floyd Bennett. It was an F6F Squadron flying Grumman Hellcats. We met one weekend a month, a Saturday and Sunday. We flew a regular syllabus and kept current in all phases of our curriculum. gunnery, rockets, bombs and instruments to name a few. Once a year we would go on two weeks active duty. This would usually be performed away from our home base and would be intensive; we could expect to log over forty hours of flight time during this time frame. Our Squadron Skipper was a lieutenant commander as was our Executive Officer. We had several lieutenants and the rest of us were lieutenant junior grades and ensigns. Our Skipper was a taskmaster and any time you flew with him you were busy every minute of the flight. After take off he would contact Command and Control, break up the flight and two planes would be given one vector and the other two a second vector to separate us. Command and Control would then vector two planes in to intercept the others. We would make a number of intercepts until we reached our assigned area and then we would conduct our gunnery, bombing, strafing or instrument work. It was never boring and we became very proficient at intercepts.

One weekend we were to meet in the Station Theatre. We were given a piece of paper and told to explain why we were in the Reserve. Give the reason/s. No name was to be put on the paper. The papers were quickly collected and we were dismissed. It was until three or four months later that we were informed of the results of that simple survey. Over 90% stated PATRIOTISM. In all my years in the Service I have never forgotten that survey and the pride I felt then and still feel for my fellow Reservists. If anyone is interested I said the same thing. A lot of friends in that Squadron, Dibble, Joe McGinnis, Bob Booth, Jess Bellew, Ran Daniels, Dad Meyers, Scotty', Don Grey, Ray Ketchum, Artie Hassler, Tom Crow, and a whole lot more whose names escape me for now. The camaraderie on those two-week cruises made you proud to be a member of the Squadron. The members of that Squadron came from every economic status, Wall Street brokers to civil servants but they were united in their patriotism and their love of flying.

Now back to the BCI. Jim Hennessey and Mike Martin were two of my closest friends. Jim was a character but in the nicest way. He could get you anything and the price was always right. We wanted a television. The folks had one they paid four hundred dollars for a seven-inch set. Jim got us a second hand set, twelve inches, for 100 dollars in a place on Canal Street. On our lunch hour we always went shopping. There was always a bargain somewhere. Jim and Mike were my fishing buddies too. My Uncle Bill Hetzel lived in Rockaway. Bill had lost a leg but was still active both physically and mentally and loved to fish. My Uncle Bill Geyer had a boat but nobody to fish with. We solved that by Jim, Mike Uncle Bill Hetzel and myself getting together, helping Bill Geyer put his boat into the water and starting a semimonthly fishing trip. We had a ball. Mike and Jim would bring Horn and Hardart buns, Bill Hetzel the coffee and I supplied the transportation to Bill Geyer's house. It was a win, win situation. Bill Hetzel had a day out and enough fish and clams to last him for a week. Bill Geyer had the fishing companionship he was looking for, and

Jim. Mike and I had a lot of fun. Getting my two uncles out for a day on the water with two of my best friends was all the reward I needed.

Joan was happy. We did so much together thanks to the hours I was working. Our friends were delighted to be invited to the O'Club at Floyd Bennett. We had a membership at Fort Tilden in Rockaway Point and took our friends to the beach in the summertime. Fort Tilden was right next to Jacob Reiss Park in Rockaway. Only a fence separated it. Fort Tilden was almost like a private beach while Jacob Reiss was crowded. Jack Bowne, my old friend, and his wife would accompany us to the beach where the kids would have a ball. To this day my children speak of the great times they had at the beach.

# Chapter 6
# I'm recalled to the Navy for Korea

All good things must end and this had to as well. The Korean War had broken out. Two Squadrons from Floyd Bennett had already been called back to active duty. They had transitioned to F9F2 Panthers and soon headed to the west coast and a carrier. Dad Meyers and I received orders in September of 1952 to report to NAS Norfolk for reassignment. Joan was surprised but I think she knew it could happen. We packed all my clothes and uniforms and Dad Meyers and I were on our way to Norfolk. We were given two Squadrons in Air Group Four. Dad went to VF62 a Banshee Squadron and I was assigned to VF43 a F9F5 Panther squadron.. Both Squadrons were in NAS Jacksonville.

When we arrived I discovered my Squadron was still flying F4U 4 Corsairs. The F9F5 were there but nobody had checked out in them. Each of us was given a handbook and told to become an expert on one of the systems. Mine was the hydraulics. I was also assigned as the Administrative officer of the Squadron.

After a week of flying F4Us the Skipper decided I should get ready to fly the F9F5 Panthers. He was the first to fly a Panther. We all gathered on the runway to watch him take off. It seemed like it took him forever to lift off. Once he was air born he climbed out nicely. When he landed he remarked how long it took to get flying speed. Runway temperature was the problem. The XO (executive officer) flew next and we watched him have the same problem. Flight time wise I was the third pilot scheduled to fly. I checked the jet over very carefully. It started just as advertised and after getting an up from the plane captain taxied out to the runway. I held the brakes, advanced the throttle to 100%, released the brakes and started down the runway, I'm glad the Skipper had warned us it takes a long time to get up to speed. It seemed like forever. As the end of the runway was approaching I lifted off. The climb out was easy and the plane responded to the controls very nicely but if I had to wait for the four hundred knots the Skipper said was our climb speed I would have flown across Florida. It was a pleasure to fly the jet and it was so much faster than any of the props I had flown. I was careful to watch my fuel and headed back perhaps a little sooner than I might today. Landing was easy. The jet was heavy and stuck to the ground once I touched down. Thank God for good brakes though because it didn't want to slow down on its own. The Skipper, XO and myself compared notes and briefed the rest of the Squadron on things to look for on their first flight.

Dad Meyer's Squadron ,VF62, lost their Admin Officer. He received orders and the rest of the Squadron was going to Korea. My Squadron was not because we had just gotten the new airplanes and would not be combat ready in time to deploy. VF62 was looking for volunteers. The Korean War would be a test of all that I had been trained to do. The North Korean Communists had invaded our allies in South Korea. The United States had come to the aid of the South Koreans and a full-scale war had broken out. I wanted to volunteer as I had not had the chance to fly combat in Word War 2. I talked to my Skipper and even though he wasn't pleased he gave me permission to talk to the CAG. (Commander of the Air Group) Commander John Sweeney. I made an appointment and after some questioning he approved the transfer. I reported to LCDR Bill Kelley, the CO of VF62 and he was happy to have me on board as the new Admin Officer. VF62 had a two-week familiarization course in F2H2 Banshees. You knew the airplane before you sat in the cockpit the first time. When I returned to the Squadron I flew the Banshee for the first time.

Dad Myers was still in the initial phase of his training. Bob Murphy was our ops boss and he would lead Myers and myself. My first flight was a section take off. I was surprised but willing. When we lined up and Bob gave us the nod I was amazed at the power and the responsiveness of the Banshee. I was able to hold position with no trouble at all and even though Bob took off with only 97% power we were off the ground much sooner than the F9. The climb out was exhilarating. I couldn't believe the power and responsiveness. Bob would later put us in a tail chase and I was able to maintain my position as though I was chained onto his plane. I came back from that flight and told the folks what a difference this was from my first flight in an F9. I'm sure I was the only one at the base that had flown both of these jets and could make the comparison. Dad and I flew often because we had to make up time in the Banshee. Most of the pilots were second tour. Dad and I were the only Lieutenants that were first tour in Banshees. The new Ensigns, like us, had to fly more often to get qualified in all phases before we hit the boat (Carrier Qualified). Soon we were field carrier qualifying. Shortly after we were carrier qualifying on The Roosevelt (aircraft carrier) and preparing for our Korean Tour.

Joan had come down to join me and to take the car back home. Judith, her sister and Fran Decker, a friend had accompanied her. I took a small apartment at Jacksonville Beach with and adjoining room for the girls. We had a kitchen, for breakfast but I think all evening meals were at restaurants There were no many good ones

*CDR. Jack Sullivan USNR*

Blue convertible Joan drove home from Jacksonville.

so why not.? The girls were both good looking so I had no problem getting them dates. Also because we were on the beach everyone wanted to visit. The sand was hard, you could drive a car on it, and perfect for touch football. We had games going all the time when we were off. Our motel room had a huge picture window and after the football we would return to the motel room and have beer. We would put the empties in the picture window and stack them up. If you knocked a beer can down from the window you had to buy a case. No problem until the window was nearly loaded with beer cans then everyone would watch you carefully to make sure you didn't disturb the order of things. Knocking over a beer can would provoke howls of laughter and

*Shields of Honor*

the clumsy person heading for a new case of beer.

When we flew, the Squadrons in the Air Group would fly low over the Beach for the girl's attention and thrills. The girls loved it!! I had to go to Cherry Point to pick up one of our Banshees that had completed rework. It had no identifying marks and wouldn't have until our Squadron insignia was put on at Jacksonville. When I returned via Jacksonville Beach, naturally, I put on a show for my wife and the girls. Loops rolls and everything else. I saw a beach chair being waved and took it to be my wife. When I finished my last run I headed to the Base and later that night discovered that my wife and Fran had gone to get their hair done and only Judith had witnessed my exploits and it was she that was enthusiastically waving the beach chair.

Time to get ready to fly to our new home, The Lake Champlain. Joan and the girls had the car and started out for home. Dad Fay was nervous as a cat as neither Judith or Joan had driven any great distances before and he wanted a phone call whenever they stopped for the night. Judith started and drove as far as the first bridge then stopped. Joan had to drive over the bridge and drove the rest of the way home. I can imagine three good-looking girls in a beautiful blue convertible with the top down. How much attention they must have attracted on the road. They made it home safely and now we had to try to do the same thing aboard the Carrier.

We taxied out to take off and I lost a tire. I had a flat and had to watch my Squadron take off without me. Some of the rascals even smiled at me as they passed me bye. The Base Operations had to find a tire and wheel for me and I lost my window to the Carrier. I had gotten back to Operation when the XO returned. His gun bay doors had opened. We both would have to get permission to try again the next day. I had no money, no clothes other than my flight suite and G suite. When he came back I was saved because his wife came and picked the two of us up and I had dinner at his house in borrowed clothes. I will always be grateful Mrs. Griffin. The next day we received a message giving us a time to land and we launched. No problems this time until we arrived over the ship. The Carrier was on the continental shelf meaning big ground swells. The Carrier was rising and descending as much as forty feet. We made our approach and the LSO had to time it to catch us when the ship was fairly level. I took my cut with green water between the deck and me. Thanks to you Johnny Goodens (the LSO) I was aboard safely.

We pulled into Norfolk the following day. We all looked forward to a day in port and a night at Breezy Point bar. (the famous NAS Bar). We all had a great time and since we didn't have to fly aboard we all consumed more alcoholic beverages than was necessary. Hey the band was great, the food delicious, the girls enthusiastic what else could we do but drink and have a great time since tomorrow the nine month Korean Cruise began.

The next day we were on the way across the Atlantic We were seated in the wardroom according to rank. My seat was next to the Public Affairs Officer. He was amazed that I had been a Detective in the New York City Police Department and was heading for the Korean Police action.

. . He would listen in rapt devotion to tales of my experiences. Lastly, and certainly not the least important, was my office. I was the Administrator and responsible for all the Squadrons reports. While we were in AIRLANTS ( Commander Naval Air Force Atlantic) control we had many more reports than when we transferred to AIRPACS( Commander Air Pacific) Control. AIRPAC always referred to the difference as their being the fighting Navy and AIRLANT as being the peacetime Navy In any case our workload was greatly reduced when we transferred to AIRPAC. While in Norfolk we picked up two VIPS (very important person) The Mayor of Buffalo, New York and the author Mitchner who was writing a book called " The Bridges of Toko Ri". They would accompany us to The Mediterranean.

My old Buddy Mickey Robillard was flying with Hal Joines. They returned from a flight and Hal missed the wires and flew into the barricade. It was going to take longer to repair the barricade than Mickey had fuel. It was decided to place the big crane Tilly across the deck to prevent Mickey from plowing into the planes parked forward.

Tilly wouldn't move much but Mickey probably wouldn't survive if he didn't catch a wire. It was done and we all prayed for Mickey. He made the nicest landing to the cheers of his Squadron Mates. That event made it into Mitcner's book. We dropped Mitchner and the Mayor at Gibraltar and moved through the Med at 25 knots..

The next experience was the Suez Canal. We were the biggest ship in size and displacement to make it through the canal. We had the best navigator the canal had on board. He had a platform made so he could walk across the flight deck on the elevated platform and see both sides The Carrier was dragging the buoys down ahead so he had to see those well down the canal and make his course corrections as required. Watching him made me nervous because he appeared to be calling for the wrong correction. He knew what he was doing and we transited the canal without incident.

The Indian Ocean was next and Phil Davis told us about the size of the sharks in that ocean and had us all referring to whatever books we could find on the subject. Later on I found out he was right as I now have pictures of a 25 foot hammer head shark that lives near Diego Garcia. This monster even has a name, "Herman". We stopped in Ceylon and I even got to play a little golf.

Johnny Goodens, the LSR (Landing Signal Officer) was my partner on most of the golf trips but Bob Murphy, our Operations Officer, would join us on occasion. We found ourselves welcomed at most of the overseas Golf Courses and generally stayed to have a lunch.. We enjoyed playing Golf taking caddies, most of who claimed to have low handicaps. One told us he had only three clubs, a wood, a putter and a two iron. We asked him to show us how he hit out of a send trap with a two iron. He dropped a ball into a trap, took my two iron, opened it up and popped the ball out within four feet of the pin. We were satisfied that they spoke the truth!

From Ceylon we went to Japan where we replenished in a hurry. There was liberty but we were apprehensive about our reception from the Japanese. The waitresses at the O'Club were all Japanese and from the time we entered the Club they made us feel welcome. We had a fine meal and probably more to drink than was good for us. I remember Phil Davis, with tears running down his cheeks, telling me how sorry he was for perhaps killing some of these fine girlsans.(Japanese Slang for girls) Phil had been on some of the thousand plane raids at the end of WW2. Instead of treating it as a joke we consoled him, which testified to our sobriety. Not much chance for more liberty as we were to be on the line in a short time.

We sped to the war at 25 kts and arrived in time to launch an all out assault. Everybody flew that first day and our ready room was loud with war stories. Tours on the line was usually four weeks and then back to Japan. It was amazing how quickly we became accustomed to the Korean landscape, the features that were distinguishable, the mountains, roads and railroads were quickly memorized and I never heard of anyone that admitted to being lost. The work was broken down in phases. Phase one. Close air support. The help we gave to front line troops was most important. Sometimes the enemy was as close as 100 yards and that made our job tough. We would go to tree top level at times to ensure our accuracy. Our soldiers and marines needed the help and we provided it. Phase two. Cherokee Strikes. Just as the Indian name applies this was usually an all jet strike made with the surprise and stealth of an Indian war party. We would hit a target with from four to eight jets before they could prepare a defense. Phase three. Interdiction. We would pick up a road or railroad at the front and follow it up north. The lead jet would be at three hundred feet (sometimes lower) and the others would fly at higher altitudes These were the most exciting because you would be flying at 500 mph looking for targets of opportunity. Train, trucks and heaven help us even oxcarts. The enemy used every means of transportation to bring supplies to the front. I had a brush with death or at least captivity during one of these flights so I will tell you the tale. I was leading a flight of four Banshees up Red 11 (what we called death valley because of all the armament on this route) We hadn't seen anything worth expending a twenty millimeter shell on when we came out of a mountain pass onto a flat plateau. Before I could bring my guns to bear I had flown over a collection of boxcars. I could see people working to unload them. I sat my Banshee on its tail and climbed up to be in position to make an attack. My wingmen were already attacking and debris was shooting up from the destruction they had caused, I came in for an attack with the purpose in mind of keeping them from moving the boxcars to the tunnel they had come out of previously. I walked my twenty millimeter cannons down the first line of cars and not getting a secondary explosion I fired a rocket into the lead car. It was loaded and the resulting explosion blew holes in my aircraft, as I had to fly directly over the explosion. The speed brakes were blown to the out position. I could not climb as I should have been able and I had to break off my attack and move out of range of their guns. My wingmen protected me and attacked again while I climbed out. I was using full power to maintain 250 kts and burning fuel at a great rate.

I called for a vector to the closest emergency field. The controller came in loud and clear and I was heading to a safe landing area. The controllers voice was strong and authoritative and did much to instill confidence. When the controller called field dead ahead ten miles I did not see it nor did any of my wingmen. I got the sinking feeling the controller might have the wrong aircraft on the scope when I spotted the field. It wasn't the marson matting (steel matting bolted together in sheets) I expected but a field bulldozed out of the earth. I dropped my landing gear and headed in to land. At 550 ft I noticed my fuel was dangerously low and made a straight in approach. I landed hot but my brakes slowed me down in time to turn off the strip and onto the small taxiway before I ran out of fuel. A jeep pulled up along side before I was able to get out of my jet and the taller of the two occupants notified me he was the Catholic Chaplain and his companion was the Base Doctor. Did I need help?. The next question was am I a Catholic? When I told him I was he asked if I wanted to receive Communion? I told him I had eaten just before take off from the Carrier. He smiled and told me those rules do not apply and the shooting I hear is from the front lines. I received Communion on the spot, right next to my wounded jet.

The strip I landed on was a medical evacuation strip and I was the only jet to have landed on it. It was also right on the front lines and you could hear small arms fire at all times.

An Army mechanic brought my speed brakes in and wired them closed. The Army brought me gasoline for my Aircraft and a start unit. I was able to take off in a matter of hours for Seoul where the Marines, who had photo Banshees, could work on my aircraft. My brakes and tires were shot so I still had to be careful both in taking off and the landing and roll out. At Seoul as I was slowing down and preparing to turn onto a taxi way a jeep suddenly appeared and I had to turn away from him. I thought I was going to taxi into a ditch but my brakes held and I didn't wreck my plane. The young airmen in the jeep waved at me and hurried on never knowing how close an encounter we had. I was directed to the Marine area where they had Banshee Photo Planes and could work on my plane. They had my plane repaired in a few days. Before I left the F86 pilots asked me to demonstrate what 20 mm cannons could do. They had a block of wood that resembled a butchers block on a chain that hung over the firing range. I aimed my cannons and fired a burst and shattered the block to splinters. They all were in awe of the results and wished they had these cannons on their aircraft as they told me their 50 caliber machine guns did not do sufficient damage to the Migs unless they had a direct shot at the Migs tail. Some even said they had seen the 50 cals bounce off the Migs The trip back to the ship was coordinated with the controller and I rejoined my Squadron. I might add that the few days I spent at Seoul were with a Squadron of South Africans flying F86 Sabers. They fed me and provided me with a bed in their area. Great guys and I learned they had bought the F86s from us to fly as our allies.

Bob Murphy reminded us, in a series of lectures, that we were becoming a little too cocky, While he didn't use me as an example he could have. We took stock and became more deliberate in our flying. We returned to Japan in four weeks and enjoyed our first shore leave in a while. Goodens and I went to the Ito Peninsular for a couple of days of golf and wound up playing with two Japanese Pros. They were using the smaller English ball and were out hitting us. We caught on and tried the English ball ourselves. It traveled a lot further than the American golf ball and we were hitting eight irons when we would have been hitting seven irons. They still beat us but the game was a lot closer. Besides the golf the shopping was fantastic. I bought dishes that we still use some 50 years later. As we were going to Hong Kong on our next in port I didn't go wild with the spending.

The days we spent in port seemed to fly bye and before we realized it we were back on the line.

Our second tour was exciting. We were veterans now and were receiving our air medals. The work was the same but we now knew what to expect. My trip up red 11 was a memory but Navy Intelligence reminded me that Jet Fighter pilots were not very well treated, in fact if you wound up with the North Koreans you would be hunted down and killed. They were having some success in shooting down the props but little or none with fast flying jets. The enemy was trying to recover lost ground and we were trying to stop them. They had the numbers but we had the firepower and the communications to direct that firepower. We were flying more and rest between hops became more important than volley ball games on the forward elevator between flights.

*Shields of Honor*

The XO had found a large punching bag and it was installed just outside my stateroom. We kept the gloves on a ledge just above the bag and this became a source of exercise and a method of letting off steam. I actually became pretty good and would be asked for guidance by some of the pilots who frequented the bag. I mention this because it sometimes prevented us from getting a nap between flights.

I took movies of our carrier ops and have about 400 feet that I will some day have to have reduced to video to show my Squadron Mates at a future reunion. My family and friends might also be interested but I remember my wife's words " don't bore everybody Jack " so we will have to pick our spots. I have to talk about one hop in particular. We were to provide fighter escort for a flight of AD's (Carrier based bombers). We also carried 4- 250 lb bombs as well as a full charge of 20 mm ammo. The AD's were to bomb a certain bridge that our troops were retreating over to prevent the enemy from pursuing them. The enemy put up a lot of flack from their position but we soon suppressed it with our cannons and the AD's made their run. The CAG was flying the first AD to make a run and dropped a span. The rest of the flight demolished the bridge and our 250 lb bombs only chipped the paint on the bridge. I had personally seen what a 1000 lb bomb can to a bridge and how valuable the AD was. It was a prop but in that war a workhorse. It wouldn't be till years later the A6 would take its place.

*CDR. Jack Sullivan USNR*

    Another story I have to tell about another interesting flight. We had launched a predawn flight of four Banshees. Our task was to spot for the Battleship New Jersey. There was a road and railroad that met on a small plateau. To the north, behind a row of mountains, was where the road and railroad worked its way north. That area was protected from the sea by the mountains themselves. The New Jersey could not bring her guns to bear on the lee side of the mountains where the supplies would be stored pending surface transportation. That would be the job for the Jets. She could do considerable damage to the road and railroad on the flat plateau. Our first job was to spot for the New Jersey. They would bracket the desired aiming point by firing one-shot long and one-shot short. We would call the distance from target on both shots and they would fire a broadside. This happened and our Skipper Bill Kelly, who had been trained in spotting, would call the distance and any misalignment to the New Jersey. We were flying at 15 thousand feet and we observed it all. When Bill called in the locations of the first two shell hits the broadside was launched. We could actually see the shells coming, and they looked like a squadron of airplanes pulling contrails. We watched in awe as they demolished the road and railroad and sent debris up to two or three thousand feet.

    Bill called us back from our amazement and now we had to perform. At 15000 ft we had daylight. Behind the mountains we were in darkness and our runs were made in trail and our recovery was to be 5000 ft. While we were going down their tracers looked like rockets with long tails and their ordinary shells like tracers. There was so much of it you couldn't believe that it would be possible to make a run and escape being hit. Here is where discipline and training paid off. We each made our run and concentrated on aiming point and drop point. None of us were hit and we did considerable damage as attested by the secondary explosions. I returned with newfound admiration for the strength and firepower of a battleship. I also was proud of the way the whole flight responded to the most firepower that I remember flying through. Bill Kelly was our Skipper but also our hero. I no longer had any doubts as to how I would respond to any future engagements I would keep myself in the State of Grace, as a Catholic, and do my job as requested by the US Navy. I might cheat a bit on the Stated of Grace while in port but not while I was on the Carrier. Carrier landings were always dangerous but also fun. We would watch one another come aboard, not out of curiosity but with admiration. We all knew this was difficult and as a Squadron we were proud of the 29-second interval we maintained. Cat shots on the other hand were pure joy. We used to say the only way they could be more fun would be to have our favorite actress sitting in our lap at take off. Zero to 150 mph in two seconds. That actress would sure make a lasting impression on you.

Now lets get onto the next inport, Hong Kong. Every one of us had bought a camera or two in Japan and I think every one not on duty was on the flight deck when we pulled into Port. We wore our whites coming into Port and lined the flight deck. After quarters we went for the cameras and everyone took pictures. I had both movies and still pictures. Joan loved them and vowed to see the place for herself. Later in this narrative I will tell the story of how and when she did get to see Hong Kong. It is good reading. Well liberty was worth the wait. Johnny Goodens and I went to the golf course and it was great. We met an Airline Captain and his wife at the course and that was fortunate for me. I wanted to buy some Mickey Motto pearls and the wife took me to the Jewelry store she favored and I purchased two strands. Joan loved them and I couldn't have made her happier. We also bought some Japanese currency as the exchange rate was much better in Hong Kong.. This would be used for our next inport in Japan. The food and restaurants were super and when I mentioned them to Joan after I returned she remembered them by name and insisted we revisit them on our second trip. We also visited the Correspondents club and whenever I saw movies that depicted the club I remembered the fun times we had in that location. Hong Kong was soon a distant memory as we steamed back to the line.

*Shields of Honor*

    The third tour was memorable only because we almost lost Hal Joines. He was returning from a bombing run and passed over Wonson and Yodo Pando when he was hit in the left engine by a 37 mm Shell. The engine caught fire and Hal attempted to extinguish it to no avail. Mickey Robillard reminded Hal there was a destroyer some twelve miles off the coast of Wonson and they headed out to sea. The fire reappeared and Mickey flew above Hal and kept an eye on it. When they were over the destroyer Hal ejected from the burning plane and soon disappeared into the overcast that extended down to some 300 ft. Mickey descended into the overcast and made wide turns until he broke out at 300 ft. Hal came down in his chute and Mickey spotted him and vectored the destroyer to Hal. Sounds great but when we got Hal back on board the Champ he was livid. He said he heard Mick fly by him in the overcast missing him by feet. We all laughed at the tale because we had Hal back safely but this wasn't the last we would have of the Hal and Mick harrowing experiences. Later in the cruise they would fly a bombing hop together. Hal called for speed brakes now and poor Mick's brakes did not come out and he slipped under Hal's aircraft and before a word could be exchanged Hal had dropped a 200 lb bomb that landed in Mick's aircraft behind the cockpit in his fuel tank. Mick had a bomb in his plane sticking out halfway. The flight was aborted and Mick was directed to a Marine base in South Korea. Mick made a good

*CDR. Jack Sullivan USNR*

Returning from photo flight to Yalu River in North Korea. 1953 - "Banshees"

landing and tells of two jeeps closing on his aircraft when he slowed down. When the drivers saw the bomb protruding from his aircraft they both turned away and sped off in different directions. Mick was told to shut down on a taxiway away from the runway and the Marines approached his aircraft with care. The bomb was removed when Mick told them there wasn't enough airtime for the bomb to arm. The Plane was repaired and Mick returned to us. The Skipper said enough is enough and they were separated and put into other divisions. Sometime luck is unpredictable but there was no sense of tempting fate, at least that is how the Skipper felt at the time. The rest of us thought it was funny, but again because it ended well. One more flight that was exciting was a photo escort along the Yalu river. We had four Banshees escorting a photo Banshee along the Yalu at twenty thousand feet. We saw a Mig on the other side of the Yalu but he didn't want any part of fours Banshee fighters and he didn't track us for long. It was exciting seeing him though as it was the only time I remember seeing a Mig.

Singapore was our next inport and Johnny Goodens and I, plus the rest of our golf team were scheduled, by our Embassy, to play a British team at the Royal Singapore Golf Club. We arrived early in the morning and found the course to be wet and lush. It was easy to stop the ball on these greens and we all played fairly well. Johnny and I shot in the seventies and the rest of the team in the low eighties. We had lunch and went out for another 18 holes. It wasn't the same course because the hot sun baked the course and the balls not only wouldn't hold, they bounced on the greens as though off a concrete road. The scores skyrocketed and everyone shot much worse than the morning round, to the amusement of our British hosts. We finished the golf and went to the clubhouse, showered and changed, and attended a cocktail party in our honor. I was thirsty and treated the gin and tonics as though they were soft drinks. While I didn't get sick I did become a source of amusement for my British hosts and my teammates. We had a fine meal and later that evening was jolted when a series of alarms went off. There was a flurry of activity and several of the servants were given guns and they scurried off toward one of the holes. On the peaks of the clubhouse roof spotlights were lit and the servants moved toward one of the greens. My British playing partner told me that a tiger had been spotted on one of the holes. It seems the golf course had been built on the edge of the jungle and every once in a while a tiger would come onto the course and make a bed on one of the greens. He would circle just like a housecat and tear up the green to make him/her self-comfortable. A green is hard to replace hence the urgency to drive the tiger back into the jungle. Great story but we all wondered how many of us looked appetizing to that same tiger as we passed his territory in the jungle. The Brits laughed at our concern and their reassurances didn't quite sell with us. My father-in-law would later quip he heard of a lot of lion (lying) on the golf course but the first time of a tiger. The tale was told later on to the wardroom crowd and they had a million questions as though they didn't believe the story.

Another tale has to be told. Again Johnny Goodens and I were together and doing a little club hopping. Someone suggested to us that we visit Bill Baileys place. It was a hangout for Americans that were working in Singapore. Good idea! We took a cab and soon arrived at what appeared to be a house. The bottom floor was a bar and the old gent behind the bar was the famous Bill Bailey himself. Those of you who are old enough will remember Jimmy Durante, a famous comedian of the forties and fifties. Well Jimmy used to sing a song called Bill Bailey won't you please come home. This was that Bill Bailey. They had been Vaudeville companions and Bill Bailey had gone on a tour of the far east with his wife, liked Singapore so well that they decided to stay. Their bar was famous and always packed. Bill was a great guy and when time permitted told us tales of the old days in vaudeville that had us bent in two with laughter. He knew everyone and while he never had a bad word to say about anyone he sure knew all the funny events in their lives. While I was sitting there at the bar I overheard a conversation the couple next to me were having. They were obviously Americans and surely from New York. They were getting ready to leave and he said" lets bounce over to Lucky's". That prompted me to ask "are you a policeman?" He looked at me funny and said "I was a New York City Detective" When I told him I was as well and that I'm a Navy Pilot that had been recalled for the Korean War the conversation started. He was Johnny Reardon and I knew his brother Jimmy. His wife asked me where I lived and when I told her she was in utter disbelief as she lived only a few blocks from me in Brooklyn and we knew a lot of the same people. They were disappointed to hear that this was our last night in Singapore. We spent the rest of the night with them and wished we had more time. John knew the city like the back of his hand and I suspect he would have enjoyed having me around to back up some of the Police stories he had told to some of the expatriates. We said our goodbyes to Bill and the Reardons and headed back to the ship. My father-in-law loved hearing about Bill Bailey as he had seen him on the stage many times. Years later I would read a story in Time or Newsweek about a reporter who had stumbled on Bill Bailey while in Singapore and it was refreshing to hear the old gent was still active and his bar as popular as ever.

The next line period was exciting, the war was ending or at least that was the scuttlebutt. The North Koreans and their Chinese allies were trying to take back as much of the territory as possible since the 38th parallel would not be the new boundary but whatever territory the side held at the armistice. We were called on to bomb bridges, interdict troop movements and in general hold up an advance the enemy might attempt. The truce talks continued while this flurry of activity continued. I led a strike over the beach and we dropped bombs with time-delayed fuses on an airfield. It was a milk run by comparison to earlier strikes. I'm not even sure the enemy fired on us. When I returned to the ship I had lots of fuel and was asked to relieve the cap.(carrier air patrol) The F9s didn't have our fuel capacity, or our time on station so this was a common occurrence. We singled up.(cut one engine to conserve fuel) and flew at 25 thousand feet over the fleet. When we were called down

My wounded jet and me heading back to carrier.
1953 - "Banshee" Jack's Plane

we lit the other engine and prepared to land. I made the first pass and while I had a Roger pass I was waved off. The rest of my flight landed uneventfully and I made my final approach and landed. While I was still in the wire I noticed pictures being taken of my aircraft. It turned out the war ended while we were flying the cap and I had the honor of leading the last strike and making the last carrier landing of the Korean War. New York Cop Blows Whistle on the Korean Police Action was the way it was recorded and I was flown from the ship that night on the COD to appear on television in Tokyo later on. Fine by me, it was an extra night of shore leave in Tokyo and financed by the US Navy. I wrote a story for the New York City Police Magazine "SPRING 3100" and it was published in the December 1953 issue.

*CDR. Jack Sullivan USNR*

What was great was that my old buddies in The Police Department at least knew I had made it through the war thus far.

We returned to Japan in a few weeks. We had been scheduled to return earlier as our relief had arrived on station but the Navy decided to keep five Carriers on the Line until everything settled down. I'm sure the North Koreans and the Chinese had a problem getting the word to their troops that the war was over. I think we were not trusting the other side and five Carriers were a big stick.

After a farewell to Japan, and a big buying spree we headed out to sea. The plan was an around the world cruise with stops in several South American ports where we were to put on air shows for the folks. Rio was one of them and plans called for my Squadron to be hosted aboard a big private yacht belonging to a friend of our engine reps. This all went out the window when some of the crew of one of our Navy Ships visited a temple in Ceylon and took some of the artifacts. We had to rendezvous with that Ship at sea and collect all the artifacts. The South American cruise was cancelled and I don't name that Ship because even now I'm still mad at the turn of events that caused us to lose that part of the cruise. We had to return to Ceylon and hand over the artifacts to the legitimate owners. We stayed several days in port at the request of the Embassy. Our Carrier had a good reputation and the Government welcomed us. Again we went to play golf. This golf game I will never forget. One of the gang had to stay behind to finish a report. When he finished he would join us at the golf course and perhaps play nine holes .I was on the eighteenth green when Bob caught up with us. He gave me a telegram announcing that my son John had been born on the first of November. I can't remember being so happy. Joan was fine and my son was a handsome baby. I don't remember much after that as we retired to the bar and I became the recipient and sponsor of numerous rounds of drinks. Son you were toasted more that day than any day save your wedding. More than one toast wished that you would resemble you mother rather than your homily old dad. I can say, with pride now, that you turned out just fine

We had to return to the States via the same route we had come over. We made one deviation to make sure we crossed the equator and we all were initiated in to the realm of King Neptune. We all sported bruises for a week as those that had been initiated on an earlier occasion were anxious to make sure we remembered the crossing. It was fun! Anyone who has crossed the equator on a ship will remember the experience as it has been an initiation practiced for ages. I would imagine it is more civilized on a commercial ship. On a Navy ship the old salts made sure you remembered .

We visited ports in the Med and on one of these we went to buy some perfume in Nice. We had inported in Cannes and Dad Myers rented a small Fiat automobile. Mickey Robillard, Dad, Johnny Goodens and I were in the car, believe me we filled it. We had to transverse some mountains to get there. The factories were in these mountains. Dad wasn't interested in buying perfume so he went to a small bar alongside the factory while we shopped. When we came out Dad was toasting with some Frenchmen he met in the bar. I don't think either Dad or the Frenchmen knew what the other was saying but the toasting continued until we were introduced. We headed back with Dad at the wheel. Mickey was amazed at how well the little car held the road in the turns and asked Dad " I wonder what this little car can do?" That did it. Dad stepped on the gas and we flew around curves. Johnny and I looked at each other in disbelief as any wrong turn would catapult us over the small guardrail. We both yelled and Dad let up on the gas to make the rest of the trip sort of uneventful. Mick looked like he was disappointed the thrill was gone.

 The Captain of the Lake Champlain was a golfer and on more than one occasion he would ask the CAG to get Johnny Goodens and me and go plays some golf. It happened often enough that Bill Kelley, my Skipper would anticipate it.' We played in Cannes and teed of behind the Prince of Monaco. The Captain was invited into the Clubhouse to have a drink with the Prince. While we met him at several tee boxes only the Captain was invited into his conversation. Later we went to the casino and tried our luck at the various tables. I played black and red on the roulette table and won a bit. When I had doubled my money I quit knowing the story I could tell would be worthwhile. Not many people can say they doubled their money at Monte Carlo. The Lake Champlain did make a formidable presence in the harbor and when we told people at the Casino we were pilots on this Carrier they were impressed. The trip home was uneventful, not much flying and I had to prepare the same reports that I had successfully avoided while reporting to Air Pac.

When we approached the Coast the airgroup prepared to depart. As my wife wasn't in Jacksonville I was selected to remain aboard and see to the mundane task of offloading the Squadrons material. It was sad to watch them all leave. We would tie up inport the next day but the gang was gone and it marked the end of some of the most exciting days of my life. I remember reading a book called "SHORE LEAVE" and in it the author said Chorus Girls and Navy Fighter Pilots will always live in the past. I understood what he meant. I have had jobs that required more responsibility, but for sheer adrenalin flow nothing compares to that experienced by a wartime fighter pilot. In the quite of their own thoughts I think even our most distinguished Admirals will admit those were the days. We followed up a successful flyoff with an orderly transfer of Squadron materiel to dockside and hence to the Squadron spaces in Jacksonville.

We were in a stand down which meant not too much would be going on in the Squadron. Leave had been requested and granted. I asked the Skipper if I could take a Banshee and go home and see my family and newborn son. He really didn't want any airplanes away from the base but as I had given my seat up to one of the Junior Officers to fly off in my stead he said OK. I had two days I could keep the aircraft on the ground at Floyd Bennett Field. I called home and was welcomed by the sound of my son crying. When I told them I was flying home they asked when and at what time. I would be leaving the next day and at about 10 AM. They were going to have my folks over for dinner that day so it would be perfect. I would fly over the house to let you know when I arrived. Joan allowed as she could tell the wail of the Banshee and would take off for Floyd Bennett to pick me up. I had tremendous tail winds and the radar station informed me I had ground speed of 700mph while going up the coast at 40000ft. I kept my speed to within 10kts of my mach and asked for a high speed break at Floyd Bennett. I passed over the field at 500kts and headed for the gold dome of Brooklyn College. This would take me over the Fays house. I passed over Dyker Beach golf course and landed some 8o minutes from take off at Jacksonville. Did they hear me you ask? Everybody I spoke to the next day heard me, One woman in the butcher shop overheard me telling the story to the butcher. She asked "was that you? I prayed for you because I thought there was going to be an accident." Yes Joan heard and jumped into the car and headed to Floyd Bennett. She met me in Operations as I was explaining to a bunch of pilots how I maintained that speed. A joyful reunion with Joan and I drove my car home to the Fays. My folks were there and couldn't believe I had made it that fast. We had a joyful reunion all around. Joan looked at me and said "don't you want to see your son?" I ran upstairs and there he was smiling and having a good time in his crib or was it a bassinet. Anyway he looked handsome and he certainly wasn't afraid of me. He smiled at me as though to say hey I like everybody. I held him for the first time and that beautiful boy smelled so good. Babies have a scent of their own. I could tell, from her expression, that Joan was proud of her work in making this baby. My joy at seeing him for the first time was reflected in her eyes that were filled with tears. We hugged and John was in the middle of that hug. Those moments were precious.

Since John was awake now we decided to take him downstairs with us. More love awaited him there, the grandparents. I suddenly became as invisible as the fly on the wall. John was the center of attention and I was no longer there. I wanted to remind everyone that I had flown up from Jacksonville at great expense when John looked at me. My mother said "look he sees his father". I became visible again. We sat down to eat and every gurgle, coo or groan from John drew everyone's attention. With all this attention it is amazing he never was spoiled

The brief time I had at home was soon gone and I had to fly back. The whole family drove down to Floyd Bennett to watch me take off. There were no jets in the Reserve at this time so my take off attracted attention from Station Personnel as well. I taxied out to the end of the runway, received my clearance, held the brakes and ran the engines up to 100%. Releasing my brakes I held the jet on the runway to well past flying speed and hauled it up and rolled it as I climbed out. Joan told me my mother was scared but everyone else was thrilled. She said even the mechanics were talking about it. The Banshee could perform. No record time on the return. I had to buck some of those winds on the return.

When I returned to the Squadron I had to complete the check out of my replacement. I elected to return to civilian status as the war was over. Both the CAG and my Skipper tried to talk me into staying but my son had to spend his early years near his grandparents. The CAG told me he had orders to Shape Headquarters in Paris and if I was interested he could have a set of orders cut putting me in his Command. I didn't tell Joan about this but when the CAG visited us in our little apartment in Brooklyn later on he told her about the offer. Joan looked at me and I knew I was in trouble. She told the CAG she had always wanted to see Paris. Later, after he had left, she said I had made the best decision. Little did she know what fate had in store for her.

We were in a stand down mode in the Squadron. Not much work and Johnny Goodens and I found time for some golf. Jack Harvey, the Jacksonville Pro, even talked me into buying a new set of clubs. One of the Station Pilots flew me up to Floyd Bennett in a TV2 (two place jet) and I spent the night with Joan and drove the car back to Jacksonville the next day. Joan could borrow my sister's car during the day so she didn't miss it that much. My last days were filled with parties. The CAG and the Skipper had some nice things to say after my Squadron Mates had ribbed me about my coffee drinking, my nagging them about getting their reports in on time and my insistence that when they used the punching bag they return the gloves to my desk draw. The Skipper had a lot of real nice things to say and then he ended by saying "Sully you are the only Naval Officer that I ever met that was in the Navy on a golf scholarship" The CAG was complimentary and then he wound up with "Bet you are going to miss those little martini parties you guys had aboard the ship" That brought gales of laughter from the crowd and we thought we had a close knit group of martini drinkers that met in secret for our one martini each night. Heck we even kept the stuff locked in our safes. Soon I had said my last goodbyes to a gang I had fought a war with. I was on my way home with their names forever etched in my memory. My Skipper Bill Kelly, my Exec Ted Griffin, Homer Morrow (we shared a stateroom) Dad Myers (my old Squadron mate from the Reserves and a fellow NYC Cop) Jock Geannakouri, Johnny Goodens (my golfing partner), Bob Murphy (our ops boss), Norm Claeys, Hal Jouines, Will Chard, Al Rowe, Phil Davis(my other buddy in a three man stateroom),George Watters, Ken Coleman, J.W Smith, Charlie Chech, Bud Murray, Bill Bickert, Mick Robillard, Bob Newman, Dewey Powell(my wingman) and Ed Amende. I was honored to have flown with these men and they will always be remembered as FRIENDS. My fond memories will always include the CAG, Cdr. John Sweeney who was not only a friend but a golfing companion as well. Many of us would meet again but that is for another part of this story. I think I speak for all Navy pilots when I say the people you go into combat with will always enjoy a special place in you heart and memories.

# Chapter 7
# Back to the Police Department

Now I return home to soon rejoin my family and friends. My wife awaited me in my little apartment on Troy Avenue. There was now a small bassinet in the room filled with a life I helped produce. I say that filled with humility as God and my wife did all the heavy lifting but I couldn't help but admire the result. It seemed he always had a smile for his Dad and took all the love and admiration he received without expecting it on a continuous basis. He was content to amuse himself with the beams of light that played across his room and the shadows they formed. He was never alone for long but didn't demand attention. In short he was a pretty special kid and worthy of being loved. Many of the items I had brought from my tour of duty remained in boxes. There was no place to put them in our small apartment. Joan had not gone back to work since John was born and was now a full time mother and wife. I had to report back to the Police Department.

I checked into the Military Service Bureau and filled out the required paper work. I soon had my badge and gun back from the Property Clerk and reported into the BCI. I was welcomed back by all my buddies. The representative of Naval Intelligence, came by to see me .He had worked out of our office and was considered one of us He told me that when I was called back to active duty in the Navy he had been tasked to update my Secret Clearance. He remarked it was the first time he had to update a clearance on a friend and had added a little verbiage in the remarks section to indicate personal knowledge of the subject. He laughingly remarked you won't go beyond Lieutenant, Sully.

While I was in the Navy I thought about my work in the Detective Division and decided I would apply for a Precinct Squad when I returned. I had a warm chat with my Captain and received his permission to speak to the Chief of Detectives. An appointment was made and in a few days I found myself in his outer office chatting with his Captain and Chief of Staff. He was fascinated by my stories of flying Jets in Korea and must have told the story to the Chief of Detectives because when I was ushered into his office, a few minutes later the first thing the Chief asked me was my rank in the Navy. He had been in Naval Intelligence in Word War 2 and we swapped war stories for a few minutes before I could state my request. He listened and told me he would like to assign me to BOSSI (Bureau of Special Services and Investigation) . He explained this was the Squad that investigated subversives, corruption in labor unions and was tasked to serve as bodyguards for all vips that come into the City including the President and Vice President of the United States. I really wanted a Precinct Squad and he finally agreed but told me I would be put on BOSSI's list of people to call whenever the President or Vice President came to the City. He was true to his word because I guarded every President from Truman to Nixon. I worked with the Secret Service and had a chance to get to know some of them real well. My Navy experience bonded me to many of them and there are a few stories to tell about my experiences with some of the Presidents, but all in good time.

The Chief had me assigned to the 61 Squad in Brooklyn. It was located on Avenue U and East 15 Street. The Squad Commander was Lieutenant Ed Murphy, a giant of a man some 6 feet 8 inches tall. I was very impressed. He assigned me to a team. Tom Scully and Jim Ryan were to be my partners. Your partners in the Detective Squad are like you wingman in a Fighter Squadron. Even closer, because Detectives work with their partners for hours on end and have to count on them for full time help In Detective work you are always at war. There are always bad guys out there and your partners are your backup. I don't say this lightly and any Detective will tell you your partner becomes as close as a brother. You know his reactions to any given situation and you adjust accordingly. Scully and Ryan took me under their wing. They recognized that I had adjustments to make, routines to learn. Paper work in a Detective Squad is complicated. For months I had to ask questions and make corrections to mistakes I had made. Scully and Jim were patient and with a lot of study and hard work I mastered the paperwork. In time I even became something of a resident scholar and others would come to me with questions. While learning about the paperwork I was also learning about Squad work. Jim Ryan was the more experienced of the two and watching the way he would handle a complainant, the question he would ask that would be pertinent to identifying perpetrators would always be valuable to me in the future. Jim was a professional, he reminded me of the old timers I had worked with in uniform. He had a lot of the same characteristics. He was smooth, put people at ease, if that was his purpose, but could always alter his mood and conversation, if required. He was a study. Tom recognized Jims ability but could play the bad cop to perfection when needed. They were a good team and I stayed in the background unless physically needed.

Although it was hard work I gradually became part of the team and within a year could act on my own. I should explain this a bit further. I did catch cases and I did work them much earlier than the year I mentioned but I had my partners to back me up. At the end of the year I had enough experience to go out on my own and work cases without assistance. I had the knowledge and self-confidence to handle any situation that might arise. We were often so busy that it became necessary for each of us to work independently. In other words at the end of the year I was a full-fledged precinct Detective and could work with anyone.

In one important case four young men held up a beauty parlor thinking there was a safe containing a great deal of cash. It was misinformation but thinking the Beauty Parlor owner was holding out on them the inflicted great pain on the owner and some of her clientele. When we arrived we found twelve women in a hysterical state. Seperating them and questioning them we obtained a description of these men for an alarm. Two of the women agreed to go to the BCI to view the mug shots of men previously arrested for similar crimes. Two of the perpetrators were identified from mug shots. We looked at those listed on their sheets as having been arrested with them on similar crimes. Armed with these names and addresses we mustered a force of Detectives and made a series of raids on their homes. While this reads like a well-oiled machine let me say that it took several days to accomplish. Addresses had to be checked to ascertain whether they were current. One mistake and we could lose the arrest because if they were forewarned in any manner they would flee. We made the arrest and they were identified in a lineup. They were convicted in Court and wound up in Sing Sing Prison. Usually you learn a lot about the case from different sources. From a different source I found out they had learned that a bookmaker had financed the beauty parlor and that it was their understanding he had a safe put in the parlor to keep his money. He did indeed finance the beauty parlor but he did not put a safe in it.

Another case, while not as violent, turned out to attract more attention. A young lad came to the precinct to report his bike was stolen. He didn't know the name of the thief but could identify him if he saw him again. We put him in the Detective car and drove him in the direction the thief had gone. Sure enough the lad saw him and we caught him. After questioning him at the Squad Office he admitted to having stolen a number of bikes. He would sell them to classmates at high school or anyone else at school who wanted them. Everyone, including his teacher thought he was repairing old bikes and selling them. He had a good reputation and a list of would be clients waiting for cheap bikes. His memory was phenomenal and he identified all the people he had sold bikes to at school. We had a police truck go to the school and collected the bikes he had stolen. All the buyers cooperated and the bikes were turned in without any arguments. Over fifty bikes were collected that day, the serial numbers were taken from the bikes and compared to the bikes reported stolen in our precinct. Some came from outside the precinct and the neighboring precincts were notified to search their files. The newspapers got the story and the human-interest aspects of the case were great news. I was billed as the Detective who broke up a Bicycle theft ring. It was one kid with an idea that would earn him money and make him popular with his buddies. In those days not everyone would lock their bike when they went to a store and if they didn't he would grab it an drive away with it . Juvenile Court made him grow up in a hurry.

Jim Ryan was put with another Detective whose partner retired so Tom Scully and I became the team. Tom's brother was the chief of security at an apartment complex called Beachaven. We would visit his office often because it was in our Precinct and because Tom wanted to make sure his brother had no problem he couldn't handle. We often took care of some of the minor problems he had just by showing up when he visited the offender. One day we had just come from Tom's brother's office and were sitting in the car at the corner of Avenue X and McDonnell Ave. A radio message informed us of a robbery in a liquor store in Coney Island, our neighboring Precinct. The license and the description of the car were given and we were made aware the car was heading down McDonnell Avenue towards Avenue U. We were in the perfect place to intercept and waited for the car to make its appearance. Sure enough the brown Cadillac came speeding towards us, made a high speed turn on Avenue X, almost hitting us and preceded down Avenue X. We turned and followed him at high speed. We were now directly behind him. If he remained in a straight line he might have run away from our old Plymouth but he turned and we closed. On a side street with nobody on it I fired a shot and saw a puff from his roof. A second shot and the car went out of control smashing into a parked car. The driver of the Cadillac was bleeding from the loose flesh in the front of his neck. We pulled him from the car and put him in our car and sped to the hospital with me holding my handkerchief to his neck. The Police cruisers were behind us with sirens blasting so the hospital personnel were waiting for us when we arrived.

The prisoner was taken to emergency and only after he was examined and treated did we hear that my second shot had gone through his neck avoiding hitting his windpipe, jugular vein and spinal cord. He was lucky to be alive. He was out of the Hospital in ten days and I took him to Court for arraignment. On the way he thanked me for not shooting to kill. A chase at 60 mph on bumpy streets and me taking aim with my arm extended out the side window and sighting through the windshield and he thanked me for not shooting to kill. My partner could hardly contain himself on hearing that and the Detectives at the Squad were hysterical with laughter when he told them the story. However the best is yet to come. When we arrived at the Court and I filled out the arraignment cards we waited to see which Judge would be sitting. When he came in we knew it would be an interesting day because he was very demonstrative behind the bench and very seldom sat down. He would take over the questioning of a prisoner or complainant if he was not satisfied. When my case was called it attracted a lot of attention because of the shooting and the violent crime that had preceded it. The District Attorney was questioning me on the chase when the Judge interrupted him. Just a minute Detective you told the court that the car was approaching at 60 mph how could you read a license plate at that speed. I answered. Your Honor I have just recently returned from Korea where I was a Navy Jet Fighter Pilot and the Naval Intelligence interrogators expected me to see things at 600 mph and report. The judge threw his hands up over his head and turning to the court reporters said "did you hear that, did you hear that." This man is a Navy Jet Pilot and I'm asking him how he can see a plate at 60 mph. This is a story. Copy it all. The poor Perpetrator and his lawyer realized their case was through. He was held on no bail and the Judge asked me to come to his chambers He then declared a lunch recess and took me to lunch. When I came back Scully said to me, "Sully you could step in dog doo doo and come up with a fifty dollar bill". Anytime I went into that Judge's court after that and he saw me he would interrupt the proceedings and introduce me as an outstanding example of the people the Police Department attracts. I took a lot of ribbing from fellow detectives but it was in good humor and they all would admit it was unusual for this Judge to harbor good thought about any Policeman.

## Chapter 8
## My Reserve Squadron

When I went to my Reserve drills I would have to tell my Squadron Mates about the cases I was working on and this one had them in hysterics. It was funny, most of these fellows were WW2 types. They had good jobs, some on Wall Street, some in their own businesses but my stories interested them. I guess I had more action in a week than they did in a year and they were genuinely interested in hearing about it. Some of the wives I met would ask my wife if she wasn't terrified every time I went to work. I didn't tell Joan all the stories I told them for that very reason. We were getting ready to check out in F9F6 Jets (Cougars) but people considered my job as a Detective dangerous. My fellow Detectives worried about me flying supersonic Jets and thought that was dangerous, I guess when you have an outsiders perspective you see only the dangerous side. As a Detective I enjoyed the challenge of the job. It could be dangerous but you learned to anticipate the problem areas and took precautions wherever it was possible. Flying jets posed similar problems but again you learned to anticipate problems. As a backup you studied your emergency procedures and were prepared to execute them at the first sign of danger.

We went to ground school for two weeks when we transitioned to the F9F6. Having flown Jets in Korea I was in a position to help my Squadron Mates check out in this new Aircraft. They were all amazed at the speed and rate of climb of the Jets. It was a marked improvement over the war weary props they had been flying. After they had a couple of fam hops (Familiarization flights) I took them up for combat training. The heights the Jets can reach, their speed and rate of closure when performing combat maneuvers troubled them in the beginning. They imagined they would never be able to keep track of the other jet. After a few hops they became more accustomed to the speed of closure and began to perform almost as well as they had in props. Like my old Squadron Commander Bob Dibble, I worked with them on intercepts. They remarked that it was more difficult to spot jets at a distance than it had been props but again after several flights they improved. Flying a jet was easier in many ways than a prop. There was no mixture control or RPMs to worry about . The throttle and computer controlled your power. The aircraft was infinitely smoother. A jet engine has almost no vibration and the power much greater than a prop. My Squadron Mates progressed quickly and while there was a certain apprehension on the part of some it gradually faded with time. By the time we were ready for our two week cruise they were looking forward to the adventure.

We went to Olather Kansas and were to drill there for the two weeks. Olather was a base the Navy had used for checking out pilots in Jets so they were well equipped to handle our Squadron. We worked hard and made tremendous progress.

Our Skipper had his own Contracting Business. He bid on a program in South America that would have more than doubled his business. He made several trips to the site and discovered he could not count on transportation back and forth in a timely manner. It would have meant giving up the Squadron and the Reserve. He turned down the project and elected to remain in the Reserve and hold onto the Squadron. It was an outstanding tribute to the man and his dedication to the Naval Reserve. Jim was a true leader but this didn't prevent us from playing a joke on him. We had a storm projected to hit us in two days and drop at least 20 inches of snow on the Base. The storm would halt our flying for several days so I suggested that we fly around it and return to the Base after it passed. Our route would take us to El Paso in the south to Las Vegas in the west and Colorado in the north . We would R.O.N (remain over night) in each of those places and send the Skipper a RON message from each of those Bases signaling our safe arrival. We landed in El Paso and as we taxied in we saw a group of stewardesses walking across the taxiway and signaled for them to wait for us. The girls waited till we had gotten out of the jets and we discovered in our conversation with them they were proceeding to Mexico City, We gave them our Skippers name and where he could be reached in Colorado. We then provided them with our bureau numbers and asked that they send the Skipper a telegram RON ing (remain over night) the planes in Mexico City. A true RON was sent to Olather with the airplanes RON in El Paso. The Skipper had flown ahead with our Navy Advisor to attend a conference in Colorado. The girls did as requested and when the Skipper received the message at the BOQ the Navy advisor said the paper jumped in his hand. He couldn't believe it and handed the paper to the Advisor to read. The Advisor told us he couldn't believe it. They can't leave the country with out permission. They will be court marshaled. I can't believe this. The Advisor said a telegram isn't official lets check with Olther. Oleather's answer settled the matter but the Skipper would find a way to even the score. We weren't through with our fun yet. We had a great night in El Passo and an even greater night across the boarder. ( R rated)

The next day we were on our way to Las Vegas. We flew across the Grand Canyon, low enough to admire the years of erosion necessary to form this most spectacular site. We landed at Nellis Air Force Base at Las Vegas and were treated royally by our Air Force counterparts. Three of us were Lieutenant Commanders and Jeeps were sent out for us. All of us climbed into the Jeeps. The junior officers kidded us and acted like the aides to the Lieutenant Commanders. One took the cord from a Venetian blind and braided it to resemble an aide and hung it from his left shoulder. He then went to the bar, to the head of the line, and bought drinks for the Commanders. With a little instigation he went to the front desk and ordered transportation into town for the Lieutenant Commanders. To the amazement of all transportation was provided and we headed to town in our Navy Green Uniforms. We went to one of the Casinos featuring a Minsky Burlesque review. Naturally there were no seats but the young JG with the Venetian Blind Cord told the managers that the Lieutenant Commanders had been flown in from the east at great expense and would he please provide ample seating for the Squadron. Again it worked and a table was hastily provided in a choice part of the room for the Lieutenant Commanders and the Squadron. The show was spectacular, the girls breathtaking and then out came the comedian, Moe Raft. I had seen Moe Raft perform at the Brooklyn Star in 1938. Margie Hart was the headliner. When Moe was finishing his act he asked the audience if there was any act they had seen him perform before and would like to see again. I yelled" the drugstore act where he is going down to the cellar ". He stopped and said I haven't done that one for years but set up the table with the table cloth hanging to the floor and promptly performed it. He would walk and bend his knees to imitate walking down steps until his head disappeared behind the table. Then he would come back up again in the same manner. It brought the house down just as it had those many years ago at the Brooklyn Star. After he finished the show he came back to our table and asked who had asked for that act. I told him of seeing him in the Star in 1938 with Margie Hart. He sat with us and asked where we were from. When we told him New York he stayed with us and told us stories of the old Burlesque until he had to get ready for his next show. What a guy and what stories he told us that night. After the show we went to the casino and played the slot machines. . Nobody won but we had a lot of fun. One of the gang had a little luck at blackjack but again, in time, lost it all back. While we waited for him we ran into Jimmy Durante in the lobby and he thought we were Marine Flyers and wouldn't let us correct him so for the time he was in the lobby we were Marines. He is just as funny in person as he is on the stage. One of the elderly gents was sleeping on a couch, Jimmy woke him and said "when Durante is awake everybody is awake" It was like a floor show and he had the whole lobby laughing. When he left he said so long Marines and we all said so long Jimmy. We had transportation back to the Base and took off the next morning for Colorado.

The JG with the Venetian Blind Cord still had it on and kept it on through out the trip. When we landed in Colorado we were in for a surprise the runway was 12000 ft long. This was a snap because we could land on one 5000 ft and have plenty or room. Heck we could even turn off at an earlier intersection. Imagine our surprise when we passed through 6000 ft without slowing down for a turn off. The altitude of the airport was over 5000 ft and the air was thin at that altitude. More than one of the Cougars took the whole runway and turned off at the last intersection. When we parked the Skipper came over and caught us in the operations department. He started to read us the riot act for our first RON in Mexico City but couldn't carry it out and burst into laughter. He told us he couldn't believe it but wasn't certain till he checked El Paso and found out they closed our flight plan there. We had a good laugh and told him of some of out high jinks in the Mexican border town. I won't repeat them to keep this story from getting an "R" rating (or worse). We checked into the BOQ and went to dinner. The JG still wearing the Venetian blind cord . At the bar later he ordered all the drinks telling our Air Force counter parts he was the aide to the Commanders. He had done such a good job in braiding that everyone of them thought he was an aide and nobody called him on it. He even got first call on drinks and the other Officers deferred to him.

The storm had passed Olatha and the runways were clear of snow. Preparations were made to fly back to Olatha. The trip back was uneventful and we landed in Olatha and checked into our ready room. The enlisted men had been enjoying themselves while we were gone. No planes to take care of and the maintenance officer had given them some liberty. Word got out about our trip and some of the adventures we had. They wanted to see the JG and the Venetian blind cord braid. You are probably wondering why I don't name the JG, well future events will supply the answer. We had a syllabus to fly and had lost several days because of the weather. We flew into the night to recover the lost time. The airplanes stayed up and we lost little flight time to maintenance. A day before we were to return we had completed our syllabus and had even more time than originally scheduled because of our flight around the storm. It was a successful two weeks. All we had left was a flight to Memphis. We would RON there and then head back to New York.

We landed in Memphis, checked into the BOQ. I felt a strange emotion. I had gone to E Base here as a Cadet. The BOQ was a place I had never set foot in before. It was the Holy of Holies, the place where the instructors lived. Now I was entering it with a rank superior to any of them. After a shower we headed over to the O'Club for a Squadron happy hour. While we were drinking a Commander noticed the Venetian blind cord on the JG. Instead of seeing the humor in it he was going to call him on it. He addressed him and berated him for mocking the Aides. We gathered around when the Skipper stepped in and asked the Commander for his date of rank. One Commander to another and happily he was junior to our Skipper. The Skipper took him aside and in a few minutes they were both laughing. The Skipper told him the whole story, particularly the part in Nellis AFB where the JG had jumped the line to get drinks for the Commanders. He waved to us and departed for parts unknown leaving the aide to do his job. Smitty had been worried and had asked us if he should remove the braid while the Skipper was talking to the other Commander. Silly as it sounds we all had a lot of fun with the Venetian blind cord. If I were on active duty I don't think I would have liked it but we were a lot looser in the Reserve. When we returned to Floyd Bennett he removed the braid and everything returned to normal. I have talked a lot about the reserve but in post WW2 it was different. My Squadron Mates came from every walk of life. We had lawyers, wall street brokers, businessman and Airline Captains in our Squadron. All of which lost a lot of money being away from their jobs for two weeks. It didn't matter to them. The thrill of flying a high performance jet and the camaraderie were what counted. They wore the uniform as patriots. I think ww2 was the last time the Country could count on all classes and economic strata to be in uniform together. The all volunteer force changed that and the economic elite are under represented. In my Squadron that was not true.

Now on the personal level Joan was pregnant with our second child. I had an accident and had something in my eye that had to be removed by the doctor, It caused me to wear an eye patch and I could not drive because of the drops I had to put in my eyes. One morning Joan announced that her water broke and I had to notify her Doctor. He insisted she be taken to Midwood Hospital immediately. I called her sister Judith and she responded at once with her car. Judith suffered with back problems and as luck would have it this was one of those times. You have to picture Judith driving, Joan sitting in the middle and one eyed Jack sitting on the outside as a lookout. Joan was hysterical with laughter saying she was the only one fit to drive. We arrived quickly and safely and Joan was ushered into the labor room. A few hours later the Doctor came out to tell Judith and me that Joan had a beautiful baby girl. Maura was the name we had given her and although she was early she was over eight pounds and as beautiful a baby as you can imagine. From the moment of her birth she was an independent force. After John and his docile nature Maura was a tiger. John was crazy about her and there was no sibling rivalry. They enjoyed one another's company. A funny story

*Shields of Honor*

has to be told. One night my mother in law was baby sitting for us and Maura's crib broke. She fixed it but it broke a second time. Maura was upset so Mom brought her out to the living room with her and held her. John woke up both times the crib had broken. When Mom brought Maura back to the room after quieting her John was nowhere to be seen. Mom put Maura down into the crib she had fixed a second time and looked for John.. Calling his name quietly she went through the apartment until she noticed the gate to the top of the stairs had been opened. She went down stairs and heard our landlady saying your grandmother is calling you John. He had gotten out of his crib and gone downstairs to "Honey" ( Our Landlady's name given to her by our two kids). The door to her apartment was open and he had gone in and crawled into bed with Honey. She had not woken up until she heard Mom calling him and there he was laying next to her. Our landlord was in the same bed and he never woke up and had to have the story told to him the next day. The Levesques were our landlords but they were more like family. Mom told us the story when we got home shortly after the events had taken place. We all had a good laugh as did the Levesques and yes I did repair the crib. Maura and John became the center of our lives and every move revolved around them.

# Chapter 9
# Jet Fighters are eased out of Floyd Bennett

Irv Levine was a Commander in the Reserve. While not in my Squadron we all knew Irv. In civilian life he headed up the control tower at JFK International Airport. There was great concern when the Reserves at Floyd Bennett transitioned to jets. Floyd Bennett was only a few miles from JFK and our traffic patterns would overlap. In props we were not that much of a problem because our pattern was tighter but with jets our speed was a factor the controllers at JFK would have to consider. There was talk of moving the Jets to Lakehurst. This would be a disaster as so many of our Squadron lived in the greater New York area. Irv Levine was our spokesman at the meetings the FAA had on this subject and the jets stayed at Floyd Bennett at least for the foreseeable future.

It became apparent that this issue would not go away and decisions would have to be made. The Navy elected to bring in the S2F2 Trackers, an antisubmarine aircraft. It was a twin engine aircraft that did most of its work under a thousand feet and would be an ideal aircraft for Floyd Bennett. I didn't realize it but I would be part of the last Jet Fighter Squadron at Floyd Bennett. The S2F, "stoof" as we called it arrived and some of the other Squadrons transitioned. The Chief of Training called me into his Office and had a long talk with me. He allowed as how I had had more recent combat time than most of the others but the jets would be going to Lakehurst in the very near future and he wanted me to transition to the S2F. He also informed me that I had screened for Command and if I got into the Anti Submarine program early I would probably have a chance of Commanding one of these Squadrons in the future. One advantage I had being with the Police Department was I had thirty days leave as well as thirty days military leave. In a few months my Jet fighter Squadron was decommissioned. Some went to Lakehurst to fly jets there but for others there were no billets and they scrambled for non pay billets. They wanted to serve and money wasn't the object.

I was transferred to VS837, a S2F Squadron of Anti Submarine Aircraft The Skipper was disappointed that I had no ASW experience and sent me to a two week course in Norfolk to learn about ASW. I worked hard at school and aced the course. Coming back with the best course grades helped me with my Skipper. I then was given a two week transition course in the S2F by Frank Schaufley. Frank was a commercial pilot who was given active duty orders to train me. Frank and I logged over eighty hours in that period and I felt very familiar with the aircraft. The Skipper flew with me on the next drill period and I could see he was impressed with the work Schaufley had done. I volunteered for the next Slamex (an Anti Submarine exercise) and flew over forty more hours of simulated combat. I would fly every chance I got. The Base would ask me to fly with pilots that needed time and because of my hours in the Police Department I could often accommodate them. In the next year I had flown over three hundred hours in the S2F and had two Slamex Exercises under my belt. The Skipper was getting ready to retire and called me into his office one day. He told me that he had not been happy to have me placed in his Squadron by the Chief of Training and had put me under the microscope. He said three things had impressed him. One, my grades at ASW school. Two, the way I had flown the aircraft after my two weeks with Frank Schaufley. Three, the work I had put in the last year, flying two Slamexes and the amount of flight time I had logged. He told me he expected me to be the CO some day in the future. This made me feel much better because I sensed that he had not liked the way I had come aboard.

Sig Bajek was our next Skipper and Sig was a friend. Bill Clark was our XO. Bill was an old friend who was the Admin Officer that had briefed me in Korea on the Air Pac reports. We had both been in the Reserve at Floyd Bennett before being called back for Korea and even though we had not been in the same Squadron we knew each other. There was no tension as there had been for me until my old Skipper called me into his office that day. Sig was a joy to work for and Bill Clark was a good friend. The rest of the guys were great and many were in one of my old Squadrons.

I'm neglecting Joan. My wife never minded me being in the reserve. I came home one day with an invitation from the Commanding Officer of the Base for our wives to attend the next wives club meeting. Joan was going to go, then she got cold feet. When the day arrived she gritted her teeth and decided she would attend. When she got there she met Bam Newell, the skippers wife and they had a lovely chat. It turned out that Bam enjoyed the opera but had no one to go with. Joan belonged to the Metropolitan opera Guild and obtained tickets for she and Bam. Thus began a friendship that lasted as long as the Newells were stationed there. The wives club wanted to get tickets for a play in New York City. Joan was working as a secretary on Wall Street and frequently had to get tickets for clients of her firm. She contacted her broker and obtained the required number of tickets for the club. Her fame grew and she was elected President of the

Floyd Bennett Wives Club the following year. She planned more social events during her tenure as President and more and more of the Reserve Officers Wives joined the Club. Captain Newell told me how pleased his wife was that Joan had joined the Club and how the membership had increased during her term as President. When the wives are happy it makes the Officers life a lot easier. He told me to remember that.

# Chapter 10
# Police Cases

Now back to the Police Department. In the past I have told you of different cases I worked on. Now I'm going to tell you of an important one that was on the front pages of all the papers in New York and was carried by the news services. We had a man who was planting bombs in crowded theatres. Some of them had gone off and injured people, some were discovered in time to save lives and prevent injuries. There was a common theme, he was consumed with a hatred for Consolidated Edison in New York. Letters would be received warning of future bombs. These letters and bombs became more and more frequent and the Press and the public in New York became more and more frightened. The Mayor directed the Police Department to put an end to these bombings and to apprehend the perpetrator. To this end the Police Commissioner and the Chief of Detectives formed an elite Squad of Detectives to investigate these bombings and to assemble intelligence from interviewing possible witnesses and people that had contacted the Police on the hot line offering possible clues. Each Borough was to offer two detectives to this task force. Brooklyn West nominated Jimmy Murphy and myself to represent our Borough. Jimmy had caught the case of a bombing in the Brooklyn Paramount Theatre. Murph and I reported to Manhattan West Detective Headquarters and were assigned to a Detective Captain who was the new Squad Commander. His name escapes me but not his zeal and dedication. He believed nothing is unimportant and any fact should be compiled, studied and analyzed for authenticity . He had a huge chart on the wall listing what was known thus far.. Murphy and I were a team. He then had us go out and interview each of the witnesses. We had to be cognizant of the information on the chart before the interviews. Each interview was examined for common threads that would provide a modus operandi (method of operation). Each morning there would be skull session on what information we had obtained from the previous days interviews. The Captain insisted we remain current on the chart. We could see the results of each teams interviews. Leads were passed out to each team for investigation. This probably sounds like a reasonable way to operate and it is for a case of this importance. In normal police work it doesn't happen this way. Each of us would get swamped with cases. We would have to devote attention to those with leads that were active

*Shields of Honor*

and had promise of resulting in an arrest. The others we had to put on a back burner. This didn't sit well with some complainants that took an active interest in their case and could care less for anyone else's. You had to develop personal diplomacy to be a good Detective, a trait that would stand you in good stead regardless of you future career. Now at least you have an idea as to why this case was being pursued in a proper but extraordinary way. For teams of good detectives to be able to concentrate on a particular case, review each other's work and then proceed was extraordinary. No other cases were even discussed unless they had a bearing on this one. Let me digress a bit and tell you some thing of my partner, Murphy. We had come into the Police Department right after the war. Murph had gotten out of the service before me in 1945 and had taken the first exam in 1945. He was a year ahead of me having been appointed in 1946. He was a Lieutenant in the Army and had seen action in the European War. He served his time in uniform in the 23 Precinct (Harlem) and while traveling used to tell me stories of Police Work in Harlem that would terrify the average citizen. He was the subject of an article in Life Magazine that chose to depict the veterans of World War Two that had chosen to become policemen. After my experience with Murph I don't believe they could have chosen a finer example.

We Americans are filled with a sense of mercy and compassion. We believe in fair play and honesty and want to believe the best in everyone. We extend that belief to foreign nations and different creeds which is why it is so hard for us to believe stories that do not match our belief . The average Police Officer has had experiences that make him a realist not a noble philosopher and we act out of our experience. Our lives are lived between the seamy side of life and the noble side. We are aware of each and act differently when exposed to each. They say a conservative is a liberal that has been mugged. There is more truth in that than the average person wants to believe. We interview victims every day and recognize there is a dark side. I am going into this in a little more depth than I planned but I know that some of you have disagreed with my observations. I know that if you walked in my footsteps you would understand and most of you, if you were honest, would agree with me. Murph talked to a seamy side of life that was prevalent in his precinct not the exception. My precinct was different. We didn't have the same crime rate and our crime was not the violent type he experienced. The Police reaction in his Precinct was almost that of self preservation. Rodney King would be recognized in that Precinct for what he was and the actions of the LA Police understood. This is not the " Delehany" answer to this question. An in joke that any New York City Policeman would understand. (A Delehanty answer is what we had years ago and a fore runner of political correctness) Delehanty was a school that instructed Police candidates on the correct answers to civil service exams. Some times these answers would be what the Civil Service exam wanted to hear rather than the true facts. Some times the truth hurts but it shouldn't be covered up.

Murphy was a good cop and a good Detective it was a pleasure to have worked with him . We had a number of bombing case interviews that were odd. We interviewed an American Indian that claimed to have seen the perpetrator in his letter to the Police Department. Before any revelations on his part we had to see his clippings proving he had led the parade for Franklin D Roosevelt in New York. He waited for our congratulations before continuing the interview. His sight of the perpetrator was in a dream and Murph and I looked at one another. He had to unlock three deadbolts on his door before letting us out. We were polite and thanked him for his information before we left. Another took us to Sing Sing Prison. A prisoner told us of hearing a plot between his two cellmates to have theatres bombed and if we could just arrange to have his case brought up before the parole board he would tell us of all the details. We questioned him as to when the plot had been hatched and he gave us a time frame that did not match. We checked on the cellmates and obtained copies of their records. Neither of them lived in NYC. Both were from upstate New York. None of the people they had been arrested with were from

New York City. There were some interviews that required further police work. Most of these were dead ends or proved inaccurate. Finally one of the teams struck pay dirt and a former mechanic for Consolidated Edison was unearthed. Investigation proved him to be a solid suspect and a search warrant was issued for search of his premises. Bomb making equipment was found and it matched a bomb that had been found in one of the theatres. We had our man and he confessed when confronted with the evidence. The case was closed and received headlines in all the papers. "The mad bomber" was found and everyone could breath a sigh of relief. The Chief thanked us all personally and we returned to our respective Squads. The Captain who was our boss lived in Brooklyn and I had the opportunity to get to know him personally. When we finished our work at night each day I would drive him home as it was on my way. He told me some stories of" the Job" during Prohibition . Stories that I hope he wrote down because they make a wonderful movie. The roll the Police Department has played in society has evolved yet stayed the same. Evolved because social engineers and lawyers have made us change our tactics but the same because it's still the bad guys against the good guys and the good guys are still the Police despite the Al Sharptons of this world who think otherwise.

Shortly after coming back to the 61 Squad Brooklyn West we had a shake up. A lot of

Detectives were transferred to different Squads. I went to the 72 Squad in south Brooklyn. My new Squad Commander welcomed us and made us feel wanted. He was a grandfatherly man and easy to get along with in every way. My old Squad Commander had been quirky and you had to interpret his mood before speaking to him. We had several arguments and even if proven wrong he would never admit it or apologize . This made for a difficult situation and I was always relieved when he wasn't around. Lieutenant Louries was not like him at all and the atmosphere was pleasant. I had several partners while at the 72 Squad. They were all good Detectives and a pleasure to work with on cases. At the 61 Squad we were assigned cases on a rotation basis. The first case was mine the second my partners and so on. In the 72 Squad it was broken down by time frame. It didn't make much difference, it was only the persons name on the Complaint report (UF61) because we both worked on each others cases. The neighborhood in the 72 Precinct was poorer and more drugs were being used here. While it doesn't compare to what we see today it was certainly more prevalent than what I had experienced in the 61Prcinct. It meant a little more home work and instruction from the Detectives familiar with drugs.

A year or so into my tour at the 72 Squad we lost our Squad Commander to retirement and our new Commander was a great personal friend of mine, Joe Mooney. Joe and I had worked in the BCI together and were good friends there. He had been a Sergeant in the BCI and I heard that he had made Lieutenant but hadn't seen him since he was promoted. He relied on me to fill him in on the precinct and the Detectives he had working for him. This was an easy task. The precinct wasn't complicated and the Detectives were all the kind he could work with and trust. The work became extremely pleasant because Joe was the kind of a fellow we used to say would give you the top card every time. He was honest and loyal and I saw him on many occasions go to the Boro Commander to bail out a Detective who had been the subject of a false complaint. Joe remained a good friend of mine for the rest of his life .After he had retired I visited him in Florida whenever I went to see my son John and we and a couple of other Detectives from the BCI would have lunch together with our wives. He was a good man in every sense and a friend to the end. He died several years ago without me knowing it or I would have gone to his wake.

I remember that Joe was eager to have his Squad perform and would schedule meetings at least on a semi-weekly basis. This did not set well with the Detectives that had the day off and there was some griping. Going over cases that required review or could prove to be a problem in the future and tracking repeat offences that could be traced to the same perpetrator. Each Detective was responsible for his own cases. His partner was familiar with them as well. Joe wanted all the Detectives to be aware of these cases as many of them could have been the work of the same perpetrators It became apparent to us that he was right and when we took these cases more seriously our arrest rate went up, Joe was vindicated in most every ones eyes and when the results were noted at the Division and Boro levels I think all of the Detectives in the Squad were willing to give up part of there day off to attend these productive meeting. We also talked about what we had heard from informants and everyone gained by being privy to this information. Detectives are no different than anyone else when it comes to innovation. We sometimes get set in out ways and it takes a while for a good idea to catch on and become accepted. It taught me something that I never forgot if what you want to do is right and will improve operations you sometimes have to buck the inertia. Do it and persist and when it has happened nobody will look back. It's a form of leadership. Joe Mooney had it and I tried to emulate him.

    One of my most serious trials was to befall me. We had a Detective come into our Squad directly from, the uniform ranks. He had made a award winning arrest and was assigned to the Detective division as a result. Joe Murray reported in while I was on duty and I had the chance to talk to him first. Joe Mooney was out and not expected back to the Squad till later in the day. Joe would not be assigned a partner until Joe came back so I took him under my wing and brought him out on some cases with me. I learned a lot about him. He was an excellent cop and had more time in the job than I had, having come into the Police Department from an earlier exam. He was a vet and had come from a busy Precinct so he knew Police Procedure but wasn't familiar with Detectives paper work. I gave him the basics and by the time Joe returned we were friends. He was assigned to one of the old timers and scheduled to begin work in two days. It was a couple of months before Joe Murray got his gold shield and was officially a Detective. During that time period Joe would ask me questions on how to proceed on various cases. His partner was an old timer with an alcohol problem. On occasion Joe was on his own.

One day he called me at home. It seems two partners in a heavy machinery plant had a falling out. One had gotten word that his partner was getting ready to dispose of the machinery without his blessing and compliance. He wanted to move the machinery to another place for safekeeping until the two could agree on final disposition." Jack how do I handle this" was his question. I told him to originate a UF61 (Complaint form) and to call the District Attorney on duty for clarification on the way to proceed. Get the District Attorney name, time called and advice on the complaint form before you take any action Follow this up with DD5 (Detective action taken since the UF61). Keep the DD5s current by describing on paper the latest action taken. I told him this is the kind that can bite you so cover your actions with paper. Was I ever right. It took close to six months for this to fester before the Detective became the problem. The other partner was politically connected and the problem was brought to the attention of the Boro Commander. He looked at the paperwork and realized it was going to be a hot potato and ordered Joe back to uniform. There was no Police trial thus if the case became red hot it would be a uniform matter rather than a Detective Division problem. The only catch was Joe would be named as a Detective in the case and when the Jury saw him with the white shield of a Patrolman they would assume the Police Department had already tried, found him guilty and had demoted him. This is exactly what happened. He was put on trial after the second partner perjured himself in Court.

The District Attorney was a friend. We had a number of cases together, had lunched together and would greet one another when ever we met on the outside. I placed a formal request to talk to the District Attorney. It was granted but my Squad Commander, the Boro Chief or his representative, and the Chief of Internal Affairs had to be present as well. This covered all Bases. We were not allowed to testify in Court as a character witness for another Police Officer so the Department was curious as to what I had to say. When I entered every one named was already seated. I began by reminding everyone that a Detective, because of movies and television is looked on as someone with a stature beyond what actually exists in the Police Department. Here we are mortals with feet of clay and can be removed for little or no reason with the consent of the Boro Commander. Joe had been reduced to Patrolman without a Police Trial and it will appear that he has already been convicted of malfeasance by the Police Department. Everyone agreed I was right. I then asked the District Attorney to mention this to the jury before the trial as a matter of simple justice . He had been sacrificed to save the honor of the Detective division. The Boro Chief was not there, his Deputy was and he became angry. "Are you blaming the Chief for this" he asked angrily. I asked "who did it?" He stormed out of the room my Squad Commander right behind him asking him" who did do it." They held a heated discussion in the anteroom that we could all hear. The Chief of internal affairs told me you had it won until he thought you were blaming the Boro Commander. He also added there were some nice things said about you by all of them. It seems the Mad Bomber case the Chief of Detectives had asked for the two best detectives from each of the Boroughs to be assigned and I had been selected by the Boro Commander to represent our Borough. Now I'm in deep trouble but morally right. What I said was true and the only satisfaction I can take is that the Chief of Internal Affairs talked to the Chief Inspector and the Police Commissioner and they decreed that shall not happen in the future.

A Detective that has to appear in Court to face charges shall remain a Detective throughout his Court appearances. I was called in to the Boro Commanders office a few weeks later. I was asked to sit down and tell him what part, if any, I had played in this case. It turned out that the second partner had filed a complaint stating that Joe Murray had threatened to arrest him unless he pay Joe a large sum of money. He lied so convincingly that the Judge believed him and Joe was arrested. I told the Chief that I had advised him to make a Uf61 explaining the case, call and get the District Attorneys opinion and act accordingly. Make frequent DD5s stating the progress of the case. He then tuned his swivel chair around and with his back to me asked how do I know you are not part of the plot to obtain money from this man. My friends when you get to this part of the story you will recognize the guy you know. The hair on the back of my neck stood up and in a loud voice, heard in the Chiefs office by his staff, I demanded he turn around and face me when I answered that question. He did and I looked him dead in the eye and said if anyone even suggested that he's a liar and I would take a lie detector test to prove everything I said was the truth. He changed his attitude and demeanor and spoke nicely to me after that. He said he had to ask questions because he didn't know what direction this case would take after that.. When I got back to the Squad I was met by most of the Detectives and my Squad Commander. They all thought I would be going back to uniform and were mad. I told them exactly what had happened and when I told them of the part where the Chief had turned his back on me and what I had done and said they were even more amazed the axe had not fallen on me.( I am writing this some 45 years later and am somewhat detached looking on my younger self as almost a different person but my friends believe me when I tell you that I am proud of that person and the way he conducted himself then and hope I will always do what I think is right and honorable).

Everything was fine for six months and then I got the word that a teletype message had been received at the Squad and I was to report to the seventh Precinct. To this day I do not know what caused the change and what made the Chief take the action he did.. When I was called back to the Navy in l961 for the Berlin Build up and held on Active Duty I eventually was stationed in Keflavic, Iceland. A C130 manned by Reservists came in one day. A warrant Officer introduced himself to me and told me he had been a clerk for the Boro Chief the day I was in to explain my role in the case. He said they could hear every word that was said in the outer office. He said Sully you are a legend in the job the way you handled that. No names will be mentioned but his words filled me with a warmth that I can remember today. I also learned that Joe Murray was acquitted of all charges and received back pay. Joe retired rather than come back to the

Police Department. We remained friends until his death.

One final word on the Police Department. While I was in the Detective Squad the work completely absorbed you. There were so many things you could do to help people. A word dropped here or a threat of further action could change people's behavior. Friends you made in the business community that stood by you. Arrests that got real bad guys off the street and into prisons where they belonged. Complainants you met on cases that became friends. You could build up a reputation in the precinct and among your fellow Detectives in neighboring Squads that would follow you wherever you were assigned. To illustrate this I'm going to tell you a story about a Detective in a neighboring Squad. Fitz was an old timer compared to most of us. He had almost twenty years in the Detective Division. Joey Gallo was a hood, part of the Mafia, although the Mafia wasn't proud of him as he was a loose cannon. "Crazy Joe" had testified before congress and in his pure Brooklyn accent had become the poster boy for the Mafia. Joe was not careful and Fitz had locked him up on various charges. Each time Joe Gallo's mother would go down and bail him out offering her house for his bail. Fitz would ask her why she kept bailing him out. "He is a bad guy" Fitz would tell her but she would always reply "but he is my son Detective Fitz." Fitz would the hang around and drive her home since

Gallo lived in his Precinct. Fitz was tough but had a heart of gold and we all loved him.

This must have happened a dozen times. One night Fitz and his young partner were riding In the Cruiser (Detectives car) and came across a robbery in progress in a liquor store. Fitz pulled up and telling his partner to watch his back entered the store, got the drop on the perpetrator and disarmed him. Seeing this the young partner entered the store to assist Fitz . The perpetrators partner then entered the store and shot the two Detectives. Both died in the hospital of gunshot wounds. The Detective Division went to general quarters and every Detective was called in. We arrested all known felons or at least questioned them all. Harass them until someone talks or makes a mistake. The Boro Commander was questioning Joey Gallo himself and we could hear him. He told Gallo that were are going to get these guys and we all heard Joey say" You better get them before I do Chief because they are fish bait if I get them. My mother has not stopped crying since Det Fitz was killed" He wasn't kidding about the fishbait and his mother really loved Detective Fitz and was at his wake and his funeral mass. Whether Joeys feeling for Fitz were prompted by his mother alone the result was the pair surrendered to Police soon after rather than face the ire of "Crazy Joe"

Now for my last months in the Police Department. When I reported to the Seventh

Precinct I had an interview with the Captain. I told him I wanted him to know that I wasn't here for misdeeds or because I had my hand in the till. He stopped me by saying I usually get a report as to why an ex Detective is being assigned. In your case I got glowing reports from your Squad Commander and your Precinct Captain of the Uniform Force. Reading between the lines you stepped on somebody's toes or rocked somebody's boat. You are starting with a clean slate here so report to the Lieutenant for assignment. My uniforms still fit so there was no expense. I had seniority and could pick my vacation time to correspond to my two weeks active duty and save my thirty days of military leave for my week ends. I also decided I would study and advance through the ranks. This I did and passed the Sergeants test with test scores high enough to be promoted quickly. Things were going well but the Berlin Buildup came along and my life was to change dramatically.

# Chapter 11
# I'm recalled to Naval Service a third time

The Berlin build up resulted from actions taken by the Russians to inhibit our entry into West Berlin. Reserve squadrons were called to active duty to indicate our willingness to resist this action. It was during this timeframe that photographs taken by U2 aircraft revealed that the Russians were placing Missiles in Cuba.

Sig Bajack was the Commanding Officer of my Reserve Squadron and he received advanced notice of our Squadrons recall to active duty. He called us over to his Office at NBC Television and we met in the conference room. He told us we would be receiving orders some time in the next two weeks and would flying out of Floyd Bennett for the foreseeable future. He then announced our biggest problem would be in our maintenance department and told me I would be the Maintenance Officer. Everyone was amazed because I had done all the scheduling in the Operation department and had kept us qualified in all phases. I talked to the Lieutenant who had been our maintenance officer and he took the demotion in stride. He warned me that our Maintenance crew was poorly trained and that the station keepers at Floyd Bennett had been responsible for the aircraft maintenance and our people had merely assisted them.

Training was needed. I took some military leave and flew to Memphis and talked to the training detachment there. I asked if we were called up would I be able to get some people in schools there. Even if we had to put extra chairs in the class was the reply. I touched base with all the job descriptions and various rates and got the same answer. I kept track of whom I had talked to and their phone numbers. I then flew to Quonset with similar requests and got the affirmative answers there as well. Sitting down with Merv Chopen (Former Maintenance Officer) we then decided who should be sent to school and where. The orders came as expected and we reported to Floyd Bennett. Phone calls were placed to the Maintenance Schools at Memphis and Quonset and orders cut for what must have seemed half the Squadron. We were given planes from the Reserve Fleet at Floyd Bennett and we were to maintain them ourselves. This caused problems for several reasons. One, we had insufficient people to man them. Two, even if we did have the people they were not sufficiently trained to handle them. Most of our enlisted people were trained in other aircraft and not familiar with the aircraft we now flew.. Our pilots were ready but the Maintenance men were not. A major check was impossible. They had never pulled one as the planes we used on our two week cruise had come fresh out of major checks and didn't require that type of maintenance. To compound our problem the base expected us to allow the reservist on week end duty to fly our aircraft and for us to keep the aircraft in a high operational status. The Skipper knew what my plan was and tried to prevent me from taking the heat. I turned to the Maintenance Officer on the Base, explained my problem and asked for help and assistance. He did help but his men thought they were getting rid of a Squadron full of aircraft and were not happy to be doing the same amount of work they had been before our call up.

Another problem I made for myself. We wanted to park our aircraft outside of our ready room where we could see them. Good idea but there were no pani (tie down rings) I put in a work request but was told it would take six months for public works to get around to it. I visited Quonset the following day and by chance got to meet the CO of the Reserve CB (Construction Battalion) Detachment. When I explained my problem with tie downs he said he could do it next weekend for me as he had run out of work for his troops. The next weekend he arrived in a C130 and his men completed the task in two days, the cement would cure in a few days and we could use the tie downs. We were tying our aircraft down for a week or two before the Public Works Officer was informed. This resulted in a meeting with the Captain of the Base. The Public Works Officer had put me on report. The Captain told me I should have informed the Public Works officer of the agreement with the CBs. The Public Works Officer stated he couldn't have allowed it as it would be against the union's agreement. The Captain said well its already completed so it's a mute point and dismissed us. When I was getting ready to leave he asked me to stay for a minute. When the Public Works Officer had left he said if we ever go to war Sully I want you on my team but you realize the Public Works Officer is right he does have to face a union that jealously guards its domain.

In the weeks ahead we started to get the troops back from the various schools. We had a couple of Chiefs that had worked for Grumman on the S2F and they proved invaluable. Between the schools and these two Chiefs we started to have the makings of a Maintenance department that would make anyone proud. Airlant ordered the Squadron to Guantanamo Bay (Cuba) and we were ready. All of our people had been to schools and were advanced in their training. We could pull major checks now, a little slow at first but better each time. Guantanamo (Gitmo) is great for flying. The weather is usually fantastic and with no families around its like being on a

Carrier. Not quite because there were plenty of bars serving great Cuban Rum Goodies. If you haven't tasted one take my word for it, they are great!

The temperature, the lighting made working at night a pleasure and there was always a gang working. A funny thing, we had the maintenance broken down into day and night shifts with the emphasis on the night shift. We were still light on people in avionics and some of the flight crews had that background were needed in the Flight crews. When problems looked like they were getting out of hand the day crew and the flight crew would show up without being asked and help. Our readiness was outstanding. We flew every flight that was scheduled as well as add-ons. We were flying with five inch rockets under our wings and our job was to detect the Russian ships carrying the big missiles and intercept them. By flying across their bows we made them slow down so the destroyer escorts could check their cargo. This was funny as the deck hands would give us all sorts of obscene gestures as we passed them at close range. My sonar man was Italian and I asked Capi to come forward and observe. I told him there were gestures I had not seen before. When Capi saw them he asked me to make another pass with him up in the bubble. He flashed them hand signals I certainly had never seen before and accompanied them with verbiage that would make a Mafia captain blush.

From then on Capi was our retaliation for bad manners on the part of the Russians.

On these flights we would continue on past the straights or Windward Passage and check around the Islands for any strays that might be attempting to elude the blockade. On one of these flights we came across an old WW2 oil tanker that had been torpedoed and beached on a small island. We checked it out but the rusted hulk had been there for years. We remembered its location. When we returned from the hops we would light off a smoke flair in the gunnery range and fire our missiles at the smoke. The five inchers could do some damage if fired in anger but here they just blew up some water. The very next flight we followed a similar course and again spotted our old tanker. As it was on the way home why not see what a five inch rocket could do to a rusty hulk. Both my crewmen came forward to see. The first run was on a 20 degree angle. Land the rocket short, have it bend to the parallel course of the water and explode three feet below the water line. The first rocket did just that to everyone's satisfaction. The book was right! Now how about a direct hit so we planned that for the next run. The results were even better because we could see old rust plates leave the ship. Now how about a salvo of the remaining rockets. Every rocket hit its target and rust and dirt flew everywhere and the ship seemed to shudder. A little smoke appeared from somewhere and then much more. We circled and the smoke was 500 ft when we left. If the Coast Guard had to investigate they would have to charge it to spontaneous combustion but we went home in awe of our firepower.

Gitmo is an ideal place to exercise a Squadron and you can get more work done in a week than you can in other places in a month. We were proving that as our Squadron was able to pull a major inspection in less time than prescribed by the book. The cooperation of the crew was fantastic as this was the first time that many of them had spent this much time together. A good number of our enlisted had been attending college when the Squadron was called up. They were sharp, intelligent and eager to learn. The senior enlisted personel with greater Navy active duty time continuously praised their work ethic and were amazed at the progress they were making. Life on a rock has its downside and I spoke to the Skipper about some sort of leave for the troops. The Officers stationed at Gitmo spoke of Montego Bay in Jamaica as being a favorite of theirs. It was close and since the weather was good most of the time it could be scheduled with some certainty. I was elected to fly to Montego Bay and make some arrangements. Since their tower operated on VHF (very high frequency) and our aircraft operated on UHF (ultra high frequency) we would have to contact them on HF (high frequency). I brought a radio expert with me since HF is funny sometimes. As an example I remember coming back to the States from Gitmo on one occasion and in trying to contact Miami I was unable to reach them but was heard by New York and they relayed my message to Miami by landline. We contacted Montego Tower they were weak but readable. My radio tech said he could retune their station to where we could hear them loud and clear. We were amazed to hear a young woman's voice on the tower and speaking in a clipped British accent. When we met her a few minutes after landing she turned out to be a pretty black girl. She was Jamaican but had been trained in Great Britain. The control tower operator was happy to have our radio tech peak up his HF and it was accomplished in short order. He did such a great job that we were able to contact Montego Tower from the runway at Gitmo henceforth. It was always nice to hear that lyrical voice from Montego tower before making a liberty run. While we were on the ground we inquired as to suitable lodging and were touted on the Montego Bay Hotel a short taxi ride away. We took that ride and let me say you have not lived until you take a taxi ride in Montego Bay. One of my Squadron Buddies later quipped " can you imagine giving these guys 100 hours in an F6F and sending him out". They never slowed down and would pass one another on a narrow bridge causing sparks to jump from their respective rear view mirrors. The hotel turned out to be even better than reported and I spoke to the owner, manager. If you remember the television show Palladin and the star Richard Boone that was so named you would recognize the manager. I had to ask if he was related and smiling he just answered "you too". From that moment on he was Palladin to my squadron and would respond with the same smile. He was interested in working out a deal with me because he had a preponderance of woman at the hotel and not many men. Can you imagine how that was received at the squadron. There were secretaries, airline stews and a host of others and into that mix you put a bunch of Navy Pilots. Someone suggested it was like dying and going to heaven. He gave us an extremely attractive rate on the room we would rent for our entire stay and we shook hands on it. The plan was for one crew to fly over and a second crew would return the aircraft. The first crew would spend the day and the same night at the hotel and the next crew would overfly the hotel the next day, rev its engines as a warning and then proceed to Montego Bay airport. They would wait for the crew on liberty to say its goodbyes and join them at the airport. The liberty crew would fly the aircraft back and the landing crew would proceed to the hotel and the glorious welcome it would receive.

    We worked out a deal with customs whereby we could bring a big bottle of gin into country for each man. That afternoon these two Squadron reps would hold a martini party for the hotel in the corridor outside our room. It was the driest Martini you ever tasted because vermouth was not part of the ingredient unless some girl

*Shields of Honor*

contributed her vermouth to the party. This party was frequented by, the who's who of the hotel. Certainly every girl was there and even couples, on vacation, got caught up in the camaraderie. Remember the television show where the little fellow would call out "the plane...the plane". Well that's what would happen when the girls caught sight of the plane that circled the hotel each day. The crews would exchange a lot of information, most of it being the names of girls at the hotel. The routine went like this, upon arrival in orange flight suites you dropped off your bag in the room and taking your free drink chit proceeded to the bar on the beach where the girls would be sunning themselves. You would have your rum goodie and check out the scenery. The girls would check you out as well, your orange flight suit would make certain they knew whom you were and who would be hosting the cocktail party that afternoon. Back to the room, change into your swim suite and back to the beach. Unless you were made of steel you would soon be engaged in conversation with the girls and your name would be known prior to the cocktail party.

Not right away but later when we were able to get a larger number over to Montego for the weekend we would hire a band that played in a nearby hotel to play for us starting at midnight. We would put beachchairs in a circle around the torches the hotel would provide and have our own concert of calypso music. This really went over big and we had one of our pilots, Jim Repko, to thank for this innovation. The hotel would have a band play dance music after dinner. One of our Officers, Iggie Dawson, was of Greek heritage and had taught us a Greek dance to the tune of never on Sunday. At least once, sometimes more if the girls would ask for it the Squadron would get up and dance. To see us arm in arm doing this Greek dance was always a show stopper and everyone was fascinated. Some of the girls and even the couples would join us and we taught everyone to dance this Greek dance. Thanks Jim and Iggie where ever you are for making our liberty so enjoyable. . Palladin was happy to have us and told me that word of mouth between the girls and their friends at home had increased his reservations numbers and that we were responsible. Palladin had people come to his hotel that were well known in the theatrical field and when ever I was there he would introduce them to me. They would be vacationing and not want to mingle but they came to our cocktail parties. I used to kid him by saying if I had your job I would weigh 140 lbs and the whole back of my head would be soft. He got back at me one day when I was dancing with a real pretty girl and danced up to me and put his hand on the back of my head and squeezed.

    I had to dwell on this aspect of our tour because reservist are loose and enjoy them selves. This account certainly attests to that but I don't want to give you the impression that my

Squadron wasn't doing its job in a professional manner. I already told you we flew every mission assigned. We had back up aircraft ready to go if a maintenance failure occurred. We flew every add on flight that was given to us and all told flew more hours than any Squadron of our type during the Missile crisis. The pilots I knew would meet the test but my praise is directed to the maintenance people whose hard work made this record flight time possible.

When I returned home and attended my first conference at COMFAIR Quonset I was singled out as the Maintenance Officer whose readiness and flight time were at the top of the charts. This praise was directed at me but belongs to the men of my Maintenance Department. When Sig had given me this job before we were called back I wasn't sure I would like it but after meeting these men and watching them grow into experts in their fields I realized this is where I wanted to remain. On one of my trips to Montego I went bar hopping and found two of my enlisted men at the table of a couple old enough to be their parents. I said hello and was introduced to the couple. Both of the enlisted men had been called back from college to active duty. I said a few pleasantries and moved back to the bar. The older man came to me and said he had been in the Navy in WW2 but he was amazed at the professionalism of these two young men and what gentlemen they were. He said they are a tribute to US Navy. I told him I was proud of them

*CDR. Jack Sullivan USNR*

as well and thanked him for his remarks. I never forgot that conversation nor will I ever forget the days with the Squadron. Fellows like Sig Bajak, Bill Clark, Bill Foley, Bill Graham, Eddy O"Beid, Frank Schaufley, George Mabardy, Iggie Dawson. Merv Chopin, and some whose names escape me but whose faces will always be remembered. Thank you VS837 for shaping me for adventures yet to come

# Chapter 12
# The Navy Assignes me to Training Squadron 1

My life in the Navy continues. When I reported back to COMFAIR QUONSET I was commended on the showing our Squadron made during the Missile Crisis and in particular the maintenance effort. They were aware of the record number of sorties the Squadron had flown without losing a single flight to a maintenance problem and I was told that I would be kept on active duty after the Squadron was released. This was a tribute to the men of the maintenance department not to me but the powers to be had already decided I would remain on active duty. When the Squadron returned to Floyd Bennett I was ordered to AIRLANT and subsequently to the detailer at OPNAV. The Commanders detailer was none other than Captain Bill Kelly, my old Skipper at VF62 during the Korean War. Bill had seen my name but had never read the jacket that accompanied it.

When I showed up it was old home week for I did not associate Captain Bill Kelly, to whom I was to report at OPNAV as my old Skipper either. We sat and talked as his phone calls stacked up, then agreed to meet after he had finished his day. He had read my report from COMFAIR QUONSET as well as my fitness reports going back to the days when I worked for him. COMFAIR QUONSET had recommended I remain in a maintenance billet and Bill agreed.

I was assigned to a Training Squadron One (VT1) at Saufley Field in Pensacola as the Maintenance Officer. This Squadron had 173 (T34) aircraft and was responsible for primary flight training for the Navy. Every naval officer undergoing flight training had to start his flying at VT 1. The T34 was a product of Beachcraft, and was comparable in most respects to the SNJ formerly flown in advanced training. It was easier to fly in most respects but much of that could be attributed to being a much newer aircraft. Bill told me my orders would be cut and I could expect to report to Pensacola within the next month.

I was anxious to get home and tell Joan because she had worried I might receive orders to a ship and be gone for extended periods of time. Pensacola sounded good to her. This was her first move in the Navy and in the time I had remaining I did everything I could to assist her. The real move would be up to her. It was planned I would go on ahead and secure housing either base quarters or a private dwelling in

*Shields of Honor*

some subdivision. By this time in our lives we had two cars. The Volkswagen Bug was mine and the Chevrolet was hers. I would drive down to Pensacola in the Volks and bring my uniforms and such civilian clothes as I might need. She would pack her clothes and the children's in the Chevy and everything else would be shipped to the address I would provide. Saying goodbye to the rest of the family I set out for Pensacola. A few days later I reported in to VT 1 and met the CO. Cdr Hal Kendrick and the XO Cdr. Bob Orcut. I recognized I was meeting two of the finest Naval Officers I would ever serve under. We had an hour long talk and from what I could gather Bill Kelly had made a phone call to the Skipper telling him what sort of an Officer I was and knowing Bill I'm sure it was complimentary. We talked about the mission of the Squadron and it's importance since without its production the whole Training Command would grind to a halt. The last maintenance officer had left a few months before my arrival and while the assistant had taken up the slack there was much improvement needed.

They recognized I needed a little personal time to check into the Base and to find housing for my family and provided me a junior officer to assist me in checking in. Until I had quarters I would have to reside in the BOQ so I made those arrangements first.. Anyone who has ever checked into a new Base will recognize there is a lot of paperwork to be filled out and many

*CDR. Jack Sullivan USNR*

From top to bottom:
L-R: father-in-law George Fay, my wife Joan, my mother Catherine Sullivan, my dad Cornelius, Maura - John

My sister Marian.
My mother Catherine.

signatures to obtain. Every Department of any importance must know you are on board, where you can be reached, what your new phone number is and what activity you are assigned to, Thanks to the young Ensign I found all of these places without much trouble. That same evening I was out house hunting with a real estate broker. I wanted to rent a home as close to the Base as possible, I also wanted a three bedroom house in a nice subdivision. I tentatively asked what the price might be and was pleasantly surprised when I found Pensacola was not a high priced community. Coming from New York I expected the price to be much higher. In two days I had picked out a house, signed the contract and in a week had the keys. I notified Joan and she set up a date for the packing and shipment. John and Maura were attending a Catholic School in my old Parish "Our Lady Help of Christians" (remember some of the wild tales about the tennis courts…..The School was built on these grounds) I inquired as to their attending Catholic Schools here in Pensacola and was told school officials would have to see their records, but it looked promising. Within a month Joan was packed out and three days later she arrived in Pensacola. We lived in a motel for three more days until the movers arrived. They unpacked us and we spent the first night in our new home. John loved it but Maura was not overjoyed at having her own room and came in with us the first night. The next day she was busy decorating her room and from then on she loved the privacy. The neighborhood was nice and quiet. The kids came calling shortly after the moving vans had departed and our kids became part of the gang early on. Most of the families were Navy and the kids were practiced at making new friends in a hurry. Ours were fast learners and in no time were on little league teams. When your family is settled and happy you can go to work with a clear conscience and peace of mind. We were fortunate to be able to get John and Maura in a Catholic School and they picked up right where they had left off in Brooklyn. Catholic Schools insist on discipline and that is exactly what we wanted for them. They were in school to learn not to spread their wings and exhibit any conduct they desired. They loved the new school and each of the teachers made certain they met their new classmates and ensured each of them they were welcome at school. Joan had to drive them since they were out of the public school district but she didn't mind.

My new Squadron was large both in the number of aircraft (l73) and in the number of instructors (76). It was subdivided into four flights, each with a Flight leader that acted like an Officer in Charge. Three of the flights were Navy and one Marine. The flight Leaders reported to the Commanding Officer via our XO. The Skipper, XO, Ops Officer and Maintenance Officers were all Commanders and as such could conduct Speedy Boards (Evaluation Boards) on students that weren't measuring up to the standards prescribed. I should explain a speedy board is comprised of five officers. A commander is the senior officer and instructors from the various flights make up the rest of the board. This board is convened when a student receives a down (failing flight grade) and the purpose is to decide whether further flight training is warranted. As maintenance Officer I had five Division Officers all of which were supposed to carry a student load. When you consider how many aircraft were coming out of scheduled checks each day and had to be test flown before a student could fly them I realized I had a problem. One of the first things I had to do was get my division officers relieved of their student load .I had to ensure my test pilots were qualified and conducted the flights how and when I wanted them to ensure maximum readiness. The Operations Officer was convinced the old way of flying test flights when pilots were available was the way we should continue. We sat with the XO and CO and I outlined my plan which I estimated would add 5% to the operational Readiness or I would go back to the old plan. I had the green light to try it for two months and the plan would be subject to reevaluation. Each morning my pilots tested the aircraft according to the plan. I flew test hops as well and we soon reached the 5% I had promised. The Operations Officer agreed the plan had worked and was grateful for the additional aircraft he could now schedule. My pilots flew all test hops and had more time for Division Officers work. Everyone was happy it was a win-win situation.

Our operational rate was the highest in the Training Command but there were still improvements that could be made. Our radios were not good. TheT34 was a small aircraft and the Navy did not spend a lot of money on the radios. It was thought they only had to speak to the tower and expensive radios were not needed. If a student could not contact the tower he could not taxi, if he couldn't take off a flight was lost and the pipeline for graduation from VT 1 was slowed down. We would not get new radios but could we change them in time to ensure the completion of the flight. We devised a hot spot for aircraft to taxi to and have a new radio put in their aircraft. We picked up another 2% on our operational readiness. We had 154 aircraft in operational status and 19 more in B status(not to be flown). We could change operational Status on these with a message to higher command. If an aircraft had extensive work we could place it in B status and place a good aircraft in A status for flying. This added a couple of percentage point to our operational readiness. The more aircraft we had the more flights we could schedule and the faster the pipeline completed primary training. I have used the term pipeline now let me explain its use. When I joined VT1 we needed 1700 new pilots each year to replenish the number of pilots that were retiring or being released from active duty. The pipeline was the number of graduating pilots the Navy needed each year to maintain its goal. This number would increase to 1900 then to 2100 during my time in VT1 as the war in Viet Nam expanded.

My Division Officers were now relived of their student training schedule and devoted all their energies to making the Maintenance Department work more efficiently. We devised a plan whereby enlisted men could accompany us on test flights and record numbers for us, This speeded up the time required for a test flight by enabling most of the paperwork to be completed during the flight. It also enabled the enlisted men to experience the fruits of their labor. They loved it and morale was sky high as was our reenlistment rate. We would get suggestions from all ranks and rates on how to save flights or cut down turnaround time between flights. The difference was noted at headquarters and we were singled out for praise but more importantly the whole department took pride in itself. Each man felt, and was, needed and while every suggestion was not employed the originator was thanked and an explanation was given as to why it could not be implemented.

The social life of the Squadron was handled by the wives. Here Joan once again proved her worth. Admiral "Dog" Smith headed the Basic Training Command. "Dog" was his nick name and while I might sound disrespectful using it believe me that is the farthest thing from the truth. The Admiral was to become one of my best friends. Anyone that could sink a Japanese Cruiser single handedly by dropping a bomb down the smoke stack and was the recipient of the Navy Cross deserves the respect I always awarded him. He plays a role in my future as well. A formal party for all of the Training Command was scheduled and each Squadron was to have a theme. The Skippers wife was at a loss since we were so big when Joan said she had it. We have John L Sullivan and our theme would be the "Roaring Nineties" and all the characters of that period would come alive. The Skipper would be Diamond Jim Brady, his wife Carrie Nation. Joan would be Lillian Russell and I and the Marine Major of Flight 4 would play John L Sullivan and Gentleman Jim Corbett. The rest of the Squadron and their wives would pick out notables of that era. Any of the pilots without imagination would be handlers to Gentleman Jim or John L. It worked out well as Joan found a dress shop in Mobile that supplied the dresses as well as the outfits for the guys. We won first place and the whole theme program worked so well that it was used again the following year.

Joan was, again assigned the task of dreaming up a show stopper for the following year. She contacted Ringling Brothers, Barnam and Bailey and they sent her material and pictures of the circus and its performers. She later asked for and received large advertisements the show used for promotion purposes. Somewhere along the way she developed correspondence with the promoter and as she revealed what the Squadron was attempting to do he offered beneficial suggestions. We won again but the rest of the Squadrons were a lot more competitive this time. I remember I was Frank half a Buck the lion tamer and I had a small chair and two of the young wives on leashes. One was a tiger and the other a leopard. The abbreviated costumes they wore attracted attention as we paraded around the Club and more than once I heard the comment made "you really don't beat them with that whip do you Sully". My Father in Law George Fay was visiting with us and he dressed as J. Phillip Boozer (the band leader) and led the band around the Club. Joan was a snake handler and had a huge python wrapped around her. That python was around the house for years to come. The Squadron and particularly the wives got into it and again Joan was the leader. Some of the women were handy with needle and thread and their costumes were spectacular. The girls worked on their costumes for three months and their work was rewarded with the first place prize There were individual prizes awarded as well and some of the other Squadrons proved they had individuals with talent as some of the costumes were works of art. .In those days most of the wives were homemakers and had time to prepare for events such as this and the morale of the Squadron was sky high. These events were fully attended and enjoyed by all concerned. It's an era gone by and most of the wives are working today. The social life has taken a back seat to financial independence.

Another event we had that was supported by most was our bowling league. We took up the whole alley for the evening and while the Squadron only produced a half a dozen real good bowlers the rest fit into the category, "I'm getting better each week". It was enjoyable and Dad Fay bowled with us as a suitable sub. If someone couldn't make it Dad and his average fit in to take his/her place. He loved it! The family loved his visits.

Now about my two children. John and Maura loved Pensacola. They were both into sports and both played little league baseball. John played with an older team but Maura was accepted by the boys and she held her own. John had trained her and she threw the ball like a boy and batted like a boy. She stepped to the plate expecting to get a hit. Her coach was amazed and when some of the boys brought her to their practice the first time he expected to tell her she couldn't play. He said that was before he saw her hit and throw. Now she is a regular on the team and it is the opposing coaches who are amazed. Their schoolwork was great, both were on the honor roll and I was happy I was able to get them to a Catholic School. Here is why. The Skipper of VT1 had replaced a Skipper who had gone to the Staff at CNABATRA (Chief of Naval Basic Training). His wife had produced plays in College and later on for traveling Companies. She was a professional. She was attempting to put on a play using Grade School children. She spread the word around at the wives club meeting and asked for volunteers from all the Squadrons to help in the production and to screen for children with some experience. Our executive officers wife. Kay Orcut, asked Joan to stop by after school and assist her with her task. Joan had John and Maura with her and they sat and watched the children try out for various parts. The lead was Princess Maybloom and was to play opposite the Directors son. One girl after another read for the part but none were satisfactory. Kay. suggested Maura read but the director thought she was too young. After Kay insisted she relented and Maura read. The Sisters had done a good job because Maura read like a champ. The director was amazed and before long was reading the other parts herself to see how Maura would relate to these. Even her inflections were perfect and it became apparent to Joan and Kay that Maura had the part. Later the director told them she was dumbfounded how someone that young could not only read the part but become one with the character she was playing. Both my parents and Joan's came down for the play. Maura especially, since she had the larger part, was studying her lines every day after school. I was amazed at her abilty to memorize, not only her lines but the inflections they required.

The play was a hit and the local TV Station requested that it be taped and they be allowed to program it. The program received great reviews and Maura became our little Sarah Bernhard. One of Maura's talents was her ability to function before an audience. This ability served her well later in life

Things were going well for me as my maintenance department was establishing new records for operational readiness. Our pipeline for producing Naval Aviators was increasing and our number of Vietnamese students was increasing as well. These students were sent to us by the Government of South Vietnam to be trained and would, upon graduation, fly aircraft in defense of their country. This required more of our aircraft be put in " A " status (active flight status) and was an additional load on our maintenance troops. The Vietnamese students had trouble with our language to start with but they also lacked the mechanical skills of the American Students. I had a number of speedy boards(consideration for washout) for Vietnamese students. They were all eager young men. Really the cream of the crop from Vietnam. They were well educated, could speak English and were determined to earn their wings. Like any nationality there are people who just can't master the rigors of flying. One young man stands out in my memory, not for his lack of competence but for what he said to me during the Speedy Board. I had told him the voting in the Board went against him and we were going to recommend he be terminated from the flying program. He had tears in his eyes and he told me his Country had invested a lot of money in his training and education. He went on to say that if he were to graduate and advance to AD Skyraiders and to fly in combat in his country his life expectancy would be five months. He would be proud to fly and die for his Country if only we would reconsider and grant him additional time. He said those words and every member of the board knew he meant them. We reconvened and decided to give him extra time. He made it through the rest of the program at VT1 but I'm sorry to say I don't know how he made out in the advanced Squadrons. He earned my respect and admiration and certainly my best wishes for a long and fruitful life. Speedy Boards were not my favorite moments but certainly when you have someone's future in your hands you must take it very seriously. I only remember overruling the entire Board once. As senior member I had that prerogative. I could tell the younger members were not happy with my decision but the young man was so determined and wanted it so bad that I granted him special time. Years later when I was at Cubi Point, in the thick of the war years, a young Lieutenant came up to my office and told me I had made a profound impact on his life. He was the young lad I had given the extra time He had done well in the program from that point on. He was a helicopter pilot and his ribbons showed me he was a good one. We shock hands and I wished him well. Within a week one of the pilots from that Speedy Board came by and I told him of the young Lieutenants visit. He told me after I had left the Squadron the other members of the Speedy Board had agreed I had been correct. Those two visits I will always remember. The young instructors that served on the Speedy Board were the ones that had to fly those extra hours I was awarding, not me. That young student was begging for the right to become a Naval Aviator. My instinct proved correct and the decision I had made gave the Navy a decorated Navy Pilot. A Speedy Board ending that few of us get to see.

When we deal with other peoples lives, it behooves us to act with discretion and if we err to do so to the other persons benefit. I have always believed that my first duty in the Navy was to help, advise and report accurately on those under my supervision. Any of my enlisted men receiving marks of 3.0 or less were to be scheduled to meet with me in a private session. We would discuss the mark/s and I would schedule the individual to meet with his reporting senior for explanation and what the individual must do to correct the problem. This worked in two ways. First the individual sailor knew I had an interest in his welfare and secondly the reporting senior had to explain what the individual was doing wrong to merit the low mark. I then would ask for a special report in thirty days to ascertain whether corrective action had been taken. This worked so well that our enlistment rate showed a marked improvement I also worked with my Officers. If I thought they needed improvement in any particular line item on their fitness reports we would discuss it and I would suggest ways and means of improving them. I guess I remember my days in the novitiate when my fellow novices would advise me of my faults and areas I needed improvement. It worked then and it worked in the Navy as well but I admit to being extraordinarily tactful in my approach. I wanted all my troops to improve themselves, Officer and Enlisted as well. Unless I have deceived myself all these years I believed I was successful. I can honestly say that I tried to the best of my ability.

Now back to Squadron activity.

The war in Viet Nam was heating up. Our Squadron was flying more hours than ever to keep the pipeline open. VT 1 was the only Squadron every naval aviator had to complete.. Helicopter, single engine and multi engine pilots flew together at VT 1 then they split and went into their specialties. The carrier group continued on in single engine aircraft. The elite group went to Jets and the rest to higher performance prop aircraft. One day an instructor called in an emergency. He had lost half of his horizontal stabilizer but was able to control the aircraft. We cleared the field and he made an uneventful landing. Upon examination we determined the stabilizer had cracked over a period of time. We searched the area for the part that was lost and managed to recover it. It too showed the same results. I called in my Officers and Chiefs as well as all the first class airframes mechanics. We all examined the crack and agreed it could be happening to other aircraft as well. We devised several plans to attack the problem but they all included grounding the fleet of T34 aircraft. The pipeline for all of Naval Aviation would grind to a halt. We also determined how long it would take for an aircraft to be examined before it could be certified for flight. With this information I asked for a meeting with the Skipper, XO and Operations Officer. I laid out the problem along with the solution and gave them a time table for an interim solution. They were real concerned and the Skipper stated we would have to explain to the Admiral why we were closing down the pipeline.. His phone call to the Admiral resulted in our reporting to the Admiral forthwith (immediately). The Skipper was concerned that the Admiral would ask question for which we had

*Shields of Honor*

no answers. The preparation my Officers, Chiefs and senior metalsmiths had made at my earlier meeting made me aware that I could answer any question that might be asked.

The meeting with the Admiral went very well. He had invited the senior engineer from the Narf (Naval Air Rework Facility) and he turned out to be my strongest ally. We explained that a number of aircraft could be in the same condition and if it had been a student with little time in the aircraft it could be a fatality. The Admiral then asked how long it would take to check all the stabilizers and I had an answer that satisfied him. I then asked for assistance from the Narf. I wanted asssurance that a service change be made to beef up the stabilizer in that area and again Harold Yesness, the head engineer at Narf, was my ally. He told the Admiral that I had worked this out in the same manner he would have and that both an examination and a fix would be required to keep the T 34 operating in a safe manner. The fleet was grounded there and then, and I sent a message out to all operators of the T34 informing them of the action and detailed the examination required. When I returned to the Squadron we immediately broke the workforce down into teams that would alternate shifts to ensure twenty four hour of work. Mechanics and Electronics worked with metal smiths in teams. Over the weekend we supplied operations with enough aircraft to maintain a basic flight program. Each day many aircraft were added to the workforce but sadly we discovered about twelve aircraft that had cracks that were serious. We had guessed correctly and by now Harold Yesness was a daily visitor and congratulated me on being as forceful as I had during the meeting. Beechcraft engineers were in at the meetings now and Harold showed them the design of a doubler (the fix) the Narf had engineered and they all agreed it was the answer. We now had to rework the aircraft to install the doubler. We did this over a period of time so Operations could fly the scheduled flights.

One more problem occurred. The S2F Fleet developed a problem. Being a Fleet Aircraft they had priority over training aircraft and our doublers would not be coming to us as scheduled. Again I went to the Skipper, Hal Kendricks, and asked that a meeting be set up with the Admiral and Harold Yesness to discuss this problem. He did so but wasn't optimistic as Fleet always came before training. My advantage was that I had been a S2F Pilot and recognized the problem was not as severe as imagined and shouldn't be considered as serious a safety of flight item as our horizontal stabilizer. The meeting with the Admiral went well and this time the Admiral was my ally and convinced Harold to keep the doublers coming as scheduled. The same week the pipeline of Naval Aviators was increased from 1700 per year to 1900 per year. I talked about Admiral "Dog" Smith before in this narrative but this emergency is where I met him and when we became friends.

I was invited to many functions the Admiral had and by the tone of the introductions he made in my behalf I knew he was a friend.

Where I failed. The pilots were flying three hops a day in the T34B and the heat of the day in the summer was wearing them out. There was no air conditioning in the cockpit. The pilots would get out of the aircraft soaking wet and tired after the first flight. What could be done? My Maintenance Pilots were talking about turbo props. I asked Beechcraft for an unsolicited proposal to convert the T34B into a turbo prop. Our Beeccraft Rep, John Stewart, took all of our thoughts back to the plant and they submitted to me a plan to convert the T34B into a T34C (turbo prop) .The additional power would allow for air-conditioning to be added and this would help our instructors fly additional flights. Later on I would go to Pax River for two tours. If I had that experience earlier in my career I believe I could have made a difference. The Staff at CNABATRA wasn't all that interested in my proposal and I didn't have the knowledge to pursue the plan in the correct manner. The fact that the T34C arrived on the scene much later proved the idea was sound but the guy that was pushing it didn't have the smarts to make it work earlier. I still have the original proposal and I chuckle when I look at it. The maintenance crew was great. All I could do for them is make sure the letters of appreciation the Squadron received were made part of their official record and where possible give them some free time. The operational readiness of the Squadron was the Navy's highest and I made sure every white hat in the Squadron recognized the fact. We flew the increased hours with aircraft to spare.

The Squadron was blessed to have two outstanding Skippers in a row, Hal Kendrick and Bob Orcut. Both were easy to work with if they thought you were doing your job and would back you up to the hilt if you needed assistance. My tour was coming to an end and I was due for orders. Hal had gone to the staff at CNABATRA and he and Bob played a trick on me that had me going. They faked a set of orders sending me to Adak Alaska. Joan wondered whom I had offended and even the kids thought it was the end of the world.

Within the week the true orders came in. I was going to Iceland. Bob and Hal both. promised they had nothing to do with the new orders. They were legitimate and in a few days I had received a welcome aboard notice from Naval Station Keflavic Iceland. I don't think Joan was enthused and the fact that most of the Squadron was feeling sorry for us didn't help.

# Chapter 13
# My tour in Iceland at Naval Station Keflavik

What awaited us was one of the most memorable tours of duty I ever had. We would remember Iceland and the friends we made long after the tour was up. Joan again would shine and as President of the wives club would make everyone's stay in Iceland a memorable one. The only trouble was there was no concurrent travel. Joan would have to remain in the States until I had housing in Iceland. If I went alone, without dependants, it was a one year tour. This was an option and we considered it. The welcome aboard notice spoke to off base living and there were problems. You could only take so much food and drink from the commissary off base each month. The Icelandics had allowed us the use of the land for a NATO base. They reserved the right to police it. If you drank and drove aboard the Base you were subject to Icelandic law. Anything over two drinks was proof of intoxication. The Icelandic Police could stop you and ask you to take a breathalyzer test If you refused they would forcibly require you to give blood at the Base Hospital or if off base at their hospital. The fine was one months pay if proven guilty. This, probably more than anything else, was the bane of some peoples existence. Joan being a none drinker was the duty driver whenever we went out in town to a party. How many people can fit in a VW Bug you ask? More than you imagine if one months pay is the forfeit. Joan could tell you of returning to Base and having to unload four or five just so people could reach for their ID at the Guard Shack. Despite that obvious problem the plusses far outweighed the negatives and Iceland was a most productive tour. When we left Pensacola it was a sad day because we were leaving so many good friends. There were so many farewell parties and our two children were leaving friends they had grown to love. At least Joan and the kids were going back to Brooklyn where they had family and friends. The grand parents eagerly awaited their return and so did many of their old friends from the neighborhood. Both my Dad and Joan's Dad were active in the Church and our children were accepted back into our Catholic School. Joan and the kids would stay with her parents but my parents were just across the street from the school so both grandparents got to see them.

I arrived in Iceland on a DC6 and was met by my new Staff of Maintenance Officers. Bob Laurienzo was the first to greet me and the warmth of his welcome made me realize I was going to enjoy this tour. He and Bill Hackett both made me feel as though I was greeting old friends. I had releaved Carl Deutche. Carl had been the Maintenance Officer at Keflavik and while he had to leave to take a new post at NAVMAT (Naval Material Command) he had left his room with all its extras for me. The extras included a fully stocked liquor closet, a striped rug, a mural of a naked lady hidden discreetly behind a drawn drape and many of the other necessities a bachelor would enjoy. I laughed and remarked it looked like a brothel but I soon found myself enjoying the response of strangers seeing it for the first time. My new found friends enjoyed the ambiance of the room and the nurses loved it. It soon became the meeting place for bachelors, real and geographical. It became the unofficial capitol of the wine mess and later on as our tastes changed the Irish Coffee Mecca. We became known as the answer to the Air Force's infamous bar known as the "Whiff "I can't leave the impression we were a bunch of lushes for that is not the truth but it was a place to relax with a cigar and spirits. Everybody who was anybody wound up here at some time or another even our Skipper, Bob Sparks.

Back to work. After I had checked into my now famous room I reported in to the XO, Cdr James.

## CDR. Jack Sullivan USNR

I liked him from the first time I met him. He gave me the low down on the Base and some of the problems I would soon discover. He was a problem solver and gave me advise that stood me in good stead for the rest of my stay. He then took me into see the Skipper, Captain Bob Sparks. Again I was impressed by the frank and open ways of this man. You knew you were always going to get the top card from Bob and that later saved me a lot of embarrassment. I also had orders to COMFAIR ICELAND. Duel orders meant duel allegiance and even worse two bosses that sometimes want opposing outcomes. This happened early on when the chief of staff asked for something that was opposite to what Captain Sparks wanted done. I went to Captain Sparks, told him of my problem and he went to the chief of staff and settled it. This sort of problem never came up again. The Chief of Staff was an intelligent man and excellent at expressing himself in writing. As a reservist I had not been called on to write official reports and this area of my training was greatly enhanced by the efforts of the Chief of Staff. He worked with me in this regard and would explain both the format and language to be used in these reports until I became proficient.

One of my earliest problems in Iceland was the phasing out of P2 Neptune aircraft and preparation for P3 Orion' arrival. I asked AIRLANT (Commander Air Force Atlantic) for a meeting of all contributors to be held at my Base as soon as possible. AIRLANT set the meeting up and all the players were notified and present at the meeting. This was important since the arrival of this new aircraft was of utmost importance to the fleet and could quickly become a deterrent to the free operation of the Soviet Submarine Fleet . When all players were in attendance I opened the meeting by listing the support equipment I had on hand to support the new aircraft. I then listed the equipment still to be provided. Next to each piece of support equipment to be provided I listed the name of the provider and the timeframe each of the providers listed for delivery. I even took the names of those speaking for the various activities. When the meeting was over I had a complete listing of time, dates and activities responsible. The various activities owned up to their responsibilities and the others agreed. When the meeting was over I put the minutes in writing and sent to each of the activities a copy. I also had taped the meeting so I had the arguments and the resolutions offered by each of the players. Every piece of equipment required was pinned down to a particular activity as was the time frame of its delivery. My Detective training came in handy here. If delays were to occur the guilty party was open to criticism. I sent each of the parties a complete list of agreements along with the timeframes for delivery. I kept phone numbers for each of the participants just in case there were delays. Two vans with required avionics arrived first. We would eventually relocate the avionics into our shops but for now the P2 Venturas were with us as well. The rest of the support equipment arrived close to the scheduled timeframe and few phone calls were required. The transition was a success and I sent out weekly updates to AIRLANT and to the other participants announcing the arrival of the equipment. The P3 s arrived and we had complete support for them.

Glitches occurred not for the lack of support but for the lack of maintenance at their home bases. Inertial Navigation was a problem. The range and speed of the P3 required it to be working since the aircraft would be operating in the northern zone with little or no radio aids. The proximity to Russia was obvious and required the aircraft to be aware of its position at all times. Stateside the radio aids were plentiful and not enough attention was paid to the inertial. My techs were busy, too busy really, bringing the first aircraft up to speed, peaking their inertial to prevent international incidents. While I brought this matter to the attention of the P3 Community little was done Stateside and my tech had to work overtime to peak the gear when the aircraft arrived in Keflavik. Not just the first Squadron but the ones to follow as well. I asked for and received permission to send a second tech to Inertial Navigation School. It consumed 16 weeks of training and was as expensive as sending a student to Harvard but at last I had some backup in that field. The P3 was an instant success and its exploits were legendary. The crews of the P2 had been good and their experience made up for the limitation of the aircraft but the avionics and flight characteristics of the P3 was far superior. COMFAIR was happy with the results and praised all concerned for the smooth way the P3 was transitioned at Naval Station Keflavik..

The Fleet had been maintaining a Radar Barrier. To supplement the fixed radar stations it was necessary to fly aircraft to complete the ring. This was done with Super Connies and they flew in all kinds of weather. These birds did heroic work screening aircraft traffic for unknown and unfriendly aircraft. They completed the loop of a radar net around Russia. The Russians would probe for a weak link and each time they came within our alert range they would find a US Fighter or two on their tails. It became almost a game. I flew with the AirForce F102 Delta Jets until the operations officer became desperate for Navy Pilots to fly the C47 and C54 aircraft. It was fun intercepting the Russians Bears and Bisons. You never understood how the Russians would react, some would wave and some would greet you with obscene gestures. I remember one time the rear gunner activated his guns and swiveled them around to follow us. My wingman turned on his radar gun sight and slipped behind the Bear. The rear gunner turned off his guns immediately and they were put in the upright and stowed position. We later remarked that when the plane commander saw our radar come on he yelled at the rear gunner and the act was over. When we departed we got a friendly wave from the plane commander. One point I have to make. The ocean in this local is not friendly. The temperature is some 33 degrees. A man in that water would last some 30 minutes even in an exposure suit. We had nothing in Keflavik that could reach him in time. You would have to depend on a fishing boat being close enough to pick you out of the freezing water or you are dead. Those Airforce Pilots of the 57th literally were depending on the Pratt and Whitney J57 engine for their lives. They flew day after day and only the Super Connies and their radar knew where they were. Anyone who flys in the Artic has my respect. When I stopped flying with the Airforce they presented me with a picture of the F102 surrounded by the Bear, Buffelo and Bison (three Russian Patrol Planes that probed the Radar barrier each day looking for holes im our Radar net). I have the picture hanging in my den to this day. They also initiated me into the Whiff bar and made me an honorary Air Force Fighter Pilot.

The C47 Skytrain has been around since WW2. It has two fairly dependable Wright Engines and while not the most powerful they were capable of taking the aircraft off from unimproved beaches. The tires were wide and the plane could literally land almost anywhere. The Skipper asked me what airplane could take their place and the only one I could think of was the C130 and that was in short supply and would never be sent to Iceland for our use.

We supported two outlying sites with the C47 and both of these sites literally depended on periodic flights to maintain a tolerable lifestyle . We brought food and supplies and they would make their way to the airport to pick them up. Sometimes this meant plowing the roads to remove snow and ice to reach the airport. The northern site had a radio beacon and we would make IFR approaches relying solely on the radio beacon and our radar altimeter. The site would measure the ceiling by means of a balloon and we would make the approach. In the winter months with almost 11 hours of darkness we would have to time the flight to arrive with the little daylight available. If we missed that window we would have someone from the site go to the end of the runway and hold a light. We would take off and aim at the light. The safety center would have had a ball with this procedure but we never had a problem and all the flights got off safely. Each approach to this site required us to cross the artic circle so each passenger was awarded a blue nose certificate on his first trip.

C54 and the Super Connie( C121) were our R and R aircraft. (Rest and Recreation) The Super Connie belonged to the Admiral but Admiral Weymouth had it configured to hold the max passengers when he wasn't on it and it would rotate with the C54 on flights to Scotland, London and Frankfurt. I served as flight commander on the C47 but only 2nd Pilot on the 54. Following rotation we would have to take one trip per month to Germany. The flight left on Thursday Morning and arrived in Germany on Thursday night. We would have Friday and Saturday in Germany and leave on Sunday Morning for Keflavik via London and Preswick Scotland. The flight crew would be deluged with requests from people to pick up items for them and you would spend a lot of your time shopping for people. That pretty much describes the flying the Base Pilots performed but I have to mention flying over Glaciers and breaking off ice on the wings and props wasn't exactly normal flying for guys used to Stateside flying. You adapted rather quickly because it occurred regularly and the pilots with experience taught you the ropes. Another local problem was the high winds. Eighty knot winds would come up almost from nowhere. I had to land in one in a C47. It was right down the runway and I literally got to pick the spot I wanted to sit down. When I landed I put all passenger in the tail of the aircraft to keep it on the ground. I needed a big Booder tug to tow me to the parking spot and even then I had to park into the wind and tie the tail down. It was as close as you could come to flying a Harrier in those days One flight in particular I have to mention. We had a group of girls come to entertain us. They were from Clark College in Dubuque, Iowa. It was a small Catholic College specializing in music and arts. They were accompanied by a Nun who acted as their manager and director. I flew them to the two sites on two separate days and sat in on their performance each day. They were wonderful, friendly girls and performed like troopers. I had the Nun up in the cockpit and allowed her to fly the airplane. I had her keep the small airplane in the gyro horizon level and then showed her how to make small turns and changes of altitude. She got the hang of it real soon and thoroughly enjoyed flying. I then brought the whole group over the artic circle and told them they were now crossing the Artic Circle and they were now bluenoses. When I said we were crossing the Artic Circle they all looked out the window expecting to see a line on the ground and we laughed about it later. On the way home I took them to see the volcano, called Surtsi, that had recently popped up and announced on the intercom that this is what hell must look like. They were all impressed by the volcano. The Nun asked me to bring my family to the performance they were to give at the Base on Sunday and introduced my family to all the girls. Maura was delighted and during intermission asked permission to borrow a guitar. Before I could stop her she was playing and singing for the girls. I had no idea that she had been taking lessons from our neighbors and was dumfounded when she sang the ballad of the Green Berets. I was also amazed at how well she sang and played the guitar. Now she is a professional and has performed in many places and Cities in this Country as well as the Voice of America.

*CDR. Jack Sullivan USNR*

Big NATO ( North Atlantic Treaty Organization) Exercise. Not long after I arrived we had a big NATO exercise and we had to make the 600 man camp ready for use. The camp was made up of a series of quonset huts that were inhabitable but crude. The Skipper came to me one day and asked me to accompany him on an inspection of these huts. The electrical system in several was unsat and he asked me to take my men and repair them. I had my electricians look at the huts ,draw the supplies from Public works and make the repairs. They did it without questioning but when it was finished I told the Skipper it really wasn't my job. He laughed and said it was done and that if left to Public Works it would be completed after the exercise and that is why he asked me to do it. I remembered my experience in New York and laughed. These exercises brought many of the NATO Nations together and as I interfaced with them all I met some interesting people and learned a lot of their customs and method of operating. The Base would be loaded and the various Clubs would be taxed to provide food and entertainment. They were summertime exercises and the long days made for a lot of flying. It was also the time of intense Soviet activity and the various nations had a chance to operate with the enemy as a target. The Op Center was busy keeping tract of the various aircraft and confirming Soviet contacts. The briefings each morning were informative and well attended. The Canadians would visit several times each year so we got to know them by name but the Brits and Danes and Norwegians were strangers and we would only see them on occasion. In the midst of the exercise the Barrier aircraft maintained their role as did the 57th Fighter interceptor Squadron so we had various and sundry aircraft taking off and landing all day. We had a NATO Command at the Base and while they were technically in charge of the operation and did the planning the whole Base was involved and expected to cooperate fully with NATO. When the operation was complete and everyone had left the Base the clean up began. There was almost a let down following such hectic flying and you could almost imagine a general sigh of relief.

The Barrier aircraft received the highest priority and we were expected to cooperate with any and all maintenance requirements. Captain Larry Bounce was the Skipper of one of the Squadrons. When ever he arrived I would be on hand to meet him personally and I can still remember him coming down the ladder of his aircraft, seeing me and giving me the big " God D—- it Sully where are my engines" We were required to maintain two engines for the barrier air craft, built up and ready to go at all times. We did that but they also had the privilege of removing parts from a built up engine to repair one in service so we had a logistics nightmare. Their reports would always show a partially built up engine rather than the fully built up engine

I had delivered to them. I would explain the problem to Captain Bounce and he would be understand. (until next time) We had a good relationship and it served me well in the future when he was my Boss at AirPac.

The first year seemed to fly by but my family was still in the States and I was what we described as a geographic bachelor. This fit in with the Skippers plans and he called me into his office one day and introduced me to a civilian I had never met before. It turned out that this civilian worked for the State Department and Dean Rusk in particular. Dean was going to the NATO Countries to set up a civilian fleet of ships that would carry nuclear missiles and be deployed to various places. He would be visiting Iceland and would have twenty two secretaries and aids with him. The American Embassy would host his visit but could not handle his aids. The civilians task was to make plans for the twenty two women that would be with Dean Rusk. My purpose was to plan for and entertain the women. What a job for an old fighter pilot. It so happened we had a formal party planned for that night and the girls would be invited. The varied in age but no problem because so did the escorts I provided them. We wore our mess dress and the girls had formals with them. They checked into the Loftlieder Hotel and changed into their formals. We then escorted them to the Officers Club and we really had a marvelous evening. They were all great girls and Navy Pilots know how to entertain. After the dance broke up at two in the morning we brought the girls back to my room for Irish coffee. No problem since I think I had the corner on the Irish whiskey in Iceland and everyone had a coffee pot in their room. The Icelandic Cream has to be the best in the world and whips up in no time. When we returned the girls to the Loftlieder Hotel it was to change into their traveling clothes as there was no time for sleep before take off. When the Skipper came down to say goodbye to Dean Rusk half his Officers still in their Mess Dress uniforms met him. He asked if we had partied all night and then answered his own question with " you son of a guns" Some weeks later the Skipper and I were playing liars dice in the bar when he was called out for a phone call. He returned a few minutes later with a surprised look on his face and said Sully that was the Ambassador on the phone. He just received a phone call from Dean Rusk. It seems that Dean was interested in discovering what part of the trip the girls had enjoyed most. Iceland was the unanimous choice and your name was given to Dean Rusk. He notified the Navy and you have a commendation from The State Department in your jacket. We both laughed but I can honestly say it was a great party and these girls were ideal dates.

The Skipper wanted me to stay the full two years and hurried up the transfer of a senior officer in quarters so I would have an apartment on Base. Joan agreed to come and the children wanted to be with their Dad so it was settled. I took the apartment and agreed to stay for another year. Joan spoke to the Navy and was booked on Pan American vice the DC6 the Navy flew. Logistically it was easier for everyone as we were only minutes from JFK International Airport where Pan Am was based. I was ready for her arrival when the Pan Am agent in Iceland (a good friend) notified me the flight would overly because of weather. He transmitted a message to Joan via the Planes' Captain that I would follow her progress and meet her whenever she returned.. Joan and the children landed in Scotland and were put up at a very nice hotel on one of the golf courses. She then was flown from Scotland to Reykjavik on Icelandic Air's DC6. The Captain lent me his car and driver and I met her in Reykjavik. It was cold and blustery but the family was together again. The kids took to the new base and were soon surrounded by new friends. They couldn't get over the amount of sunlight they had during the long days of summer. Their friends soon introduced them to the amenities of the Base. Free movies, a youth center and scheduled bus rides to any place on the Base. Our apartment was just across the street from the O'Club and the school. Joan too was welcomed by the wives and soon became engrossed in the wives club functions to the point where she was elected President. Her imagination and intuition resulted in the Embassy wives of the various nations being invited to a formal dinner at the Club. This was so well received that the Ambassador asked her to have another such event. The second event she asked all the embassy wives to wear the native dress of their countries. This was spectacular and the Club was packed, even the geographic bachelors attended and the Ambassador and the Admiral both complimented Joan on the event. The Embassy wives invited Joan to their teas and were eager to attend the Clubs functions. Because of the social life in Iceland both on and off the Base we thoroughly enjoyed our tour.

The city of Keflavik had a nine-hole golf course and even before I arrived my sponsor had me signed up as a member. A number of military on Base played golf and we convinced the people in charge of our recreation fund to lease a sheep farm we could turn into a nine hole golf course. A number of us helped plan the holes and we literally turned that farm into a pretty nice golf course. It was about a half mile from the Keflavic course. The agreement we had with the owner called for the fish racks to be left in place and the sheep to be able to wander on the course. As the sheep kept the grass cut this was no problem, the fish racks were just obstacles as trees would be on a stateside course. We played around them or over them depending on your skill. As I belonged to both courses I promoted the first Icelandic American Golf tournament The first nine holes would be played on the Keflavic course the second nine holes would be played on the Navy course . Invitations were sent to the golfers at the Reykjavik Golf Club, the Akuari Club, and the club in the Vestman Islands. As we had already played those courses as guests of the various golf clubs we knew all concerned would gleefully accept the invitation. They arrived by plane and Buss and we made arrangements for them to spend the night at lodgings aboard the Base. The turn out for the tournament was even larger than expected but we were able to handle it. The camaraderie between all the players made the event a tremendous success and the party that night at the Chiefs Club was a real hit. The chairman of the Vestman Island Golf Club came to me with what appeared to be tears in his eyes and told me that if I ever visited Iceland in the future to please contact him and he would send a plane for me so we could play golf in the Vestman Islands together. I knew he meant it and I was touched. To a man, Americans and Icelandic alike the event brought us together like few events can. God bless golf!!!

The airport manager, Peter Gusterson, was already a friend but this event made us even closer. We were working on a Status of Force Agreement that would give Loftlieder (Iceland's commercial air carrier) space in one of our hangars. They had acquired a new and larger aircraft (CL44) a turbo prop that was too big for Reykjavik Airport and would land and be maintained at Keflavic. We closed off a bay and a half in the large hanger that had been built originally for B36 aircraft and gave it to Loftleider. The land the Base was built on belonged to Iceland. They lent us the land but according to the agreement all buildings we constructed on the Base would be given to the Icelandic Government, whole and complete when we (NATO) left the Base. This would include housing, schools, movies and the swimming pool. We paid no rent but the Icelandic's maintained the privilege of policing the Base. The Icelandic Government maintained a strict policy of not drinking and driving. They were heavy drinkers and the policy made sense. Two drinks could get you a fine of a months pay . You had to submit to a breath test and should you fail that you must give blood for a final test. Your blood would give you away and there was no appeal. This was the hardest thing for Americans to understand and I guess because of my Police training I was elected to give the lecture to all new arrivals. We are accustomed to lawyers representing us in all our problems but here it was only truth that could defend you. If you were over the blood alcohol level your blood would testify against you, if not it would indicate your innocence. This is how I explained it to all concerned. It was easy because I truly believe this is the way we should handle it in the States as well.

Arlis 2 Ice Island. The Artic Research Lab had been maintaining a program of experiments on an Ice Island in the Artic Ocean. There were many experiments. Some were secret and some can be discussed. The Island was made up of clear fresh water glacier ice. It was over 200 feet deep on one side and some 80 feet on the other side. It was over a mile wide and over a three mile long. It made an ideal landing site for supply aircraft. It was held in place by artic sea ice made up of salt water and fresh water combined. The Island had been circulating in the Artic Ocean for an undetermined number of years before it was discovered. It made a suitable floating base for the experiments the Artic Research Lab wanted to pursue and was manned by an international crew of scientist hired for the purpose. They drilled through the ice to enable the scientists to lower probes below the ice to measure the amount of heat released through the earths surface. They also measured the distance from the bottom of the ice to the surface below. Max Schindler from the Artic Research Lab had asked for a meeting with the Admiral because the Ice Island had broken free from the Artic Ocean and was going to float over the northern coast of Canada and would float down the Eastern Coast. They were going to abandon it but realized they had little data on the ocean floor on the eastern coast of Canada. This could prove invaluable. The logistics of supplying the Ice Island from Alaska were almost impossible and Iceland would become a better Base of support. The Admiral decided I was the one who should manage this operation and called me in to the meeting with Max Schindler. Max informed me he had a C47 they had been using to supply the base and he would need Maintenance support for this aircraft. It was a reasonable request and the matter was closed. I invited Max Schindler back to my Quarters where he had dinner with my family. Max fascinated the kids with tales of wolves the artic research lab kept. He told them about how friendly they were to the keeper and his family and the keeper had no qualms about letting his family go in among the wolves. He told us about how agile they were and would leap over one another's back just for the fun of it. He also told us stories of artic survival and how the Eskimos would survive under almost impossible circumstances. He departed that night leaving us with adventure stories to remember. My family still talks about his visit to this day.

The aircraft would be flown to Iceland on schedule and I would maintain it. The plane arrived and the civilian pilot was very compatible and a seasoned artic pilot. I flew to the Ice Island as copilot on the first trip and learned about landings made on ice. The sea ice will support a C47 if the ice is at least 19 inches thick. The problems encountered were ice mounds formed by winds and in the summer months the temperature some times get above freezing and a thin layer of water will form on the ice causing hydroplaning. Both of these events are tough on the aircraft but ground observers were trained to locate and warn the pilot of their existence. When I arrived at the Island I met the scientist stationed there. They were very interesting and I listened to their every word. One humorous event involved an incident where the scientists had just bored a hole some three feet across and one hundred eighty feet down through the ice. . The probes were lowered and the equipment to monitor the results was placed in a room honed out of the ice in the surrounding area.. One day a seal came up the hole from the depths below and both the seal and scientist monitoring the probes met face to face. Both were terror struck. The seal made a one eighty and disappeared down the hole and the scientist fled in terror back to the main cabin to tell of his encounter. It was a standing joke on the Island.

We would bring food and clothing and the necessary equipment out to the Ice Island. They had a large supply of fuel for our aircraft that had been brought out earlier by a C130. We would take some fuel to give us loiter time in case the Base at Keflavik was closed or weathered in at the time of return. I made a number of the flights and flew the C47 out to land on the ice several times each week.. As I got to know the scientist better they would tell me of their experiments.

One day I received a message from CBS (television) they wanted to film the Ice Island and tell the tale of its existence and its use by the Artic Research Lab. Max Schindler was agreeable and I set the program up. I flew a team of reporters and filmmakers out to the Island and they spent the day filming and reporting on those unclassified projects. They sent me pictures later on showing their work and it is still fun to look

## Shields of Honor

at the pictures of the scientists that had become my friends and the ice island that had been their home.

The gang out at the Island gave me some ice that had been taken from the glacier when they bored the hole. It was reputed to be two thousand years old and I brought a chunk back with me on the airplane and used it for ice in a cocktail party I had. When I told everybody they were drinking cocktails with ice 2000 years old everyone stared at their drink. We toasted the crew from the Island and the work they were doing.

Another one of the marvels on the Ice Island. The Eskimos provided the physical labor, driving tractors, plowing the runway and maintaining the shelters. They would work in the coldest of weather and when they would get warm would shed layers of clothing to maintain body temperature. They instinctively knew what to do in this weather and if they told you to do something regarding the weather you better pay attention because it would happen. I remember one telling me to take off within the hour, which I did, and a radio report from the Ice Island that we received on the way back reported a white out they were experiencing. We couldn't have taken off in those conditions.

Instead of evacuating the Island by air it was decided to send the icebreaker Edisto up to remove the crew. The sea ice was breaking up and the Island would be in that local before the month ended. The Edisto came up and we met the captain and the crew. The Icelandic Government had asked the American Ambassador if the ship could clear a couple of the Icelandic Ports before going to the Ice Island. The Admiral agreed and the Edisto made points with the Icelandic Government by breaking the ice in those ports before going to the Ice Island. The scientist were evacuated in plenty of time and the Ice Island became a floating Iceberg of serious dimensions that required Maritime warnings. The equipment was expendable and because of the shape of the glacier was thrust into the sea when it turned upside down. Centuries in the future some underwater explorer will wonder how they got where they did. The research scientists were welcomed to a party in our Officers Club and were feted for their work before returning to their own Countries. It was another exciting job for me that was outside my job description.

We lose the Barrier Aircraft. In my second year the word came from higher authority our barrier aircraft were no longer needed to maintain our radar network and would be phased out. The many pilots who had worked tirelessly to maintain that Barrier have to be given a special place in Naval Aviation. The weather they launched in had to be seen to be believed. Ice, high winds and almost zero visibility failed to keep them from maintaining their vigil in the sky. The Super Connies were old and required a lot of work so their maintenance people shared in the glory as well. We would have to account for and salvage the support equipment the Navy had provided. This was a huge task as the equipment had been at the Base for a long time and the records were incomplete. The Squadrons rotated and on occasion brought gear from their original Base without notifying us. We sorted it out to the best of our ability and any overages were reported to higher authority for disposition. It was a backbreaking task but was finally completed and the gear was placed in storage for final disposition.

While working on this we also worked on a task given to us by AIRLANT. We had to break the Maintenance Department down into two groups.. The men that controlled the Station Aircraft was transferred to the Operations Department. Intermediate maintenance would have to be done with fewer personnel than before. This presented a problem. The amount of personnel needed to make up two staffs was insufficient. Maintenance control and material control had been performing two functions and if separated they would not have the capability to perform them separately. It was argued but AIRLANT insisted so we had to comply. Bob Laurienzo was my best officer for the task. He took his troops down to the big hanger and set up shop as the operations maintenance officer. In deciding who would stay and who would go I had to put my priority on Fleet Aircraft, the P3. The technicians I had trained on P3 avionics, electrical and systems stayed in the shops, those that had been working and flying Station Aircraft went to Bob. The staff was fairly evenly divided. Both of us were short of people. We had implemented the new 3M Maintenance instructions and were following them to the best of our ability. The Squadrons felt the new instructions hampered them but frequent meetings helped reduce the gripes.

Everything seemed to be working out when we had a disaster. Our Skipper, Bob Sparks was killed in a helicopter accident. He was returning from a day at the fish camp along with several other senior people when their helicopter crashed. Everyone on board was killed. Cdr. J. Hahn and I were made the senior members of an accident investigation board. The pilot of the helicopter had been a friend of mine from VT1 and I knew him to be a good pilot. The helicopter evidently had a runaway throttle and landing could be made in either of two ways. The pilot could elect to make a high speed landing or he could cut the throttle, put the collective down and make a dead stick landing. They were following the road from Reykjavik to Kevlavik when the blades conned and the helicopter plunged to the ground. The Base was all doom and gloom since all the people on that helicopter were particularly loved. The Skippers son was to graduate from high school the night his father was killed. It was months before the Base returned to normal and Captain Pierre took command. He and his wife recognized the position they were in and did everything possible to restore equilibrium. By strength of will they managed to shake the doldrums and restore the Base to the congenial place it had been. He was a badminton player and we teamed up to play against some of the NATO Staff. In the winter badminton was very popular and contrary to the popular conception is an exhausting game if played by good players. The Captain was good and I had worked on it for almost two years and could hold my own with almost everyone at the Base. The Icelanders had played it since their youth and were formidable opponents. .

Soon the date of my transfer would arrive. Orders came announcing I would be going to the Naval Air Test Center at Patuxent River as the Maintenance Officer of the Intermediate Maintenance Department. Leaving a Base where you have made so many friends is always tough but is what the Navy makes you do. A new challenge would await me. I looked back at what Iceland had made possible. My family and I had traveled through Europe and visited Countries we had only seen as pictures on a map, My children had experiences that few are fortunate to ever partake of and would stand them in good stead later on in applying for colleges. We had visited my family in Ireland and had taken pictures of the homestead where my father and his brothers and sister were born. I met my uncle Frank, the Sullivan who had stayed behind and kept the forty acre farm the family owned. The family house was made with walls that were three foot thick and covered with a thatched roof and was much smaller than I had imagined from my father's tales. It was hard to believe that five brothers and one sister were brought up in it. The bathroom was outside in the unheated barn. The view from the house was spectacular as it was on the crest of a hill overlooking the lake down below. The green color of the grass and surrounding bushes was breathtaking. The flowers my grandmother had planted were in full bloom and my uncle Frank said she would have been proud to name the various varieties had she still been alive. Meeting uncle Frank was as emotional as any I have ever had. He hugged me and told me I was welcome and that I looked like my father. We both wept for the shear joy of the meeting. He embraced my wife and children telling them they were most welcome as well. And they became teary eyed as well. We met John and Mary his nephew and his nephew's wife. His daughter Bridget and her husband came over later and we all had tea. Maura and John were playing with the dog and later rode the horse. I took movies of the events. We stayed in a hotel in Limerick and spent several days with my uncle and his family and when we left my uncle Frank gave me a big hug and told me how happy he was to have met Connie's son and that we would never meet again on this earth. I was reduced to tears at his words and hugged him even tighter. My wife and children were all crying, so was everyone in attendance. I cried again when I showed my father the movies of the house he had been born in and Uncle Frank hugging me goodbye and the words he said at the time. I was working hard to blink the tears out of my eyes when I noticed my Dad was crying as well. Even now at eighty years of age, as I write this, the tears are streaming down my face. It is an emotional moment to relive. We Irish are an emotional lot, true to our God our Country and to our friends and to finally meet the uncle who had stayed behind to work the family farm was heartwarming and we bonded immediately as family. My family, my wife Joan and Son John jr and daughter Maura shared my emotions. We all felt the profound sadness at leaving our relatives. I did return twice more but Uncle Frank was right, he was gone when I next returned but his words were in my heart. Our tour in Iceland was one of the finest. The family was able to travel through all of Europe, England, Ireland and Scotland. I know it broadened their horizons and they still remember it. Living and visiting foreign lands gives you an insight into this world that others can only live vicariously.

# Chapter 14
# My tour at the
# Naval Air Test Center
# Patuxent River Maryland

We leave for Naval Air Station Patuxent River (Pax River). Iceland had been a great tour but now we would have to say our farewells to friends and prepare for our new Base. I had landed at Patuxent River several times and remembered this was the Base that tested all new aircraft. It was the home of the Test Pilots school and would be an interesting place to work. It was, at that time the home of the P3 Community. The P3 Training Squadron VP 30 was there as well as four other P3 Squadrons. I had met some of the pilots up in Iceland and had recognized the P3 Community was active and vibrant. I liked the caliber of pilots they produced and the spirit they demonstrated. I looked forward to the new assignment. I had bought a new Volkswagon Squareback sedan in Iceland and it had been shipped to the States for me. I also brought my little bug(volks beetle) back to the States. We spent a few days with our folks in New York before driving down to Pax River. The trip down was pretty uneventful until we got to Waldorf and made the turn down rout 5. The number of farms we encountered on the trip down recalled our early days on Long Island when farms were everywhere. Joan immediately liked the area. When the wife likes the place you are going to be living for the next two or three years it certainly makes things a lot easier. We stayed in a hotel for two nights while our quarters were made ready. Having billet quarters and knowing where you are going to live is enjoyable. They called our quarters the two John Circle meaning there were at least three bedrooms and two baths to each set of quarters. We found them very comfortable. Our Catholic Chaplain had written to me in Iceland and had both of our children enrolled in Little Flower Catholic School. Everything fell into place. The kids made friends the day we moved in and some of them remain so to this day. Joan met some of the wives and was taken to the Wives Club Meeting where she met more of them. Her fame preceded her and she soon found herself on various committees. I checked in and met the CO and XO and found that I too had been mentioned, in favorable terms, by the Skippers of the P3 Squadrons who had visited us in Iceland. I had orders to the Admirals Staff and was delighted to once again be working for Admiral " Dog " Smith. When I checked in with his secretary she informed me the Admiral was delighted to see my orders and I was to be ushered in as soon as I arrived. He was most gracious and arose, came around from his desk and warmly shook me hand. I have to say that Admiral Smith was to become one of my best friends in the Navy and the love, admiration and respect I had for that man knew no bounds. If I ever was to disappoint him, and I don't think I ever did, it would be like disappointing my own father (which I'm sorry to say I did).

I then checked into my own Maintenance Department. Meeting new Officers and men is easy, evaluating them takes considerable more time. Shortly after my arrival we were to have an inspection by NAVAIR . Patuxent River is under NAVAIR and their staff would evaluate us. I concluded the best way to learn about my new Department was to give them an inspection myself. This way I would learn in advance what NAVAIR would discover later on in their inspection. It would give me a few weeks to make correction where needed. The Department needed help. There were many errors to correct and much planning to do before our inspection. We took the glaring errors and tried to correct them first. Maintenance publications had to be updated or new ones ordered. New test Equipment ordered and obsolete equipment surveyed. The training programs for our enlisted personnel updated to show compliance with current instructions.

This was all done or at least put in process to be completed. The inspection came and the shortfall we had discovered were highlighted but the inspecting Office in his comments kindly noted that correction had been put in place since my arrival and that the Department was heading in the right direction. Some times it is easier to take a Department that has bottomed out and improve on it than to take a well run Department and keep it running smoothly. I must admit my Officers and Chiefs wanted to get the Department on track and they worked long hours in the beginning to make it happen. We were under a new Maintenance instructions and the first thing we did was to have all Officers arrive an hour earlier than normal. Each Officer had been assigned a Chapter and he would brief the rest of us on its contents and meaning. He had to study that chapter at home, become the resident expert in its meaning and brief us to the point we all were aware of its instructions. In a month were all familiar with the new instructions and were able to implement them in the Department. The results in the next month or two were noticeable. The moral in the Department improved and the work ethic in each of the Divisions improved dramatically. Sometimes a little pressure from the top if evenly distributed can work miracles. My good fortune was to have division officers who really wanted a smooth running outfit and were willing to work hard to make it happen. When I asked them to report an hour earlier they didn't gripe and at the end of the month were happy we had put the extra time in to learn the contents of the new instructions. They remarked that friends in other outfits were questioning them for answers on various parts of the instructions.

I was required to hold a monthly meeting with all the Maintenance Officers of the various outfits we supported. They all depended on us for support equipment and for repair of components that malfunctioned on their aircraft. These monthly meeting were pure gripe sessions in the beginning. These gripes not only had to be sorted out but we had to instruct not only our people, but their people as well, on the content and meaning of the new instructions. As my department improved the gripes became fewer and fewer. The flow of information became easier and within four or five months we had a smooth running department. I could now work on other projects. The inertial navigation problem was the first. I had a meeting with all the commanding officers of the P3 squadrons. I explained the problem I encountered in Iceland when the P3 arrived with uncalibrated inertial navigation systems. I explained how difficult it was to calibrate them in Iceland and yet how necessary it was to have navigation equipment that was working in good order as the aircraft had to operate close to the Russian border where there were little or no navigation aids. I wanted to establish a program where by the P3s at Pax would check their inertial navigation on each flight to ascertain where help was needed. They agreed and it was done. We gradually improved the inertial navigation for the whole fleet and the planes that went to Keflavic performed immediately on arrival.

The Test Center was a different problem. The project officers sometimes used test equipment that was purchased through their Programs. Sometimes it was identical to mine and some times it was brand new state of the art equipment. If it belonged to the Navy I should have been made aware of its existence as eventually it would have to be picked up on my inventory. Some times it was borrowed from the Aircraft Company that built the airplane and would make its way back to that company. Talking to all the individual project officers was impossible so I brought it up at the Admirals meeting with the Test Directors. It took some time to explain my position as most of them thought I was trying to interfere with their programs. While they agreed with my position it remained a bone of contention with the project officers for some time.

I got a break when the Admiral made me the chairman of the social golf committee. We played home and home golf tournaments with the contractors. We would sponsor them at Pax and they would sponsor us at their course. I made the arrangements and set the dates. Most of the Directors were golfers and were eager to play in the matches. The contractors enjoyed them as well. We socialized with them and got to know them in a way that would be impossible without golf. I have to say I enjoyed matches and even today I look back on them as some of the high points of my golfing days. In today's climate there might be people who would look at this socializing with jaundiced eyes but it was done above the board and I think improved the ability of both Navy and Contractor to enter into civilized conversation. I was proud to be part of it. Another task the Admiral gave me was the Chairman of the Navy Relief effort. I was to be the deputy to the Chairman the first year and Chairman the following year. There was an awful lot of planning to be done and at least part of your day for the four months preceding the drive was spent in meetings. The air show that accompanied the event was complex and the number of people required to coordinate the various events was staggering. One of the biggest money makers for Navy Relief was the sale of chance books. Each of the various activities that made up the Test Center was tasked with selling a certain amount of books. All kind of tactics for selling these books was employed. Car washes sprang up all over the base as activities tried to make their goals. Pat Hannigan was on the Admirals Staff and one of the premier sponsors of Navy Relief. He took me outside to visit the Top Businessman in the area who had sold great quantities of books for the Navy League. I met a number of them and even today count them as valued friends. Some of them are in my Rotary

Club and are still active in Navy Relief and the Navy League. The air show brought thousands of visitors to Pax River and was then and still is an eagerly anticipated event.

One of the highlights I still remember is our trip out to Edwards Air Force Base to visit with our counterparts in the Air Force. The Admiral was invited to view the SR71 and asked me to come along. It was first glimpse at the plane that was, and probably still is, the worlds fastest. The two Colonels that showed us the aircraft had flown it countless times and when I blurted out that it looked like it could do mach 3 they smiled and told me that if I were doing mach 3 I had better get out of their way. I don't know what my facial expression was but believe me I was impressed. We met and talked to the pilot who had saved the supersonic bomber by use of a paper clip. Again I was impressed. Between these two Test Centers there is so much aviation folk lore, so many heroes, so much achievement and to be in the company of these pilots was a privilege. I appreciated the work being done at the Test Center. Not only the work on new aircraft and systems but the hard work being done in the P3 Community as well. Thanks to the cooperation I received from the Commanding Officers of all these squadrons I honestly believe we sent the best P3s in the Fleet to Keflavic and Rota for actual Submarine work with the Russians. Cdr. Waller had been the Skipper of one of these Squadrons and had been responsible for developing and disseminating tactic to be used by the Fleet. When he was made a Captain he was transferred to NAVAIR as Program Manager for the P3. I visited him at NAVAIR and sought his assistance. The inertial Navigation I have harped on comprised seven boxes that had to be working, and aligned with in specified tolerances. To do this you had to remove the boxes and put them on test equipment at the AIMD. This required time. Litton was asked if they had a piece of test equipment thatcould test the alignment while the boxes remained on the aircraft. They replied it could be done in their factory in Toronto, Canada. I was invited to bring a party with me and visit the factory for a demonstration. I called Captain Waller and during a subsequent visit at NAVAIR he approved of a flight to Toronto by one of the P3s from Pax. It was set up and the local Litton Rep accompanied us to Toronto for the demonstration. The Litton Industry at Toronto proved to my satisfaction that it was feasible and even had drawings of what the finished product would look like. They had it priced and a schedule for delivery if we should be interested. The Squadron Maintenance Officer and I agreed it would be a tremendous time saver and my avionics Officer was thoroughly impressed. The Litton President told me I seemed even more anxious to get this done then his people. I explained the Russian Problem to him and he understood the anxiety. The Russians would intercept any aircraft infringing on their airspace and the

*Shields of Honor*

only navigation system we could count on was our inertial navigation so it had to be working flawlessly. I returned to NAVAIR with the drawings and schedule and Captain Waller approved of the acquisition. While I was not at Pax River when the Test equipment arrived I received a letter from the Litton Rep telling of the complete success of the cart. The AIMD could roll the cart up to the aircraft, hook it up and completely align and test the Inertial Nav on the aircraft saving countless man hours. The P3B was soon replaced by the P3C and as the P3C had a different inertial Nav the Cart was overcome by events. I was happy, the AIMD (aircraft intermediate maintenance department) was functioning smoothly as I had a year remaining at Pax River( or so I thought). Captain Tom Goben was at OPNAV and was the leading 1520 (maintenance officer designation) and worked for CNO as part of his staff. He had told us they were looking for a replacement for the Maintenance Officer at Cubi Point in the Philippines. It was the biggest job we had in Maintenance in those days as Cubi had backup capability for everything and anything they had in Viet Nam or in the Fleet supporting Viet Nam. It also had capabilities found only at Cubi. He asked me if I was interested. I had heard of a job as head of Maintenance in Viet Nam that had been listed as requiring an AEDO. I asked him for that job, he agreed and for a while I had it. One day I received a message to report to CNO at a specific time and date. When I arrived I met Captain

Goben who accompanied me to CNO's Office. I was then told by CNO I would receive orders to relieve Cdr. Hamilton as Maintenance Officer of Cubi Point. He pointed out that everything the Test Center was working on would soon appear in the Fleet and I had better knowledge of it than any other Maintenance Officer. Case closed I was going to Cubi and there really were no arguments. CNO was right and in my heart and mind I had to agree with him. What I hadn't told you was that earlier the same week Admiral Smith had called me into his office. He revealed that he was getting orders to Japan as Commander Naval Forces Japan. He wanted to take me with him as his staff security officer. Captain Goben still had me tentatively slated to go to Viet Nam and that was the job I wanted because it would put me in a position to oversee the aircraft maintenance in all of Viet Nam. When CNO told me I would be going to Cubi he told me the orders would be coming out within the week but in the meantime I was to maintain complete silence until they were published. I thought that sounded strange at the time but when the orders came out and I explained to Admiral Smith what had happened he was furious and said "that old SOB knew I planned to take you with me to Japan and he wanted you for Cubi" In this case the CNO was right because much of what I worked on did wind up in Cubi and I guess, because of that, I was the right man for the job. I attended a farewell party for Admiral Smith and wound up with a small group of his close personal staff. We laughed about some of the funnier events that occurred during his tenure. He had a wonderful sense of humor. He also had a twitch that would strike him every few minutes. The Chief of Staff had told me of one occurrence where the Admiral had arrived at the BOQ bar unannounced and found a young officer imitating his twitch to the delight of some of his drinking buddies. Instead of venting his rage the Admiral walked up behind the young Officer and said "I got mine from syphilis. What did you get yours from?" It stopped them right in their tracks and then they suddenly realized the Admiral was jesting and they broke out in laughter. It broke the ice and nobody made any more jokes about his twitch. He was a warm human being and he left the bar that night having made friends of everyone present. His self deprecating humor surfaced one time on the golf course when he confided to me and Captain O'Neil (the base CO) that if he could incorporate his twitch into his drive he could hit it with Sam Snead. What a great guy to work for and what a friend. He will appear in this narrative again. Leaving PaxRiver was tough. The XO had a party for Joan and I and I remember a hand made sign that read " the Sullivans go to Cubi Point with ten thousand Irish smiles". A take off on the distance from Pax to Cubi. Captain O'Neil and Cdr Barnet the CO and XO of Pax gave us the party and all of our friends at Pax were invited. The place overflowed with well wishers and it was tough making a goodbye speech.

# Chapter 15
# My Tour at NAS Cubi Point in the Philippines

We had to make a lot of the preparations beforehand and we decided to drive cross country in our 65 Chrysler 300 L. The kids looked forward to it and the same ground rules as previous trips applied. We would be on the road at 6 AM and would drive 150 miles before breakfast. The kids would sometimes sleep during that stretch of the trip, a blessing, and we had peace and quiet. We would drive 400 miles a day and get a hotel or motel accommodation that had a swimming pool. Everybody was happy with this as we usually were finished driving by 3 PM and the pool was inviting. The family traveled well although in later years they remarked that I was a severe taskmaster on those trips. This criticism was often mellowed by such statements as" but you were right daddy". All I can say is it worked and we arrived on the west coast in plenty of time to enjoy some of the scenery. Joan was struck at the difference between the two coasts. The east is lush and green, the west is brown and rugged. We drove around San Francisco. Down the winding streets, visited Fisherman's Wharf and had dinner at The St. Francis Hotel. Joan was fascinated with San Francisco and the kids loved the cable car. Time to turn in our car for transportation to Cubi. We rented a car for a few days then boarded a jet for Cubi ourselves. The Air Force flew us there via Wake Island. It was a history lesson and the family listened as the pilot told us of Wakes history. When we deplaned at Wake you could see the look on the kids faces as though they expected to see Japanese planes attacking at any second. We landed at Clark AF Base having lost a day during the trip. Crossing the time zone was amazing to the children and it took some explaining to make them understand how the date could change so rapidly. Clark directed us to a buss that was to take us to Cubi. Our sponsor Cdr. Hamilton had been called back to the States to help solve a maintenance problem in the A6 community and had not been able to arrange for a car. The buss ride was great because we could see more of the countryside sitting up a little higher in the buss. My whole family was fascinated with the Philippines. The trip through the countryside showed them how others outside of the industrialized world lived. Cubi Point was almost like a small piece of America by comparison. Our house was ready and when I checked into Cubi we were soon directed to our new home. The place was fully stocked with food and other items needed for housekeeping. The crowning point was the maid who had been hired by Cdr Hamilton and was in residence when we arrived. Linda was her name. A young Philippine girl who was to become part of our family for our entire stay at Cubi. She quickly had a meal on the table and we settled in to what would be a very enjoyable stay. Joan was overjoyed. She had read the welcome aboard paper long before we arrived at Cubi but I think the idea of having a maid was slow to sink in. People who are used to doing all their own work might be a bit apprehensive at having it done by others. Joan liked to cook and it took a while to train Linda to cook her dishes as Joan wanted them cooked. God bless the kids. In twenty minutes they had made new friends and there would be places to explore that would keep them engrossed for weeks. As Cdr Hamilton was not on board I could not relieve him nor was it my place to change any of his standing orders.

I had checked into the Base and made all the required stops, signed all the paperwork and was officially recognized as a legal inhabitant of the Base. Captain "Red Horse" Meyers was my Commanding Officer and we had a warm chat as he welcomed me aboard. I asked his permission to visit my new Command and become familiar with my new Officers and the AIMD in particular. This was granted and he told me of Cdr Hamilton being ordered back to the States to solve a maintenance problem in the A6 (intruder) program. He would be returning within the week but for me to visit the AIMD and grow acquainted with its size and scope. I had a car I rented from Ships Service and drove to the AIMD Admin Office and met Lieutenant Thomas the Admin Officer. He showed me my new office, introduced me to my Secretaries and the rest of the Admin Staff. He then took me to visit the various shops in the Department and I met the Officers assigned. It was immediately apparent that the workload at Cubi was much greater than it had been at Pax. Not only were many more personnel assigned but we had areas of concern that were outside those usually found in an AIMD. We had a Calibration Lab that was funded by Rep Pac but managed by the AIMD Officer. It was a program that had been worked out between the two Commands and suited the wartime environment. This Cal Lab had capabilities far exceeding any AIMD in existence and was manned by a combination of Navy and Rep Pac personnel. The engine shop did complete engine repair on all the engines found on Carrier aircraft. We had the same capability in Pax River but the number of engines reworked each month far exceeded the number reworked at Pax. There were civilians from Rep Pac working with us in the engine shop as well. They assisted in training Navy Personnel as well as working on these engines. Over 60 engines were reworked each month. Only a NARF in the

States was capable of complete engine repair of more engines. Both of these shops worked around the clock and a new engine shop was in construction when I arrived. Cdr Hamilton had greatly expanded the capability of the AIMD to back up the requirements of the Carrier Fleet. It would fall to me to continue this effort and complete the work. In this short visit I learned the breath and scope of the job . I also realized the CNO had been right. The AIMD Officer of Pax was the logical replacement. We performed similar tasks but Cubi was busier. It would be a big job and I told Joan that I would never have the free time I had at Pax. How true this was would be driven home time and time again. Before Cdr. Hamilton arrived the Base had a visit from the Maintenance Officers of the Staffs of Air Pac and COMFAIR WEST PAC. Captain Bounce from AIR PAC was my old friend from EC121 days at Iceland the Skipper of one of the Barrier Squadrons. The Captain from COMFAIR WEST PAC was a stranger and his first question was why had I not made a visit to COM FAIR WEST PAC before reporting to Cubi. The answer surprised both Captains and when I told them who had picked me and who had given me my orders they were amazed. CNO should have given me a delay in orders to visit both Air Pac and West Pac before coming to Cubi but he didn't and I followed his orders. The next questions could only be answered by Cdr Hamilton since I was not aware of the day to day operation of the AIMD, having only arrived a few days before their visit and had not assumed Command of the operation. I accompanied them both on their tour and listened to both questions and answers they asked and received in the various divisions. They would direct me to do certain things when I assumed Command and I dutifully noted them all. It was fun being in Captain Bounces company again and even in my presence he spoke highly of my competence and ability to Captain Warner of West Pac. It sure started me off on the right foot with my new boss. I'm sure they wanted more from their trip but only Cdr. Hamilton could have answered some of their question. When Leo Hamilton returned he took me on a trip of Cubi that only he could have conducted. I learned more of the history of the base from him than anyone else. He showed me all of the new construction that had been done to enhance the Maintenance capability. He had been responsible for most of it and had a lot of influence with Air Pac, Nav Air and Opnav in getting these projects through and funded. He was a proud and strong willed individual who had probably irritated a lot of people in his various quests yet the results of his efforts were undeniable. That being said I was very happy to be taking over from him instead of being assigned to work for him. I realized our method of management was entirely different. This would be driven home to me later at one of my Officers Meetings. Cdr. Hamilton and I spent a week together and completed the paperwork necessary to transfer the Department over to me. There was a farewell for Cdr Hamilton at the O'Club and was attended by the Staff of Deputy Com Fair West Pac plus the Officers at Cubi Point. He was complimented for all his achievements by all present and certainly deserved it. There was one problem. Have you heard the expression " only the bride wears white"? If not let me explain. The Captain of the base is responsible for everything that occurs on his base, The Captain get lauded for the results of his juniors and then he praises the junior. Some COs it do not mind if the juniors are praised from above. Some do and I was now working for one of these.. He was seething that Leo Hamilton was considered, by some seniors, as having run the base since all the improvements were directly related to Leo's efforts. It would not happen on his watch. I was unaware of this so I pressed on and ran my Department much the same as I had before at other bases.

I called my Officers in and introduced myself to them. I gave them a brief history of my experience and then told them if I make a mistake its their fault. I watched their faces drop. Then I explained to them, with a smile, what my philosophy of management was all about, I told them they knew more about their Divisions than I did, they knew their personnel, their equipment, their workload better than I did. Until I got up to speed I would have to trust them to do their job to the best of their ability. If they had a problem come to me for assistance and don't let it fester

*Shields of Honor*

until it became a big problem and would effect me and the whole Department. If I make a policy they believe is wrong come and speak to me. If I can't. convince you I'm right maybe I'm not and the policy should be changed. On the other hand if my decision has to be made immediately due to time constraints then I expect them to work hard to make it happen. I am there to help and because of my rank I can make things happen that they can't so they should use me to help them.

I always felt that the most important, the most private attribute a person has is his dignity. You should never attack another's dignity. If there is a problem, focus on the problem in such a way that you both are looking at the problem like it has a separate entity. You solve the problem together and never touch on his dignity. This has been the cornerstone of my managerial philosophy and has stood me in good stead. It was weeks before my Officers believed what I said the first day. My assistant came in one day and closed the door behind him. I felt he had bad news but he smiled and said the guys now believe you. He said they were talking about how it is fun to come to work again in the morning. He told me a story about how Leo would get mad and have them report in to the office in the middle of the night and berate them for some infraction. He ended by saying the ghost of Leo has gone and you are now the Boss. When he left he shock my hand. I was lucky. These were good

Officers and they became good friends as well. The moral improved dramatically and I could even see it in the enlisted men and the way they greeted me. The division officers would openly discuss their problems at officers meetings. The major problems would be put up on my board for action and we would work it together until it was solved. If in my travels I saw something that could become a problem and I mentioned it to a division officer it was handled immediately.

As I settled in I began to see things that required more attention. Our support equipment shop had a lot of potential as it was designed not only to take care of Cubi Points support equipment but to assist the Bases in Viet Nam as well. We would be asked to send special support equipment to one Base or the other and we had to track it. Equipment would eventually be received as a replacement but often we had to double up and use our equipment for two of our tenant Squadrons at once. The temperature on the ramp at Cubi was well over 100 degrees and the GTC85 Airstart was not sufficient to start our C2 Aircraft. We asked for and received a wells air storage unit. This unit had bottles that stored compressed air and could on one charge start 4 C2 Aircraft. It freed up several GTC100 air start units. These were workarounds we could use as the C2 s were the Aircraft that brought mail and needed parts to the Carriers. They enabled the maintenance crews on the Carriers to keep their squadrons flying. Each Carrier had at least one C2 land each day and often two or three. They were the workhorses of the fleet and any problems the C2s had brought the Staff to General Quarters. One week we had a C2 lost as a result of the load shifting on the cat shot. The same week another C2 lost a prop blade in flight and it was a miracle that plane wasn't lost as the blade slashed through the overhead fuselage and just missed severing the control cables. The plane made an emergency landing at Cubi and I was there on the runway to witness it. Cdr. Lou Sarosdy of COMFAI WEST PAC Staff, an old friend was on the aircraft as a passenger. He was all for grounding the fleet. Admiral Whitmore was sent out to head a special board of inquiry to examine both accidents and I was added to the board. The first accident was due to cargo shifting on the catapult launch and quickly attributed to an error in the loading of cargo and improper restraints being used. The second, with Cdr Sarosdy on board, was not easily solved. Consultation with Grumman and Hamilton Standard revealed we had a prop balancing problem at the squadron level. We asked for and obtained the same prop balancing machine Grumman used. It was flown to us and we decided to balance the prop on a new engine while both were on the AIMD test stand . Grumman assisted us and again my old friend Sal Vitale, our local Grumman Rep, proved his worth. The props and engines were installed on a C2 and the Squadron Commander Test flew the aircraft. When re returned he said he had never flown a C2 that was so smooth. He said he could read the instruments as easily as reading an automobiles instrument panel. Usually the instruments would dance with the vibration. We did the same thing to another aircraft, again with good results. Admiral Whitman was satisfied and the Board recommended using the new prop balancing machine. My work with the C2 didn't end with the Navy and later on with Grumman I would face my old friend Lou Sarosdy, now Admiral Lou Sarosdy, in NAVAIR. While as C2 Project Manager I was attempting to sell 39 new and improved C2s to the Navy to replace the old C2s that had flown themselves into retirement. Aircraft will always break and there will always be a requirement for an aircraft that can fly out to the Carrier with the parts needed to fix that broken aircraft.

When the Board had concluded its work Captain Hardy, The Deputy COMFAIR WEST PAC asked me to accompany him on a trip to Viet Nam. The purpose was to brief the Navy and Marine Maintenance Officers at all our Bases in Country on the capability of the AIMD at Cubi. This type trip would take place every six months as the maintenance officers continually rotated and the new ones had to be briefed, Each new carrier had to be briefed as well so I had to spend a lot of my time making every navy and marine maintenance facility aware of the enormous capability of the AIMD at Cubi. Capability that was always improving as each new weapons system made its way to the fleet and the test equipment came to Cubi Point AIMD. Cubi also had back up capability for all the test equipment in Country and there were daily flights to and from Cubi. If gear went down send it to Cubi for repair if they did not have the capability to repair it on site.. He also asked me to observe the way Maintenance was being conducted at all these Bases and give him a written report at the end of the trip. We flew to Danang and were met there by two Marine Colonels who had planned the rest of the trip by Marine Helicopter.

We spent the first night listening to these two experienced Marine tell us war stories. Just after a night cap at the bar one Marine Colonel showed me man hole covers down the center hall of the BOQ we were staying in and told me this had been a French BOQ. The man holes were over the sewerage system and one night the Viet Cong had crawled through the system, opened the manhole covers and had entered the rooms of the French sleeping there and cut their throats. I was armed with a thirty eight revolver and as a former Policeman could shoot as well as anyone but I must admit that if a mouse farted that night my guns pointed in his direction. The next day we said goodbye to the Colonels and boarded the helicopter they had provided for the rest of our trip. We flew to the DMZ and I remarked to the pilot that there were lots of lakes below us and he laughed." Cdr Sullivan those lakes are B52 bomb craters that fill with water this time of the year," he explained.

The Maintenance facilities were remarkable. They were Quonset huts or trailers but well equipped and manned by sailor and marines that were as dedicated as any you could find. My end of the trip report would be easy if I could find enough superlatives to describe what I had seen. Cameron Bay was our last stop and who was the Maintenance Officer but LCDR Harry Errington an old friend from Pax River and his assistant was Lt. Jim Mims my Maintenance control Officer at Keflavik Iceland. It was old home week for all of us and a perfect ending to our trip. One of the best things to come out of the trip was the messenger service we all agreed on during our meetings. They would send an escort with their avionics or test equipment they wanted repaired . We would receipt for it and the messenger would stay over night, have a liberty in town and the next night would collect and carry back to his home Base any equipment that had been completed. The escort loved it and the Base had a good handle on their property. It completely stopped the loss of items plus it gave the Maintenance Officer a window of when he could expect the newly arrived equipment to be repaired. A win win situation.

In the midst of all this another problem arose. The A7 attack aircraft was slated to have a new engine and would be designated the A7E. The new engine required special support equipment and it was to arrive and be installed in my engine shop well before the arrival of the new A7E. The dates of arrival of this support equipment kept slipping and the date I was to have support for the A7E. was rapidly approaching. I had sent confidential messages to COMFAIR WEST PAC and Info to AIR PAC that we could not support the engine unless the arrival of the required support equipment was expedited. By the time the new A7E arrived I had a small telephone book of messages I had sent to higher authority informing them of the growing crisis and requesting immediate assistance. It was not like Iceland where I had controlled the provisioning conference and knew all the players. CTF77 was furious when he realized the support equipment was not in my shop and he would soon have the new A7s arriving. My messages covered my butt however it didn't solve the big problem. Tools and equipment were borrowed from the Narf and I finally had capability but I know several staff weenies must have gotten chewed out for this fiasco

All the secret gear that alerted pilots to missiles being launched at them was repaired and kept operational in one of my shops. Each piece of equipment was serialized and we knew what piece of gear was in every aircraft.

The scope and depth of the Maintenance at Cubi was far greater than any other AIMD in the Navy. I was obliged to attend meetings in COMFAIR WEST PAC at least every other month. The scope and depth of these meeting meant you had to prepare days ahead to readily have the figures available. Capt. Warner was the staff Maintenance Officer and he was thorough. His message traffic was short and to the point but sometimes his staff would miss or misunderstand the meaning of messages sent to him. The A7 engine being an example.

Another problem, also an engine problem arose about this time. We could perform complete engine repair on all the engines of fleet aircraft. We did not have capability to repair hot sections. Only the NARF (Naval Air Rework Facility) or the engine manufacturer had this capability. The hot sections became scarce. Like so many supply problems each item manager had so much money to buy parts. Sometimes this pot of money was diverted to another product and parts became scarce. The NARF was paid on delivery of an engine so their hot sections were important to their cash flow and they could not send it to me to be used in repairing one of my engines.

A second problem surfaced when you realize the NARF is not in my chain of command and neither I nor my superiors in my chain of command have direct authority over them. Now add this to the equation. I can receive, repair and ship an engine back to the fleet in eight days. If I ship the same engine back to the NARF via the fastest method it takes an average of 131 days for that engine to be sent out to the fleet again. Eight days vs 131 days. Sounds reasonable I should have the hot section doesn't it? Now consider the NARF will not get paid if they send the hot section to me instead using it to sell one of their engines. That was the dilemma I faced when COMFAI WEST PAC decided to send me back to a meeting with the Admirals of AIR PAC and REP PAC. The meeting lasted no more than fifteen minutes. The two Admirals looked at one another after I had made my pitch and they agreed I was correct and I should get the hot sections. A small conference between my Division Officer and the NARF representative worked out the details and we were back in business. I sent a message to ComFair West Pac outlining the details and promised a complete report when I arrived in Japan. I wondered who had been reading my messages and why this could not have been worked out before my arrival. The answer probably lies in the lack of cooperation between the two commands. That and the fact the NARF is paid for an engine repair only when they completely repair one. My visit to ComFair West Pac went as expected. They were happy to hear the results as this would preclude engine shortages for the Fleet.

One day when I was sitting in my office I received a call from the Skipper asking me to come to his office immediately. When I arrived Admiral Lambert was there and presented me with a large envelope. He had been to Japan and had a visit with Admiral Smith. I opened the envelope and it contained a large 3 Dimension picture of a naked Japanese girl and on the back he had inscribed " Jack this is how things are in Japan. How are you making out in the Philippines? The Skipper, the Admiral and I all howled with laughter and I promised myself I would give him a suitable answer. I bought a wooden carving of a naked Philippine girl about nine months pregnant and I had my machine shop make a small plate engraved with "Admiral this is how thing are in the Philippines... John L". My next visit to Japan I arrived early and went to the Admirals Office. It was deserted except for a first class petty Officer. I asked where the Admiral was and he informed me that he was on the Battle Ship New Jersey that had just arrived. I told him I was going to leave some thing on his desk and when he saw the little statue he said "if you think so Commander' as much as telling me its your choice and your responsibility. I left to attend an engine conference and didn't return until sometime around 1600 hours. The office was packed with visitors from the earlier ceremony aboard the New Jersey. I sought out the Captain, who was his aide and told him that I had wanted to see the Admiral but it looked like it would be impossible due to the crowd. I asked that he relay a message to the Admiral that Jack Sullivan from the Philippines was here to see him. He jumped when I told him my name and he said stay right here I have orders to keep you here. He then went into the Admirals Office and seconds later I heard a loud voice exclaim " send that G D Irishman in here'. I recognized the voice and was ushered into his Office. He was being briefed by two CIA operatives and they looked at me as to whether they should continue. The Admiral said he has a higher clearance than you do so go on. When they were through he said to his aide call my wife and tell her we will have Sully as our guest for dinner. I informed him I had two of my Division Officers with me. He said change that we will have three guest for dinner. We left shortly after and I got to see his wife Ginny as well. He was aware of my exploits in the Philippines as Admiral Lambert had informed him by phone. Admiral Lambert and I had played golf together several times and whenever the Admiral from Sangley would come to the Base it would usably result in a golf game with he and whoever he brought vice Admiral Lambert and myself. The Admiral from Sangley hated to lose and when I saw in the orders That Captain Bill Hartung had orders to Sangley as his Chief of Staff I told the Admiral that he had a good golfer coming and that our next match would be a lot tougher. Bill Hartung had been Admiral Smiths Chief of Staff at Pax River and I had played a lot of golf with Bill. He was a good friend and a good competitor. We did play shortly after Bill arrived and it was a good match as I predicted. Everyone was pleased. Me in particular as I got to talk to Bill and hear his story as to what happened when he arrived in Japan. He came by boat and Admiral Smith was waiting for him at the dockside wearing a large coolie hat and a big sign " BILL HARTUNG GO HOME" We laughed and I told him what had happened with me and what I had done. He laughed and said he had to think of something too. Admiral Smith was a great friend to both of us and I'm sure most of the Naval Officers who have served under him respected and admired him as we both did. The Admirals in the area would always welcome a visit from Admiral Smith or enjoy a visit to him. His sense of humor was famous throughout the Navy and I remember one Admiral telling me that at a conference when Admiral Smith spoke everyone listened. His opinions were valued.

One day I was in the XO's office on some business and he closed the door. He then asked me how my relationship was with the Skipper. It was a funny question and I guess I looked puzzled. He than asked what was my perception of the relationship. I replied good as far as I know. He than told me "only the Bride wears white Sully" Cubi was a base that existed for the Maintenance of Aircraft. CNO had told me that, so did AIRPAC and COM FAIR WEST PAC as well. Superiors had talked to me directly on Maintenance matters but I supposed it had happened after conversations with the CO. The XO had informed me in a nice way that the CO was looking at me like he had looked at Cdr. Hamilton and that was something I did not want to happen He was the CO and I worked for him. I knew it and I thought he realized I knew it. The XO was warning me my perceptions were wrong. I was having a problem. How could

*Shields of Honor*

I overcome it/? I got my answer in a funny way. It was a family problem concerning one of my Officers. I was going to handle it but I decided to seek the CO's advice. I called and made an appointment. When I relayed the problem to the Skipper he suggested a plan of action that mirrored my own but it was his idea. He followed through with it and the results were perfect for both parties concerned. It had the desired effect for me too and the Skipper and I became friends. I asked him to sponsor a Dinning In. Now in the Navy a Dinning In is a formal party. It follows a formal script but as the party progresses and the liquor kicks in it gets pretty rowdy, or it can. He was reluctant for that reason but I gradually wore him down and he agreed. The party turned out to be a smash hit and the Skipper had a ball. I know that the Supply Officer and myself returned to his house in the wee hours and were met by his wife in a nightgown and a robe. We had come into his house via the back entrance. There is a steep hill on that side of the house and we told her we had parked the car on it because we couldn't remember where the driveway was. She opened the back door to look for the car and we broke out in laughter. The next day she reminded us that in the shape we were in she wouldn't have put it passed us. We all laughed at that.

The Skipper called me into his office one day and told me of a conversation he had had with Admiral Weisner. It seems though a number of Pilots were being injured in the O'Club. They had started a fad where in one of the Pilots would be catapulted down the six stairs leading from the bar to the dance floor in a captain's chair with casters on the bottom. Few were successful and a number of them were injured affecting their flight status. He demanded that something be done about it. As senior watch Officer and the AIMD Officer what could I do about it. Let me consult with my Maintenance Officers. We had a window of opportunity as the club was rebuilding the old bamboo bar. We could build a catapult in the new section. What a meeting that was and how our imaginations ran wild. We agreed finally that we would have to construct it with parts out of the bone yard (salvaged material). The enlisted troops had as much fun as we did and recommended that we start with a salvaged refueling tank. It was designed to resemble an A7. The tracks in the club house would be salvaged engine stand tracks cemented into the deck. The vehicle would run on the feet that were used to move engines on the stand. We would propel it with compressed nitrogen that we made in our oxygen plant. We would have one wire for an arrestment, miss that wire and you would land in a pool of water. The water would serve as a brake and the unfortunate souls that landed in the water would be rescued with a mechanical winch. The metalsmiths fashioned the A7. The mechs bought the tracks and the feet for the A7. The nitrogen tanks were fed into a manifold that supplied the jolt for the cat shot. The tracks had to be curved precisely to prevent binding of the feet yet the vehicle had to go deep enough and fast enough into the pool to brake the vehicle. The engineers at Straad helped us. Engineers from Lakehurst installed lights. The cat was ready. Admiral Eisman was privy to our plans and had a beautiful Bronz plaque built in Hong Kong. It was four feet square and inscribed" Red Horse Cat House". This plaque was bolted to the wall and to make it burglar proof we used extra large bolts. The Marine Pilots on detachment tried to rescue the plaque but their tools and window of opportunity were not up to the task and it remained on the Clubs wall none the worse for wear. When all was ready and I had the opportunity to certify its use as the only member of Pax River's Board of Inspection and Survey on site. The Club was packed with both eager participants and onlookers. Admiral Eisman was the first to ride the vehicle and eagerly strapped in to the cheers of the onlookers. The lights indicated the pressure in the tanks was at maximum and as cat officer I gave him the signal for launch. The Admiral sped down the tracks and dropped his hook too soon but as luck would have it the hook caught the rubber bumper we had installed to bounce the hook over the wire and tearing it off it positioned the hook and enabled it to catch the wire. The Admiral was the first to trap and was presented with a bottle of champagne to the boisterous ovation of the crowd. His name would be placed in gold letters on the" Wall of Fame." The rubber was removed from the bumper plate and we had mod one to the cat. The pilots who eagerly working to get their San Miguel (beer) level up to speed waited anxiously to man the cat. The bumper was placed some six inches before the wire and would bounce the hook over the wire if it was dropped too soon. A late drop would also miss catching the wire,. A soaking wet pilot who would be taking his next beer dripping water would be pulled out of the pool, ignominiously, to the shouts of his squadron mates. We must have launched over a hundred riders the first night and only two were successful, other than the Admiral. Both of these had ridden the Cat several times before they correctly timed their hook drops. It was tough and yet if you were successful your name was inscribed in gold letters on the WALL OF FAME, you were presented with a bottle of champaign and your bragging rights were perpetuated. The fame of the Cat grew and each of the Carriers, as they came to port, would produce an air group of pilots eager to prove their skill and anxious to have their name on the Wall of Fame. My enlisted men were hired by the Club to operate the Cat and they enjoyed seeing the fruit of their labors being put to the test by eager Navy Pilots. Seeing all the wet pilots standing around sort of reminded me of my first solo flight only nobody offered me a beer this time. The fame of the Cat attracted Air Force Pilots from Clark and they would come proudly into the Club announcing they were up to the task and every one of them got wet to the delight of the Navy onlookers. Riding the Cat didn't cost anything but if you had to be ignominiously hauled out by the winch it cost you five dollars. This money paid for the expense and everything left over went to the recreation funds of the Ships. Navy Nurses rode the Cat and this was always fun because we would outfit them with linen flight suits tailored for the crew. When they came out of the pool it was almost like a wet T shirt party but at least their cloths were dry and waiting for them. I guess I have to tell this story. As Command Duty Officer I had to meet one of our Vips as he emerged from his Jet. He was a deputy Sec Nav and while I didn't remember his name at the time I wrote the Story of the Cat for Wings of Gold the Editor of the Gosport at Pensacola identified him from the photo as now Senator John Warner. When the Deputy deplaned he told The Admiral he wanted to ride the Cat he had heard so much about at the Pentagon. Captain Myers looked at me, I nodded and set about getting a crew ready as the Deputy was slated to have lunch at the Cubi O'Club. Word of this spread and the Club was packed with Officers and wives eager to see the Deputy test his skill. We outfitted him with a set of the same suits we had made for the crew. White linen with Red Horse Cat House proudly embossed on the back. He strapped in, saluted indicating he was ready, and proudly splashed into the water. Not once but five times, with the

Skipper pushing the bumper back a few inches each time to make it easier to catch a wire. This foot play was noticed by some of the more experienced riders of the Cat. When after five attempts the Deputy announced that it couldn't be done the bumper plate was almost a foot further back than regulation and would be an easy trap for anyone with experience on the Cat. The Skipper was in his white uniform and proudly stepped forward to prove it could be done. As he approached the Cat one of the Junior Officers kicked the plate back to where it belonged. The Skipper missed the wire and to the delight of the Deputy landed in the pool. The Deputy never took off his coveralls and proudly boasted he would bring them back to the Pentagon as proof of his adventure on the Cat. We went to lunch with the Deputy and even though his words were important I had to fight from laughing when I looked at him in the wet flight suite and the Skipper wet up to his ribbons carrying on a serious conversation. Admiral Lambert, my old golf partner, would nudge me with his foot when he detected the corners of my mouth curling in a smile. The Deputy departed later that afternoon still wearing the flight suit but the heat of the Cubi afternoons had long since dried it. If Senator Warner ever reads this I want him to understand there was no disrespect intended and I must say he acted like a Naval Aviator that day. He entered into the spirit of the Cat with all the enthusiasm of a veteran Aviator and that is a compliment.

Navy Pilots work hard at a dangerous profession but they play hard as well and I honestly believe this is what keeps us going.

Another story has to be told. I was attending Mass one Sunday Morning with my family when the OOD tapped me on the shoulder. I had a top secret message that I had to read immediately. It was addressed to me by name. A plane would be landing in a matter of hours and I was to go to Supply at Subic and pick up a classified shipment. I was also to have qualified, experienced enlisted men available to assist the crew in putting the contents of the shipment onboard the aircraft and making it ready for combat. I did both and waited for the aircraft to land. When it landed I was surprised to see a plane from Pax River that I was familiar with. One of the crewmen was a friend I had known from Church back at Pax River. For some unknown reason I never met the pilot of the aircraft at Cubi and today he is one of my best friends, Captain Ed Forsman. That aircraft went on to perform heroics in Viet Nam.

I guess there are stories at Cubi that would fill a book by themselves. One concerned a C2A that had landed in severe weather and had damaged its port landing gear and could not get off the runway. This wouldn't present a problem under ordinary circumstances but the Carrier aircraft were due in a few minutes and because of the weather would have to land immediately. The Captain was going to bulldoze the C2 off the runway but Sal Vitale asked for a few minutes and got the sling on the C2 attached and the crane lifted the aircraft put a set of rollers under the damaged gear and rolled theC2 off the runway. My buddy Sal Vitale the Grumman Rep saved a C2 and the Carrier aircraft all landed safely. Stories and adventures my family had would be worth mentioning too but I'm going to stick to the adventures of this lucky Irishman and leave most of the other stories for my family to write about if they chose. My tour in Cubi was coming to a close and I wondered where I would be assigned.

My friend Captain Bounce was retiring from the Navy and had convinced the Admiral to seek me as his replacement as Maintenance Officer at AIR PAC. San Diego is beautiful and Air Pac is great duty, but Joan knew this would be our last duty station and wanted to return to Pax River and have me retire there. She had been a great Navy wife and I felt if I could I would ask for a change of orders. My Detailer inquired if Pax would take me and thank God there were enough people on the Admirals Staff who knew me that they convinced the Admiral to request me.

# Chapter 16
# My last Tour in the Navy, Naval Air Test Center, Pax River

I was the senior Commander on the Base when I arrived so it wasn't easy to find a suitable spot. I was assigned to Weapons System test as the Maintenance Officer. Captain John Whistler (later to become Admiral and the Commander of the Test Center) was my CO. Cdr Braun was my XO. Admiral Miller, the Commander of the Test Center, was the same Officer who had trained the B25 pilots that had flown the famous Doolittle raid during WW2. We became good friends and after his retirement I would visit with he and his wife. Weapons System Test was exactly as described in its title. We tested the weapons that were dropped or fired from Navy Carrier aircraft, As a result we had a wider range of the various types and inventory of Navy Carrier Aircraft. This was a Maintenance Officers nightmare. The number of enlisted men needed to man all these aircraft were not sufficient nor were the number of trained technicians qualified in these aircraft. A man would work on an A6 one day and have to assist on an A7 the next. He might have qualification for working on an A6 but none for the A7. Cross training was a necessity but it took time. Quality Control was also a nightmare as there weren't enough trained men in each aircraft type. This required men to double hat, work on one aircraft and inspect the work being done by someone else on another aircraft. To further complicate the mission the war was still being fought and the early generation of smart bombs were being updated and tested by Weapons System Test. The urgency for swift resolution of these tests was transmitted from NAVAIR. In many cases only one aircraft was wired for these tests and it had to remain in operational status to complete these tests. You weren't dealing with simply Fleet Pilots in need of training you were dealing with project Pilots that were being pressured to complete Tests so weapons could be certified for wartime use. The number of projects being worked on seem to increase on a daily basis. A civilian assigned to me was to keep up with the amount of wiring in each aircraft. Each of the Projects had different wiring for test equipment to monitor test results. Some times it was common to more than one project but most required installation of unique equipment with wiring unlike any that had been installed previously. We would try to remove old wiring after completion of a project but sometimes, due to the urgency of the new test, it was not possible. The civilian, who had the responsibility to account for this wiring, had to track the project and attempt to remove all the old wiring while the aircraft was between tests .The reason is obvious, the wiring and test equipment if left in the aircraft could change the weight and balance of the test aircraft. I have listed all these problems to acquaint you with the scope of the duties of a Maintenance Officer in Weapons System Test. It was and is an exciting job and you are well versed in what is in the inventory of weapons and what will soon be added to the Fleet. Within four months of my arrival Captain Whistler received orders to the Philippines as Commanding Officer of Cubi Point.. I sat with him for several days briefing him on the role Cubi played in the war. I also listed a number of improvements he might effect in short order that would greatly improve the moral of the troops. I heard from various sources that he not only completed the list I had given him but had made other changes that were greatly appreciated by the troops. John Whistler was a fine Naval Officer who had the knack of talking to people in such a way that you would level with him from the time you first met him. He was able to motivate people to obtain maximum results. Weapons System Test was fortunate in that Captain Joe Simones, who was Captain Whistlers replacement, was the same sort of Officer.

Whistler was a fine Tennis player but Simones was a golfer and we would team up on the Golf Course. Anyone who knows me would understand why I added that. . Admiral Miller asked me to head up the Navy Relief effort for the Test Center and I called on Pat Hannigan and several others for assistance. These were people who had served so well when I was overall Chairman back in 1968-69 time frame. Again we met with great success and Navy Relief was well served. My last year of Naval Service was coming to a close. The beautiful Quarters I had on the gold coast would soon have to be vacated so Joan and I looked in Town Creek for a suitable retirement home. An old friend, Peg Anderson, was a real estate agent and she found us one on Rison Road

My friend Don Lilienthal was working on a project to break the distance and altitude records for turboprops. We checked our fleet of P3 aircraft for the best performing engines. These were removed and put on the aircraft Don wanted for the test. After several test flights Don and I flew to Huston to get a special inertial navigation set for the trip. Coming back from Huston we flew at a fairly high altitude for turbos and pushed the throttles up to maintain flight at ten degrees under max turbo inlet temperature. When we approached Washington Center the controller asked me what type aircraft we were flying. When I told him a popper three (P3) he was amazed and told us he had us in with pure jet traffic. Don left the States and flew to Atsugi,

Japan. He then flew back to Pax non stop setting the altitude and the distance records for Turbos. This is a quick and dirty account of a lot of hard work on Don's part and I will leave it to Don to fill in the blanks should he ever decide to write a book. WST was proud of Don's feat and the P3 aircraft Don flew. Saying goodbye to the Navy was tough. Retirement means you are getting a little long in the tooth but very few retirees would admit that and I was one of those. There were cocktail parties and nice things said by a lot of people I had served under during my service. Admiral Miller even told me he had attempted to get my service extended through a congressional bill but it wasn't possible

I was going back to civilian life. Captain Tom Goben was the head of NALC and wanted to hire me to set up a program putting the Navy Maintenance program under the same system used by the Airlines. I was interested but President Nixon put a freeze on Civil Service hiring. I was free to take a much sort after vacation and play enough Golf to get my handicap down to a three. (my personal best)

# Chapter 17
# Life After the Navy

As I stated earlier I enjoyed the leave and as I had considerable savings I waited for the freeze on government hiring to be lifted, I had already put a lot of the work in on converting the Navy to airline maintenance and was ready to roll as soon as the freeze was lifted. I hadn't approached any of the companies doing work for the Navy nor any of the Prime Contractors as I thought working for Captain Goben and NALC would suite me just fine. When the first month passed and there was no sign of the freeze being lifted I began to get concerned. Even Captain Goben's insistence that it would be lifted soon didn't console me. It was at this time that Peg Anderson spoke to me and told me that Tom Waring was interested in me and would like to talk to me about future employment in his Company. A meeting was arranged and Tom spoke to me about a mortgage company he would like to set up to work with his Real Estate Company. When I told him the only knowledge I had of mortgages was from buying a house. He laughed and said he could train me but what I had was knowledge of government business that would serve me in good stead. The rest I could easily learn from friends of his at banks in Annapolis and Baltimore. I was hired and the next few weeks found me driving his Mercedes to Annapolis for one week and to Baltimore the next week. He was right it would be simple. We borrowed the money from the bank to build the houses and would lend it to the prospective buyers at slightly higher percentage. I was ready but fate was not. Bob McGee who headed up our engineering section and was responsible for reviewing future purchases of land became ill. He knew what stage of development each parcel of land was in and what had to be done to advance it before the county planning commission. Tom called me in and told me I had a new job and would have to fill in for Mr. McGee. I visited him in the hospital and he told me exactly what to do and how to do it. We became good friends and his family became my friends as well. Bob was weak but his mind was as sharp as ever. I learned more about developing land in the months I spent with Bob McGee that I could have ever learned in a school.

During these months the Federal Government took a vested interest in land development. They were especially concerned with fraud and racial discrimination. The Government developed training sessions for contactors to familiarize them with the new laws. Tom Waring sent me to these seminars and for a while I was the resident expert in Saint Mary's County on these new laws and executive orders. The County appointed John Norris as the County Engineer at this time was not appreciated by some of the local contractors because he insisted on all local developers adhering to the State laws on roads even in their subdivisions. John and I became friends as I agreed with his thinking and engineered our roads to conform to his decree. We had no trouble with advancing our projects and developments before the Planning and Zoning Commission. During the next two years we developed the upper sections of Bretton Bay Golf and Country Club. We were selling lots for future development by the owners.

Tom Waring had a vision of Bretton Bay becoming the prime development in Saint Marys County. I had found a company called Advanced Waste Treatment Corporation in New Jersey that had a program that would treat waste water and make it potable water. I visited the company and discovered the plant was contained in a building that a casual observer would consider to be just another home. The basement contained the plant itself. It was located in and serving a development roughly the size of Bretton Bay. I made an appointment for Tom Waring and Hugh Allston to visit the plant and they receive the same demonstration they had given me. After this was done we invited Dr. Bill Merrick, St

*Shields of Honor*

Marys County Health Officer and John Norris, the County Engineer to review the plant. If this Process was acceptable to the County we planned to establish our own sewerage plant and to use the potable water in holding pools for use on the golf course. We would put in top of the line condominiums in the areas between the golf course and a conference center at the top of the hill. It was an idea before its time and the County conservationists wouldn't allow it because of concern for runoff into the bay. It was frustrating because so much could have been accomplished early on and Tom's vision of Bretton Bay would have come to fruition.

Charley Young was in charge of lot sales at Bretton Bay. Charley had been a Navy Pilot and an instructor at Corpus Christi. He had played baseball for one of the fields and played on an all star team that played Pensacola. We discovered we had played baseball against one another in 1945. I played in the outfield with Ted Williams for Pensacola and would feign disappointment every time he said he didn't remember me from that game. Charley was dismayed that our plan had been turned down as he expected the sales of lots and homes to take off with the arrival of a sewerage plant. Bretton Bay is still one of the County's premier addresses but its image would have peaked much earlier had the County allowed us to proceed.

Elsworth Franklin was our golf pro and he and Tom our greens keeper worked hard to make our golf course achieve it potential. We put on a drive for new members that had good results but again Country Club living was new to Saint Mary's County and it took an influx of new people to the County before most of the lots sported homes. In those days Pete Brecht was associated with J&T homes. He would later figure in the development of Wildwood and then strike out on his own. Hugh Alston and Pete built a number of smaller subdivisions that I did the engineering for and took through the various cycles of planning and zoning.

In 1973 a good friend of mine, George Clancy asked me to join the Rotary Club in Saint Mary's County. He touted the good work the Rotary Club did for the County but reminded me that I would be expected to make the meetings. Since Tom expected me to be available I consulted him before I committed myself. Tom was aware of the Rotary Club and said it was a privilege to be invited to join and it was good for the company to be represented. I would later find out he was one of the founders of the St. Mary's Rotary Club. I joined and found myself in the company of some of the finest members of the community. He was right it was a privilege to be asked to join and the work the Rotary Clubs throughout the world do for peace and understanding has never been fully published or understood.

Our Club grew in membership and stature each year and I had the privilege to work with Hal Bishop on our first County Guide. This County

Guide has grown each year and the Chamber of Commerce and the United States Navy use it to inform new comers of the Schools, Government Agencies and pertinent information that will be important to their settling in. Tom was also right when he said it would be good for the company because I got to know a number of the people we would work with, personally. These folks were the who's who of Saint Mary's County and one or more of them could be found on the various boards that did much of the volunteer work for the County. I volunteered for any and all programs that I felt I might be of assistance. What I didn't know my brother Rotarians taught me until I had a good working knowledge of the Club's activities. Being a Rotarian then meant a lot to me. Thirty years later as I write this it still does and I hope, in some small way, I have been able to pass onto younger members the importance of Rotary and the work it performs in this world.

My work continued but the loss of Bob McGee less than a year later left me without a mentor. Bob had briefed me on every move I was to make and without his presence I felt alone. His tutelage had reinforced me and I found myself doing, instinctively, what I knew he would have suggested. I think Bob had been suspicious of me when we first met. I had the feeling he thought as a former naval officer I would imagine I knew it all and would not seek advice. He later told me that I had proven that assumption on his part wrong and he was amazed at my attitude and how eagerly I sought his advice. Bob and I became very good friends and his wisdom in these matters never ceased to impress me. I met his whole family and the friendship I enjoyed with Bob soon extended to them as well. In 1974 it soon became apparent that Mortgage money was becoming scarce and the high percentage rate the homebuyer would be forced to pay for a mortgage would slow down the building of homes. I realized my new line of work was in jeopardy and I looked for an alternative.

I received a call from Captain Watkins that Admiral Smith had died and they were going to have a service for him the next day in Norfolk. They had an airplane scheduled to fly to Norfolk the next day. He had reserved a seat for me aboard the aircraft and I got to pay my respects to one of my best friends in the Navy. He will always hold a special place in my heart and in my memory. He was buried at sea as he requested.

# Chapter 18
# I go to work for Grumman Aerospace at Bethpage New York

I sent resumes to Lockheed and Grumman and heard from them both. Grumman was the better of the two because it would require contact with the Fleet. I would be outside and interfacing with naval officers again. I visited Grumman at Bethpage and was hired beginning the first of January 1975. I would work for Ken Webster in Field Operations in operational readiness. Admiral Faulks, retired from NAVAIR, would be our reporting senior. Nick Scobo was the head of Field Operations at the time. I had met Nick on several occasions while on active duty for the Navy and while we never had done business together I had met a number of field operations representatives who worked for him. Nick would often give you a theoretical problem and ask you how you would solve it. He would play devils advocate and take an opposing view just to sound you out. Some in Field Service would object to this line of questioning but I always considered it to be a game and enjoyed our friendly bouts. When I was sent out to the various Bases to meet the Base Managers I found they were a bit suspicious as to why I was visiting. It was not quite the same as the Navy where you were welcomed immediately. Adjusting to the corporate world took time and when I returned after my first road trip I told Ken Webster of the suspicion it had aroused. Ken was a retired Commander in supply department and he laughed and said, "welcome to the corporate world". As I became a familiar face this suspicion disappeared and I became an accepted member of Field Service,

Ken and I developed a reporting service by which we were able to predict the operational readiness of a Squadron long before the numbers came out in the monthly operational readiness report. By tracking the Squadrons we could predict who needed assistance The operational readiness of the Grumman Fleet of aircraft was of utmost importance to the Company and our reports were examined carefully

My trips to the Fleet Squadrons proved that logistics support was a problem. Too much time elapsed between ordering a replacement part and receiving a new, or repaired part. There were a number of reasons any one of which could throw a glitch into the logistics system and cause a breech. This insight would enable us to monitor

*Shields of Honor*

the C2 program later on in such a manner as to track parts through the whole system, find where they were located and move them to the required Base and Squadron. It required manpower but it enabled us to bring the operational readiness of the C2 from some 30 % to over 70 %. But this is a story for later in this tale.

I had been working in Field Service almost a year when the F14 was purchased by the Iranian Air Force. The team of engineers who would go to Iran to train the Iranians in the F14 were assembled and given desks and floor space adjacent to my workspace. I met them and was intrigued that they had for the most part worked on the space program. Having gone through both Navy and Air Force maintenance schools I realized the F14 was a Navy aircraft, with Navy maintenance manuals but would be maintained under Air Force maintenance rules. I suggested to the leader that he contact the Air Force and make arrangements to bring key people to an F4 Squadron and see how they conduct business in their maintenance department. He did and in a few weeks he visited and spent time with the Maintenance Officer of an F4 Squadron. He became aware of the complexity of the task and upon his return asked permission of my boss, to speak to me about joining the Iranian Program. Roger was a good salesman and made a good presentation but I realized this would be a multi year program and would require someone with an extensive maintenance background. The people

I had met were super engineers but were expert in space vehicles not maintenance managers. I could help so I joined the Iranian Program. I was transferred to the program and began language instruction. While it would be a large program we became acquainted with one another through language school and the lectures we received from Iranians on their culture and customs. I was impressed with the amount of time Grumman spent training us in the language and customs but when I arrived in Iran later on it was not the shock that most tourist experience upon arrival in that Country. Along with the cultural training I had a chance to get to know the F14. I had flown the F4J and knew what a supersonic aircraft could do but the F14 was impressive and the innovations made since the F4 were countless.

I learned everything I could about the aircraft to the point that when a group of VIPs were to be briefed on the aircraft and the pilot that was to brief them was called away I was asked to substitute. I not only briefed them on the F14, but also spent some time telling them about the training both the pilot and the NFO receive. It was funny because I noticed in the latter half of the brief even the mechanics were listening and a couple of them spoke to me afterwards and told me they had never realized the extensive training Pilots and NCOs go through and were impressed by my briefing.

## Chapter 19
## I go to Iran with the F14 Tomcat

I go to Iran. I was scheduled to go to Iran before Christmas but my daughter, Maura, was scheduled to be singing in a Night Club in New York City at that time and I wanted to be there so I got permission to delay my departure one week. I left on December 30$^{th}$ instead. We had a night in London on the way over and flew to Tehran the following day. The Grumman Administrator met us and helped us transfer to a local flight to Isfahan. Again we were met in Isfahan and the Grumman rep there took us to the hotel that would be our home for the next several weeks. The next morning a buss took us to the base where we met Dick Barton the Grumman F14 Program Manager. Dick had been chief of maintenance in the Air Force for B52 Squadron and was one of the most knowledgeable maintenance officers I have ever met. We also met Vinny DeStefano the Grumman Base Manager at Isfahan. Vinny arranged for us to get our identification cards from the Iranian Air

Force. We ate at their Officers Mess that same day and were briefed by our Grumman Folks on the customs of the base to make certain we would not offend our hosts. Later that day we were escorted to our work places and I got to meet Major Mavashan, the Maintenance Officer (Chief of Maintenance).

The buildings had been almost completed when we arrived but the electrical work was not. There were frequent black outs and flashlights were needed. As Maintenance and Material control were in the center of the building and had no windows a blackout stopped work. I remember sitting in a meeting when the material control people were briefing us. Phill Dressel was conducting the brief and had given us a list of material that had arrived in the last week. He had enumerated all the items and just as he got to the dollar value the lights went out. A few seconds went by in total silence when a cigarette lighter flicked on and Phil gave us the dollar value to a spontaneous roar of laughter from the entire audience. But that was the way it was in the beginning. It was almost primitive.

For example a group of Iranian laborers were working near the front gate with two donkeys that pulled carts of dirt. One day one of the donkeys died and was left by the side of the road. No effort was made to bury it or cart it off it was just left there. Over the weeks and months we watched the body deflate until it was just a pile of skin, The desert does funny things to a body it dehydrates it quickly and sort of turns it into a mummy and that is what happened to that donkey.

We did get electricity but it was never completely reliable and when the backup battery operated lights were installed they were frequently used. The aircraft arrived in ones and twos. They were ferried to Iran by Navy Crews. They flew the pond (Atlantic Ocean) to Spain accompanied by Air Force Tankers then on the next day would complete the flight to Iran....I met all the aircraft and was anxious to hear if there were any problems during the flight over and if there were any gripes on the aircraft. One of the items that always amused me was the accuracy of the inertial navigation on the F14. Several pilots told me they would have hit the boundary of their intended landing site and that they had updated the inertial navigation of the tanker. We had to get the pilots survival gear and send it back to New York for a future ferry flights..

Our maintenance people went over the arriving aircraft to ensure its air worthiness and to familiarize the Iranians with the procedure. The Iranians had all been to the States for training but for some it was months since they last saw an F14. It would be a while before the Iranians flew the F14 but they had a natural curiosity and mobbed those two aircraft. Most of the pilots had been trained in F4J Phantom and some had even flown the F14 in the States. Isfahan was to be the training site for the Pilots and the crew. They would attend both ground school and for some check out in the aircraft for the first time Our people, the Grumman crew, would train them in the ground school. We had trained technicians, mostly former F14 enlisted men hired by Grumman for the task. We also had Grumman engineers that would teach both in the classroom and would solve problems that might arise from the aircraft operations.

We also had a corps of former Navy F14 pilots and NFOs that would be flying with the Iranians and checking them out in the air. General Munisaphor was the Program manager for the Iranians. He was responsible for the F14 training and as long as the aircraft and Iranian crew remained in a training status he was the man. Tactical Air Command located in Shiraz at Tadayon AFB watched as the program progressed but until the first Squadron became operational the aircraft and crews would remain under General Munisaphor.

It was interesting to watch the building at Isfahan grow. The shelters for the aircraft were made of stone and were some two to three feet thick. They had walls at either end of the shelter that were even thicker. The aircraft could turn into the shelter but there wasn't much room for anything more. It was designed to prevent skip bombing of aircraft or strafing while they were in the shelter. The Base itself was some 15 miles from Isfahan and was located in a desert. The temperatures would ease up over l00 degrees

*Shields of Honor*

and aircraft that had been in the sun for some time would burn exposed skin. It wasn't always possible to bring those aircraft into a shelter for maintenance When the training advanced to where flight operations began in earnest we began to see some of the problems that we would face. The spare parts bought by the Shah in the original contract were being delivered. The quantity bought was higher than that of the US Navy by almost 20 %. The pipeline for repair of these parts was also much greater so the quantity helped.

While the tempo of operations was increasing our creature comfit was also being taken care of by Grumman. They were renting houses in town and gradually moving people out of the hotel. For families this was most desirable and although I had seniority over some of the later arrivals I volunteered to remain in the hotel until the families had been located. My wife had not come over at this time and as a bachelor I did not need more space. Everything I needed was within walking distance of the hotel. This also included the Embassy with their American movies as well as a number of fine eating places.

When I finally was given an apartment I found that my landloard could speak English. He and his wife often invited me to dinner and afterwards they would practice their English with me acting as a tutor. Roles would be reversed and they would help me with my Farsi (Persian). My neighbors had two daughters of high school age and we would find ourselves waiting for busses at the same time each morning. Mine to take me to the Base, theirs to take them to school. They would drill me on my Farsi and correct me on my pronunciation or use of a word. The ten or fifteen minutes of exercise helped me quite a bit. Just a few months later the Villas built for the Iranian Officers were completed and it was decided to put the Americans in these homes. It probable saved the Iranians some money but I think they were concerned about our safety.

It was during this time frame I decided to buy a car. Grumman did not encourage it because of the driving habits of the Iranians. Having driven Detective cruisers on high speed chases in New York City I guess I didn't have the fear of driving in a foreign country. I bought a Citroen. Not the luxury model but the cheap one that had a torsion suspension and a 36 horsepower motor. It has to be the ugliest car ever built with the back seat higher than the front. Perfect for a woman back seat driver because she had a view of the speedometer and could accurately quote your speed. Not to worry though on the flat the best you could do was 65 MPH. Several of us bought cars about the same time and we modified them to suite the climate. The car had a convertible top that rolled back like a sardine can. We put braces in the roof and raised the top two inches which gave us a breeze through the car. Worked like a charm but we also gathered all the bugs. We modified our improvement by installing a wire mesh screen and this prevented the bugs from infesting the car but allowed the airflow to cool the occupants. Even the Iranians copied us and we would laugh as our idea spread throughout the city. A car gave me a certain freedom and I could visit Iranian friends in other sections of town. It enabled me to eat in my old restaurants that I had found while living in the hotel. The car cost me $3000. and the gas cost 14 Cents a gallon. Since the car would give me forty miles to the gallon it was not very expensive transportation. One more thing about the car and I will get off the subject. It would go anywhere a four wheel jeep would go and would give you a more comfortable ride as well. The front wheel drive and the light weight of the car combined to give you traction when traveling off roads or across the desert. Ugly,, you bet, but practical ,and how!!

The United States Military had housing further out. The Air Force had a pool table and movies every night. They had parties as well so I wasted no time in introducing my self to these gents and were quickly accepted as a retired Navy type. I could bring guests so my friends would eagerly accept invitations. We were a friendly gang anyway and I was frequently invited to house parties and dinners. Major Mavashon had me to his home several times and I invited he and his family to dine with me in one of my favorite in town restaurants.

I should dwell on the make up of the Iranian Air Force. They had a branch that was different.

*CDR. Jack Sullivan USNR*

The Homifars were almost like our Warrant Officers but not quite. They were the skilled technicians, the mechanic. metal smith and aivionic technician. They ranged from first class that received a pay equivalent to a Captain to a third class that received a pay equivalent to a second lieutenant. They paid the skilled technicians as much as junior ranks of officers and recruited educated young men as a result. They were, for the most part, eager to learn and they all spoke English far better than I ever spoke Farsi. When I would speak Farsi they would kid me and remind me that it would be easier for me to get my point across in English as their English was far better than my Farsi. Despite that one of them told me they liked the fact that I tried to learn their language. I established a great friendship with those I had worked with and it would stand me in great stead. Later on in the midst of troubled times during the revolution they would watch my back and warn me of danger at great peril to themselves. They also proved themselves to be fast learners and we gradually set up the intermediate maintenance..

The test equipment became available and we calibrated it and made it operational. The test cell for the TF30 engine also came on line and we were able to repair and test engines. The training was progressing and all but two aircraft had arrived. The total buy was eighty F14 aircraft and the support equipment to maintain them. The aircraft would eventually go to three perhaps four bases when training were complete. TAC headquarters in Shiraz would have control over them as it did for the other aircraft in the inventory. The Shah had purchased eighty and we lost one in training.

An Iranian pilot was flying the aircraft and an American (Grumman) NFO was in the rear cockpit. The Iranian got himself into an unusual attitude and lost control of the aircraft. The NFO told him to eject but the Iranian refused. The NFO ejected and lived. The Iranian pilot remained aboard the aircraft and was killed in the crash. I spoke to some of the pilots about the accident and in private and not for publication they told me the pilot of the aircraft would have faced sever charges had he ejected and lived.

This is a different civilization and they play by different rules. We Americans for the most part have never lived in foreign countries for extended periods of time and unless you have you judge everyone by our standards. Fine for life in America but if you are facing Genghis Kahn you better be ready to fight a different fight.

The Shahs anniversary was coming up and General Robied, the head of the Iranian Air Force wanted to celebrate it by having a fly over of the entire F14 Fleet of aircraft comprising 77 aircraft. Parts were needed for a number of aircraft and we were to attempt to expedite them. I was sent to Tehran along with another Grumman Rep Chuck Dilks from supply. We would go through the military channels to expedite the required parts. We also had a direct link to Grumman. For the next three weeks I worked out of the Tehran Office getting to know those people real well and receiving all the assistance we needed from Grumman as well as the Military Reps. We received the parts and at one time all 77 aircraft were ready for flight .To accomplish this all training flights had been postponed. I know that not all aircraft were systems ready but they were flyable. At the appropriate time all 77 aircraft were airborne. One had to abort and return for a serious discrepancy but 76 F14s flew to Tehran and returned to Isfahan safely. I talked to the Former Navy Pilots Grumman had hired as instructors and we all agreed we had never seen this fete duplicated by the US Navy. Even fly off from Carriers usually had a number of hangar queens.

Another fact is the Shah had bought a larger quantity of spares for his fleet than the Navy bought for an equal number of F14s. Well my stay in Tehran brought me into contact with the man who was to be the Base Manager for Grumman at Shiraz when the first aircraft Squadron of F14s became operational. I spent some enjoyable time with he and his wife and was treated to a number of fine meals in the better restaurants in Tehran. I even got to meet General Robeid, an impressive man who headed up the Shahs Air Force. When I got back to Isfahan the Base was still excited by the results of the flyover. Seeing

76 F14s has to be impressive particularly when they are in formation.

I had heard a story when I was in Tehran that is worth repeating. It seem that the Shah had attended a meeting in Russia and he was talking in private to the Russian Premier. There had been almost daily over flights of Iran by a Russian aircraft at some 60,000 ft. The Shah had asked the Russian if it was his aircraft and the Russian denied it. Good said the Shah because I just bought 80 F14s and I intend to shoot the aircraft out of the sky with a Phoenix missile. The overflights ceased!! Someone claimed General Robeid was the source of the story. The F14 could have accomplished this task and that I can say for certain!

We were getting close to having two Squadrons operational. It was rumored we would be sending a team to Shiraz in the near future. Word came that the man picked to be the Base Manager had a medical problem and had returned home. A Vice President from Grumman came over at this time and was talking to the men about their life in Country and the state of moral among the troops. We had a couple of conversations and he inquired about my background. More than just inquired he asked pointed questions about it that gave me the impression he was considering me for the Base Managers job in Shiraz. In my heart I realized I was qualified, Cubi Point alone would more than qualify me for this job but I answered his questions truthfully and completely. He thanked me and invited me to have dinner with him that evening. At dinner we talked some more and he was very interested in my Navy Career. I spoke to him at great length about Cubi, my experience in Viet Nam as liaison for Deputy COM FAIR WEST PAC and my experience at the Naval Air Test Center. Dick Barton called me in the next day and spoke to me as well and hinted that I was a possible choice for Base manager at Shiraz. He gave me a briefing as to what he considered the job would entail and asked me what I thought I would need as far as manpower was concerned. Since these Squadrons were to be operational I would not need the numbers that Isfahan employed. The people that came down with me would have to be the best as they would not have backup in some cases. Dick Agreed with my assessment and our conversation ended without anything more being said. Rumors abounded and I heard from several people that I had been selected and was asked if they could come with me. This reached Vinny DeStefano and he asked me if I was recruiting from his people. I told him no as I hadn't heard that I was getting the job. Whether this satisfied him I don't know but that was how it was left at the time.

I Get the Job!! Dick Barton called me in to his office and told me to get ready to go to Shiraz. Joe McGill who I had met in Tehran would be my personnel manager and the two of us would go ahead, stay in a hotel and acquire some 46 apartments for the personnel that would be

*Shields of Honor*

arriving within the next two months. I was to report to the head of TAC General Mehrimand and he would assign me offices and spaces for the people who would be arriving, My wife had arrived just days before and I had met her in Tehran and accompanied her to Isfahan. She brought our three cats and they had arrived in good shape. I had an apartment or villa at Isfahan and it was ready when she arrived. Sadly she took ill shortly after she arrived but the wife of one of my friends was a nurse and she looked after her while I was being briefed on my new job. I had to go to Shiraz as ordered and Joan stayed behind with my friends. The wives looked after her much the same as the Navy wives would have.

Joe and I rented several apartments and settled on a house with two and a half apartments for us and any visitors we might have. I went to Isfahan and moved Joan down to Shiraz. Thank God she had recovered and was ready for the move. Our Furniture and my car were shipped down and arrived the day after we arrived in Shiraz. Helen McGill had already settled in and helped Joan get comfortable. We had spent the first night as guests in Joe's apartment so Joan had a chance to see our apartment in the same house. She was pleased with the home and loved Shiraz so I felt good about the move. She later told me she was disappointed in Isfahan but loved Shiraz from the time she laid eyes on it. Our home was beautiful, Marble floors and all the modern conveniences. Our landlord was a medical doctor who had attended Yale University in the States and was now teaching medicine at Palavi University in Shiraz. He was a wonderful man and became a trusted friend. His wife was a lovely lady and she and Joan became good friends. She was the woman that helped Joan pick out the two Persian carpets we bought in Iran.

Joan never tired of telling the tale of going to these carpet store. She said it was like a tale out of the Arabian Nights. The outside of the building looked much the same as it must of back in the days of our Lord but when you got inside it took your breath away. The number and quality of the Persian carpets was mind boggling. Unbeknown to us at the time the Doctors wife's brother was the police chief and all the merchants knew him. Joan was in good company and she was very pleased with her selection (assisted by the doctor's wife). The next day these beautiful carpets covered two of our floors.

Joe had been working with a local real estate agent and had rented the required number of apartments. We were ready to bring the troops down to Shiraz. I had already reported in to General Mehrimand and found him to be a very competent Officer. His second in command was General Khamani. General Kahmani was the General the Shah used whenever a base went downhill. He would send him in and in a short time the Base was back on its feet and ready for a new Commander. I had a chance to watch him work and I understood why the Shah depended on him. He could be a General in any mans army.. He had a keen insight and you knew, instinctively, you told this man the truth. I always did and it paid off for me because I was always welcomed into his office once I had established myself in his eyes.

Captain Maleki was the maintenance officer and had been selected as the most promising junior officer in the Iranian Air Force. From the day I met him we became good friends, Not all Iranians liked us, some wondered why we were needed. I heard from an Iranian Homifar, who had come from Isfahan with the F14 s that someone had questioned my concern for the Iranians and Captain Malachy had almost come to blows with this individual in my defense. I could always express my concerns to him and if I thought he was making a mistake he would attentively listen to my criticism. It was almost as though we were in the same outfit. I should say that the Iranians at that time under the Shah were our friends and were considered allies. I worked under this premise and felt I should help them in any way that I could. I am certain Captain Malachy was aware of this and we never had a cross word in all the time we worked together.

The Colonel in charge of the Squadron had married an American girl when he was in the States. She and Joan became good friends and we spent many a pleasant moment together in either his home or mine. He loved racquet ball and when he found out I played he was going to build a court on the base. This was foiled when he was selected for General and it wasn't known for some time where he would be stationed. Colonel Gohary, soon to be General Gohary had taught the Shahs son to fly and as both of them are in the States at the time of this writing I'm sure they are in touch.

The F14s were flown in from Isfahan and the operational Squadron was ready to go to work. I was asked to sit in on the briefing the Squadron received each morning on what training would be accomplished that day. While it in Farsi I could make it out from the charts that accompanied the brief. I was there mostly to answer questions should they arise.

My staff consisted of Joe McGill, my Administrator, Dave Guess (supply Chief), and Carl York (maintenance Control). These three kept me aware of general operations. Chuck Vandervort worked with the contractor who was building the AIMD. (Aircraft intermediate Maintenance Department). This is the hangar where all the heavy maintenance would be done. I worked closely with Chuck because I had so many ideas of how this building should be built to assist a maintenance officer.

We built a small show and tell room housing sliding boards that covered the work that should be accomplished. We updated these boards continuously. They indicated the scheduled time each task was slated to be complete and accurately indicated by percentage the work that had been accomplished as of the date on the board. When the Generals saw these boards they requested a weekly briefing. They had nothing in the Iranian Air Force that was as accurate. When the Shah visited the Base we briefed Capt Malachy and using the same boards he briefed the Shah. He told me the Shah was impressed. I hope so. If we were falling behind our schedule we could exert some pressure on the culprit and at least have a feasible reason for the delay on the board.

Ed Shannon was the Hughes Base Manager and we would work together. His was the avionics world and special test equipment and he did his best to see that this type equipment was arriving on time and was up and calibrated. To provide for creature comfort Grumman allowed us to take out a company membership in the Pool at the Cyrus Hotel The wives and the children found this particularly enjoyable. So did the men on the weekends and it was a favorite gathering place.

Westinghouse had been in Shiraz before us and had established a club house in town. They had a chef and you could have a fine dinner there. We met the manager of Westinghouse early on and told him the size of the force we would be bringing to Shiraz. The clubhouse would easily support us and we were welcome to join the Club. Our membership provided them with additional funds and when we brought the American Consul into the equation we were provided with American movies and tapes of recent sporting events. We would sit and watch a football game played the week before and root as though it was being played as we watched.

Shiraz was a college town really. Palavi University was there and the young students were everywhere. There weren't as many Chedars (Long Veiled robes) as I had seen in Isfahan. The students certainly didn't wear them nor did most of the population. American movies with Farsi subtitles were played in the local theatres and we often went. It would be hard to tell you were not in an American theatre except the laughter took a little longer to occur because of the subtitles. The restaurants were packed, particularly the good ones but they were there and the Americans enjoyed them, The streets of Shiraz were divided by an island in the middle that was filled with roses. The town had a pleasant aroma of roses and a native of Shiraz will swear the rose was born in Shiraz. True or not the town has more variety of roses than I have ever seen elsewhere. So many of the students spoke English. Engage one by asking a question and you have a conversation. Whether they want to practice their English or are just friendly the results are the same. My next door neighbor was Japanese. He spoke very little English and my Japanese is almost non existent. We carried on small talk in Farsi to the amusement of both wives.

The American Consulate was within a block of my home and I met the Consul early on at a party at the Taft House. He and his wife were delighted to have Americans in the neighborhood and we became friends and were frequent guests at parties in the Consulate. He also was a frequent guest at our home. Later on our visits to the Consulate would be of a more serious nature.

Our days at the Base were busy ones with the exception of some of our some of our engineering tech reps. They felt the Iranians in Shiraz were not keeping them as busy as they had in Isfahan. I spoke to Captain Malachy about this and he said the Iranians would call them if they could not solve the problem themselves. They felt they were operational now and should become a little more independent. We had some people that had been working with the Iranians in a hands on way that were still being used and his answer for that was his people were used to them working side by side with them. The engineers on the other hand are consultants and except for classroom training were never out there with the workers. He also stated they were too busy for classroom work. We were gradually working our way out of a job.

About this time we had an exercise with Americans flying F111. The very aircraft that F14 replaced was coming to Iran for a joint exercise. I met the Air Force Officers that landed and had a chance to talk to them. They were curious about the F14 but understood why their aircraft could never have been a Navy Aircraft. As a bomber it was very good but not as a fighter. I can't remember the two aircraft working together but I can tell you there certainly was a difference between the two aircraft. You only had to watch the take off roll to see that. They remained for about a week and then left and I didn't get much of a chance to talk to them after the first day..

We had a sad happening. A tragic death of one of our people.. Carl York was driving up to Isfahan. Whether he was driving at too high a speed for the road we could never tell but his car left the road and he was killed in the ensuing crash. As he was close to Isfahan when it occurred the Grumman Office there was made aware of the accident and responded. As we were a smaller group and closer knit we all felt the anguish and loss. Carl was a bachelor so there was no grieving wife but I knew he was close with his parents so I wrote to them. I hope it helped. To complicate matters Carl was carrying some cash for one of the Iranian Pilots and was to give it to his wife upon arrival in Isfahan. Grumman Isfahan would have to sort that one out with the Iranian authorities.

We get a hint of trouble. In early September of 1978 there were minor disturbances in Tehran. These disturbances caused the Shah to declare a state of martial law on September 8th. It changed our lifestyle in as much as nobody was to be on the street after ten o'clock. Parties had to break up early, the clubs had to close in time to allow everyone to safely reach their home. This lasted for a few days then it was lifted for a while.

People started to get nervous and it was the first time I heard people talk of leaving.

The company TRW had employed my wife as a typist. The manager Ted Guy was a good friend and could not get anyone who could type in English. He mentioned it one night at a party and Joan said she would help him out till he could find someone. Since TRW worked directly for the Iranian Air Force Joan was working for General Khosravi the Logistics Officer in TAC and one of my favorite people. Joan told me it was cute because he always would bid her good morning and ask her how was Mr. Jack? Joan became a mainstay because none of the girls could type as fast or accurate. She also would clean up the English in their reports, American and Iranian. Take dictation from both Iranian and American, translate it into standard English and have it ready for signature in such a short time they were amazed. Joan had worked on Wall Street as a Secretary/Administrative Assistant. Her only complaint was that nobody was using any of the other girls and she was doing it all. Despite this complaint I know she enjoyed being back in harness.

Even during the Martial Law if we were attending a party on Base the Military would keep us till the wee hours and provide us with a military escort home. Now Joan was known on some sections of Base as well as I was and the Iranian women were in awe of her because of her skills with the typewriter. Ted would call me and thank me for allowing her to work. He said his bosses back in the States can now read his letters without an interpreter. Incidentally this is the same Ted Guy that was one of the long time prisoners of war in Viet Nam. He lent me a book on prisoners of war that was given to him by one of his senior enlisted men. The inscription read "To Colonel Ted Guy an Officer Who Thought More of His Men Than a Star" That said worlds to me and later on Ted would help me in no small way

Joan had been elected President of the International Wives Club in Shiraz. Despite the language problem she had the girls playing bridge. The would point to the suit and indicate their bid with their fingers . It was a little more complicated than that but it worked. She also would have guest speakers in and one in particular comes to mind. He was the son of one of the Chiefs of the traveling tribes that would migrate to various parts of Iran depending on the season. The Shah wanted everyone in Iran to be educated including these tribes. He made a deal with the Chief where in he would educate some of his sons and people of the Chiefs choosing and they in turn would teach the children of the tribe. The black tent of the Chief was always the first to be put up but now it's the white tent of the teachers and when the children saw it they came.. They weren't being taught radical Islam either but reading, writing, and arithmetic. He invited the women to visit the camp that was only miles out of town at that time. Most of the girls visited the camp in chartered busses and were received by the Chiefs wife and the ladies of the tribe. Joan said they had a delightful time and were impressed with the colorful clothes worn by these women. The higher the rank the more slips they had under the outer skirt and the more gold bracelets they wore on their arms. Joans visit cost me some money as Joan immediately bought seven gold bracelets. The Chiefs wife said this was their custom and it brought them luck. Any excuse for my wife to buy gold. The women had told them about grand tombs of Persian Kings that were located in the dessert just outside of Shiraz. The Chiefs son gave them the name of a guide in Shiraz who could arrange tours of these tombs. Joan contacted the guide and many of the women in the Club signed up for the tour. Joan said the ride in the dessert was spooky because they were not on established roads but old camel trails most of the way. When they arrived at the first tomb she had the feeling she was looking at an old movie of Egypt. The tomb resembled those she had seen in the movie. It was old but well preserved and you could easily tell it had required countless hours of sweat and tears from the laborers who built it. They went inside and the change in temperature was remarkable but Joan said it raised the hair on her arms and the back of her neck. Everyone felt it and one of the wives jokingly said if someone had said boo they all would have fled in panic. The guide was amused but told them it was a common occurrence. They visited several tombs but only the first provoked that spooky feeling among the girls. I told General Khameneh about the trip and he was amused. He named all the Tombs they visited and gave me a brief history of them. I wish I had taken notes because I can't remember their names.

General Khemeneh asked me if I had been to Persepolis and seen the ancient City. We had decided to visit Persepolis several times but some thing had always come up to prevent the trip. He told me he would set up a trip for me as his guest and I would be allowed into the Shahs personal quarters in the famous Tent City. To celebrate his Anniversary the Shah had a Tent City constructed to house all the world leaders. Each nation would have it own tent and a very large one would host the Cocktail party and the dinner he would have each night in celebration. Vice President Rockefeller had a choice tent and I could visit that one as well. He was true to his word and we were escorted to Persepolis the following week and our guide took us through the entire city When I think of tents I imagine boy scout tents but believe me what I saw there was of a style and grandeur that I had never imagined existed. They were huge and lavish beyond description. I'm sure regardless of a persons rank and wealth nobody felt like they were camping out. The Shahs bathroom had gold faucets, all of the utilities were gold. The guide watched as we were awestricken by the display of wealth and smiled as he told us in English, " the shah lives pretty good" He took us next to the large tent that had hosted all the parties. The chairs were exquisite and he told us they cost almost a thousand dollars apiece and had been hand made in France for this event. They were arranged in such a way that everyone had a clear view of the Shah but also had neighbors they could converse with during the celebration. He pointed out where the American Vice President sat and listed some of his neighbors seated on either side. We were both impressed, no that isn't the word, overcome would be a better description. Life Magazine had run an article on the event and I remember reading it and was somewhat impressed. Seeing it in person and getting the briefing the guide gave us made the pictures in Life seem inadequate. We spent half a day in Tent City and thanked our guide profusely when we left. He told us what a wonderful man General Khameneh was and he was pleased to entertain any of his guests.

We then went to the old City of Persepolis and let me divert and tell you some thing of the City. There is an entrance way with an arch that many visitors have carved the names on. We would look in awe at folks from the seventeen hundreds who had proceeded us. Our fellow travelers would gleefully point out British Sailors who had made the trip in the early seventeen hundreds and had marked not only their names but the name of their ships for posterity. I discovered our own famous reporter Stanley, of Stanley and Livingston fame, had visited Persepolis and had carved his name and the name of his paper in stone together with the date. People would cry out when they discovered a name with an early date and yet we were viewing a city over five thousand years old. Cyrus the Great had been its king and he is listed in the early version of the Bible as being a great, noble and just King. A British Sailor from the seventeen hundreds was getting all our attention This was running through my mind yet I touched Stanley's name with reverence and affection as I passed through the gates. They were digging through the sand and uncovering an ancient staircase as we arrived. I was fascinated because the staircase was covered with hieroglyphics that looked to have been cut into the staircase yesterday. Several of the workers were carefully removing the last vestiges of the sand. I asked if any of them could read the writing and one answered in a clipped British accent. He said it depicted the people paying tribute to the king and pointed out what each of the laborers was carrying. The chiseled figures of the laborers were so stark that you could picture what had occurred here several thousand years ago. In the States if we went back five hundred years we would only have the Indians to talk to and here is a Country that can go back thousand of years with recorded history. Yet our young Country has given the world the greatest form of government and the greatest constitution out lining that form of Government the world has ever seen. The same thought passed through my mind years before when I was looking at the ancient buildings in Greece Our early fathers who founded our Country deserve our undying gratitude and here in the midst of this ancient grandeur that thoughts like these passed through my mind is a tribute to that wonderful mom and dad I told you about earlier who had instilled in me a great love for my country. I pray that similar thoughts pass through my children's mind if they find themselves in similar positions and that they attribute them to me. The amount of restoration at Persepolis that was going on at the time brought us back to the site many times before we left Iran. It was fascinating to see the engineering the ancients were capable of and the running water and sewerage collection they fashioned has not been duplicated in some parts of the world today.

General Khameneh was delighted that I had found the visit so awe inspiring. He had come from humble beginnings. His father was a camel driver and the most he had ever done was get electricity installed in his home. His father would marvel when he turned the switch and light would flood the room. The General had enlisted as a Sabas (enlisted soldier) and had been selected for further education because of his aptitude. He was made an officer after graduating from college and swiftly moved up the ranks to Maj. General. I was fascinated to hear him tell this story and he then told me his son was in the States studying to be an electrical engineer. He said his father would not be able to contemplate what his grandson would be able to accomplish. Captain Maleki could not believe the General would talk to me in this manner. He told me he was not anxious to talk to him because he was such a disciplinarian. I truly liked and admired this man and perhaps because I wasn't in his chain of command he felt he could talk to me in a different way.

Chuck Vandervort worked very well with the general contractor and most of my suggestions were incorporated into the plan. These were ideas that I had developed over the years as a Navy Maintenance Officer. Ideas that would facilitate the work of the maintenance crew, Longer air hose, couplers that would hook up to different pieces of ground support. Electrical outlets with connections that could be interchanged and made compatible with different equipment. The ability to make electrical components available to aircraft out side the hangar itself when necessary. Most of the suggestions required no monetary increase in the cost of construction but would have a dramatic effect of the maintenance crews ability to maintain aircraft. The contractor would listen to everything we said and figure out a way to make them happen. When our suggestions looked like they would add to the cost I would have to take them to Captain Maleki and convince him of their worth. He in turn would have to go to General Khosravi, the Deputy for Logistics for approval. My wife worked for General Khosravi and he would sometimes kid her saying "your husband is costing me money again".

The country squire - my home in Town Creek, Maryland 1986.

The facilities were progressing nicely when the hostile activities in Tehran broke out again. The Shah declared Martial Law again and some of my troops began to get a little nervous. We had meetings to talk about the situation and decided we would have a telephone tree so that a single phone call could activate the whole team. If you could not locate the person you were to notify call the one he was to notify and then call me and I would originate a search for the missing person. We exercised the tree several times to make certain it would work. Besides the notification each family was to have a small bag containing the essentials that was to be packed and ready for immediate use, The dependants were here and each family was to be aware of the whereabouts of each of their family members. The political climate was such that this was not difficult and each family member was accounted for most of the day. The members of the phone tree would notify those responsible when they were going out in the evening and where they would be. The second Martial Law lasted a little longer than the first but it too was overcome by events and was lifted. Shiraz was not as political as Tehran and we had not seen any demonstrations in the street.

I received my first emergency call from the American Consul and was asked to come to the Consuls' office. He was planning to have the heads of all the companies in Shiraz meet once a week in his office to discuss the political problems and what was happening in their area. He asked me to keep an eye on the aircraft traffic to make certain the airlines were maintaining a schedule. I knew some of the pilots and they would tell me of any problem that would interrupt our freedom of movement. The oil companies to the south and east would report on any problems they encountered and would listen intently when I gave my assessment of the airline traffic both domestic and foreign. There was a rumor that Kohmeni was to be put out of his asylum and nobody knew where he would go. He was really at the heart of the Iranian discontent and his form of fundamental Islamic law was what was causing the disturbances. The meeting with the American Consul took on new meaning. The heads of the various companies were nervous as many of them had dependants and were looking to the State Department for answers. Answers that they did not seem to have. The oil companies were isolated and except for phone did not have any connection with the rest of us. The weekly meetings became critical and I gave them the best information I could obtain from my friends in the airline.

This excitement was noticeable in the military ranks as well. When the word came to us that Kohmeni had been exiled to France it spelled the beginning of the end. Kohmeni had a sounding board in France that he did not have in Iraq. In Iraq he had asylum as long as he remained silent and didn't preach his brand of radical fundamentalism. In France he was news and most of the press establishment followed and reported on his every word. The British Broadcast Company (BBC) would report in English what he was doing but in their Farsi broadcast they would in effect tell the Iranians what his plans were for the following day. Now we really had problems as the Iranians were hearing from him through the auspices of the BBC. The head of the Westinghouse company had advised me that they had a flight that was coming to pick up all the Westinghouse employees on the 8$^{th}$ of December 1978. He told me there would be room for all of my dependants plus any of the men I might want to send back. I alerted all my people and told the dependants to have a bag packed and be ready to leave. The flight arrived on the 8th as scheduled and I went over to Westinghouse to talk to them. I made a call to Isfahan to talk to the Grumman people there. We wound up with a phone patch with Isfahan, Tehran and The Grumman folks in New York all listening. I informed them of the Westinghouse plane being on the deck and my plans to utilize the seats for dependants and several Grumman workers. In the midst of this conversation we heard excited voices from Isfahan call out "The whole place is on fire…the whole place is on fire" then we heard something that sounded like gunshots and Isfahans phone went dead. I heard NY ask what the hell is going on and the phone went dead. I called Tehran and spoke to Jacque Graff the Base Manager there and he couldn't give me an answer but we figured that our Isfahan Office must have been firebombed, I told Jacque I was sending the dependants home and please have Grumman contact Westinghouse in the States and make all the proper notifications and determine the schedules. I told Joan, who was with me at this point to exercise the phone tree and have everyone at the airport and ready to board within two hours. Passports would be required as we had previously briefed. Joan started the tree and it worked as rehearsed. I'm proud to say my dependants were all at the airport before the

Westinghouse people and the aircraft was loaded and underway at the scheduled time

Don Anderson from Grumman was put in charge of the dependants and he shepherded them all the way to New York. When they arrived the press was waiting for them and Joan was singled out for questioning by the press. She very nicely told them that they were coming home for Christmas and that they expected to return to their husbands after the holidays. She said she was afraid if the word got back to the Iranians they were leaving it might create a problem for us in Iran. It was amazing how many of our friends caught that broadcast and saw Joan. For years after it was a matter of discussion when we visited old friends. Incidentally it would be two months before I spoke to my wife again as all hell broke lose in the ensuing months.

Joan and the dependants left on December 8 1978 and I had the three cats that I had to take care of in our apartment. All three welcomed me when I came home each night, as they knew it was suppertime. They also missed the human company I'm sure because Joan was their friend and usually was around. They spent time with me in bed at night and probably wondered why Joan wasn't there as well.

The climate in Shiraz was changing. The poorer element was becoming a bit belligerent and there were sporadic demonstrations. One of our Grumman employers narrowly avoided a mob that was protesting the American presence in town and I reported it to the American Consul. I also heard from a British pilot flying for the Iran Airline that flights were being held up by demonstrations in Tehran and he could not promise me that they would ever hold to schedule again. Our next meeting I explained this to all the heads of the various companies and they all agreed it was time to evacuate.

The Iranian Air Force was holding together and there was no sign of any break either in their chain of command or their activities on base. Captain Maleci suggested that I might consider moving my troops aboard the base and arranged suitable space be made available should I make that judgment. The companies were leaving now and we were losing them with some regularity. TRW made ready to leave and Ted Guy came to me and told me of his plans. He gave me the key to his office located in the Iranian Air Force Headquarters. He told me he had the only direct phone line that did not go through the switchboard and it might come in handy sometime if we stayed.

Only Grumman and Hughes were still in town and the demonstrations became more frequent. On the 31st of December I moved everyone on Base. I had obtained a release from the Iranian Vet to permit my cats to be sent home. One of the wives from TRW agreed to take them home with her to NY and turn them over to Grumman until Joan could pick them up. I gave her telephone numbers for Joan's parents and mine. I would

*Shields of Honor*

learn the cats arrived safely and my good friend Archie Brooks from Grumman had picked them up and put them in a vets care till Joan arrived. I will always be grateful Archie!

Ed Shannon from Hughes and I moved in with LCOL. Woody Bryant as he had a phone we could keep in touch with our offices in Country. On January 2$^{nd}$ I started to send some of the Grumman Personnel home. Collins, Wells and Roberts left for the States. On the 3$^{rd}$ Jepson. Nurmi, Thomas, Jameson, Vasely and Pitcher made ready to leave for the States and I was left with just enough personnel to make the F14s wartime flyable for a flight to a Gulf Country that shall remain nameless. Flying on base came to a halt as gasoline shortage became critical. We were unable to leave the base even though I had some Iranians that were packing out our Grumman personnel. Alderson had attempted to go to town but his car was stoned and he returned, thankfully unharmed. On the 4$^{th}$ I was able to make it into town and met the people from Tehran that were packing us out. I felt safe because these people were not being bothered and the Iranian neighbors we had were still friendly and hated to see us leave. The packers did a fine job and the work was soon finished. The lead man also had brought funds and I visited all our landlords and paid them till the end of the month. They were understanding and well aware of the climate that now existed. If in the future the regime was to be friendlier and the program was to continue I'm sure the landlords would be agreeable to renting to us again. Jepson, Nurmi, Thomas, Jameson, Vasely and Pitcher left the next day for Tehran and then home.

The next day a demonstration in town almost reached our Consul. They were threatening but the Police would not permit them to reach the Embassy. I arrived sometime later and the Consul gave me two radios and some batteries and we arranged to communicate at certain hours. These small radios came in handy in the weeks to follow. On the 16$^{th}$ an American was assassinated in the Awaz oil fields and the Oil fields were evacuated and the American departed on the 23$^{rd}$ of January. On the 24$^{th}$ our CEO of Grumman ordered all Our Grumman Personnel to return.

Woody Bryant called us in and we listed all of our specialties and skills. We broke up into teams and each team was assigned a car. Each team had a mechanic, a medical team and someone who had a smattering of the language. I had each of the cars topped off because thanks to the patches and goodies Grumman had provided me with I was able to become friends with the operators of the Fuel Farm and Mr. Jack (as I was known as to them) could always get gas. Even when everyone else was mad at the Americans.

Shannon and Gibbs from Hughes left the next day for Tehran on their way home. On the 29$^{th}$ the following Grumman personnel left for Greece, Whittaker, Pittman, DeBose, and Banger. On the 30$^{th}$ we had an international incident. A

*Shields of Honor*

Bell Helicopter employee shot an Iranian and the Mob of some 6,000 Iranians surrounded the Korush Hotel in Isfahan demanding his death. He was saved by the Iranian Police but our Consul in Isfahan, Dave McCaffery was roughed up by the mob and required medical attention. On the 5th of Feb. Cox, McGrath, Alderson, Alverado, Guess and Pigott left for Athens.

Bazergon was appointed Prime Minister on the 6th of Feb. On the 9th of Feb fighting broke out in Doshen Tappi between the Army Cadets and the Air force. The Cadets were for Khomeni and the Air force was still loyal to the Shah. The BBC continued to report on everything Khomeni was requiring and kept the mob excitement alive.

On the 11th we got the word the Shah of Iran left the Country and the same day the Homifars broke into the Armory and everyone armed themselves. People were shooting up into the air not mindful that what goes up must come down, We stayed inside the Taft House. That night at about 2 AM I received a phone call. The caller asked me if I recognized his voice and warned me not to mention his name. When I assured him I did I received the first of several warning of impending danger from my Iranian friend. This one concerned a demonstration that would ring the Taft house the following day. I was warned to keep everyone inside and out of sight and nobody would get hurt. I won't mention his name but if he should ever read this he has my undying friendship and has been in my prayers ever since.

On the 12th LCOL. Long and myself set out for The Headquarters of the IIAF several blocks away. We went to see the Generals and when we got there we found both Generals armed with submachine guns. They were not happy to see us and warned us of impending danger. The Mob was coming to burn down the building as this Headquarters contained the disciplinary records of the whole Air Force. He instructed his driver to take us back to the Taft House via another route. When we got into the car and drove a block we saw the Mob coming but were able to turn away from them and return to the Taft House another way.

We then set a radio watch around the clock. The Taft Radio was able to contact Isfahan and we could monitor their reports. The same day later in the afternoon an armed group entered the Taft House to check for whisky and guns. They were belligerent and threatened to shoot the locks off our lockers when I said to them "NO NO we only do that in the movies. Everyone started to laugh including the armed group and we became friends again. We opened the lockers for them but they took nothing but the rifles the Taft Team had for hunting Boars

We had a Lieutenant who would visit us each day and tell us what the Iranian Air Force wanted from us and would ask us if we had any questions. I had not been able to get to my Office on the other side of the field and I had important papers as well as money in my safe. He would tell me my visit was under consideration but I could not visit until it was approved. On the13th an armed team came and confiscated the Taft Radio and we lost contact with the outside world. No argument would work. We were told we were spies and could not contact anyone. Our radios we received from the American Consul had been hidden and we could communicate with the Consul at the appropriate times. He called my boss Swoose Snead at Grumman and told him what had happened and would relay anything important.

The next day the 15th Homifar Jahantegh came for me. My Office had been broken into and asked me to accompany him to the other side. I requested LCOL Bryant be allowed to accompany me. We went through six check points with the Homifar assuring the guards at each that my presence was requested by the highest authority. When I got to my office I discovered the lock on the door had been broken and my office was open to the world. My office was in the heart of their headquarters and with all the guards surrounding it I could not imagine how the break in had not been detected. The only thing missing was the safe. It was heavy and certainly could not be lifted. There were marks where it had been dragged down the hall and out the door at the end of the hall. There were small marks in the concrete steps from which it must have been lifted onto a truck and hauled away. The Iranians who surrounded me were embarrassed and knew as well as I that it had been one of their number that had committed the crime. I told them what had been in the safe, money belonging to Grumman, my money and a plane ticket back to the States. .

I returned to the Taft House and not long after our Radios were returned. I imagine they were feeling guilty about the theft of my safe. On the 18$^{th}$ they allowed me to visit my headquarters once more to pick up any papers I might need. When I returned I spoke to Col Bryant and suggested he and I ask for an interview with the Defense Council. The defense Council was made up of the local Mulah, A Captain who had worked in the C130 group and two soldiers. They had been loyal to Kohmeni all along and believed in the same radical Islam. We were told we could meet with them on the 19$^{th}$. I went to the Headquarters building that same day taking the key Ted guy had left with me. I called my Office in Isfahan and asked the Iranian who answered if I could speak with Swoose Snead. He is not here. I then listed names of people I would like to speak to but none of them was there. The Iranian then told me they had all departed for Tehran and would be returning to the States on 747 s provided by the US Government. What a lonely feeling I experienced upon hearing that. I returned to Taft House with a certain feeling of urgency. The next day we were brought to the

*Shields of Honor*

Defense Council. Waiting to be interviewed was General Khameneh in civilian clothes. He looked crushed. Whether he was expecting a death sentence I couldn't tell you but it was possible after hearing what happened to The Chief of the Air Force. A few days earlier he had been in his Office and I visited him. He greeted me warmly but I could tell he was upset. He told me there were Sabas (soldiers) guarding his house. He said Jack I don't know whether they are guarding me or plotting to kill me. If it's at the hands of soldiers that an Air force General dies it means the end of the chain of command and military discipline and our service will deteriorate. It was a sad meeting and now I felt I had to do something. I approached him and shook his hand, defense council or not, and told him he would always be in my thoughts and prayers. His eyes lit for a moment then he dropped them and said a simple" thank you". We were ushered into the defense council and I met the Mulah. LCOL Bryant and I told him we would like to get out of the Country before anything else happens and that should some thing happen to us it would be a black mark on the revolution. The Mulah agreed and asked how we could be transported to Tehran in time to catch the last 747 Pan American had sent to bring back the last of the Americans. The Captain from the C130 Group said a C130 could be made ready and he would fly us up to Tehran. Being an old Maintenance Officer I knew the C130 s had their control cables cut so none of the Generals could use them to fly out of the Country. He was going to splice the cables. This should be a test flight. We would be part of that test flight. The last orders from the Mulah was absolute secrecy, nobody was to know and we Americans were to be ready at 5 AM the following day with only one bag each. We returned to the Taft House pleased at the results but it wasn't an hour later that we were surrounded by old friends from the IIAF who had come to say goodby and buy anything we did not want to take with us. What whiskey we had was quickly bought and even articles of clothing were sought after. I gave my stuff to friends I had known for over three years and said said goodbyes to a group of guys who under the right leadership would have made great allies. The Shah had been a friend of this Country and anyone that reads this will know what a despot replaced him. Somehow there was a disconnect in our State Department and we made an error in judgment. My three and a half years in country proved to me the Shah was an ally and he had brought his country into the twentieth century and was working hard to educate his people. He believed in the motives of The United States and listened to our State Department. The reason he did not block the transmissions of BBC was because our State Department asked him not to block them. We didn't get much sleep that night and were on the flight line bright and early the next morning. The C130 was waiting and we boarded the plane with one small bag of luggage apiece. We had to wait till they cleaned the gear off the runway. They had cluttered the runway with support equipment to prevent anyone from taking off unauthorized. The plane took off and flew to Tehran where we encountered the same problem, the runway was blocked with scattered support equipment. It was eventually removed and we landed. Our identification cards were checked five or six times by different Iranian guards before we could deplane. The State department recorded our names, checked our passports and issued us boarding passes. We completely filled all seats on the last plane, so much so that the stewardesses had to sit on jump seats. I remember as I boarded telling the Stewardess " a little bit of America." Her reply said it all "a whole lot of America" After we had started the engines a boarding party came and checked our identification once more. They were looking for someone. The pilot warned them he would have to refuel if he wasn't allowed to leave at once. That seemed to do it and the boarding party left and we taxied out for take off. When we cleared the ground a cheer went up with all of us joining in. When the pilot was ten miles from the border with Turkey he called off each mile and when we crossed the border someone started it and we all joined in singing The Stars Spangled Banner. I realized I had tears streaming down my cheeks and when I looked around noticed I was not alone. The emotion on that airplane was so thick you could feel it. A little later the General who was General Gast's deputy spoke over the intercom and thanked the crew for braving the known hardships to come rescue us. His talk was short but to the point and then he asked one of the Stewardesses to rely his sentiments to the crew. A deep voice, full of emotion replied "we heard you General and there isn't a dry eye in the cockpit." "We also heard you all sing the Stars Spangle Banner and we are proud to bring Americans such as you home to the States" Even as I write this years after the flight I still get a lump in my throat remembering the events.

When we landed in Frankfort, Germany I told LCOL Bryant I was going to stay with him as I had no money and my credit card had expired. We had no mail for over three months and had no way of renewing my card.

When we deplaned the first person I saw was Paul Von Inns, Swoose Sneads deputy. I gave him a hug and to this day he accuses me of breaking one of his ribs. Paul gave me a thousand dollars and a ticket home. He and his wife took me to diner that night and I got a good night sleep in a fine German Hotel. After breakfast the next morning they put me on a plane for the States. It was something of a miracle because Paul had been in Greece and had a feeling that someone should be in Frankfort just in case I came through that city. What luck! Paul notified Grumman of my schedule and Grumman notified my wife, Joan, Both she and Archie Brooks from Grumman were waiting for me when I got off the flight. I learned of Archies adventures with the cats and thanked him for his efforts. I had to accompany him to Grumman to be debriefed by both the Company and The CIA. I was then given some back pay, a bonus and two weeks to visit with my family. The Company had taken good care of the wives while we were gone and Joan spoke in glowing terms of how generous Grumman had been. We visited my son John in Tampa Florida as well as my daughter Maura in Virginia. I spoke to the teachers at John's school and they were very interested in hearing of my adventures in Iran. There were a lot of questions from the teachers and I think they were surprised that many of my observations and answers contradicted what they had been reading in the press and seeing on television. The mob demonstrations almost began and ended with the television lights. Our reps in Tehran used to laugh at the way the crowds would behave when the television lights were on and how they immediately were subdued and quiet when the lights were turned off. I told them some Americans acted the same way and invited them to watch a live show with outdoor performers and watch how the people passing by behave. It's the ham in all of us I guess but it sure effected the Iranians and they knew enough to act for the camera in a manner the television crew expected. The fact that my son was one of them probably gave me credibility among the teachers but they listened to my every word and seemed to agree we had bet on the wrong horse and time would bear that out.

My vacation and visits to my children and friends was coming to an end and I reported back to Field Service for reassignment. I was presented with a Project Sterling from Grumman for my actions in Iran. Project Sterling is a high award granted for something the Company thinks is above and beyond. They asked me if I had found housing and as I hadn't told me to do so and return when I was situated. Joan and I must have looked at a dozen houses but what frightened me was how long these houses had been on the market. I didn't want to be stuck with a house because we both agreed we would return to Pax River when I retired from Grumman. The real Estate broker asked if I could settle for a town house on a golf course and showed me a beautiful town house. The golf course was on a nine hole executive course and I fell in love with it. I bought it immediately. My neighbor, Ray Conboy, worked for the FAA and was a golfer. In a week I think he introduced me to every golfer in the neighborhood. The club house had a gym, an indoor pool and a great place to eat. The same year I won the club golf championship and had my first of six holes in one, a 235 yd hole in one. I had died and gone to heaven but Joan was not as happy. She enjoyed the people but had wanted a one story home and the town house had the bedrooms on the second floor. Later on when I had to travel and be gone for weeks at a time she told me she felt safe in that house with friendly neighbors all around her.

# Chapter 20
# The C2 Cod Program

I felt better and when I returned to work found that Nick Scobo was still my Boss. He questioned me about my knowledge of the C2 Cod aircraft. I smiled when I recalled all the work I had put in on the aircraft and how I had been part of an investigation that had cleared the aircraft for flight after two serious accidents. We talked for several hours and he told me I was the new Project Manager for the C2 and sent me over to see the Executive Vice President Bob Watkins for further evaluation. I had met Bob before, in fact he was the one that convinced the Board to make me the Base Manager of the Grumman effort in Shiraz. He knew of my Naval Experience but now our conversation consisted of the Companies efforts to sell the Navy 39 more C2 s. He gave me a stack of proposals and asked me to read them. I would help John Stark to sell the new airplanes. The C2 was important to the Navy as it was the aircraft that flew engines, spare parts and people to the Carriers. It had good range and was used in all theatres for supply functions. This twin engine turbo was the workhorse of the Fleet.

Nick sent me over to see Dick Read, the program manager of the current C2 s. Dick was a Reserve Navy Captain who I had known from my days at Floyd Bennett. I remembered him winning the Navy Trophy for the best Helicopter Squadron in the Reserve and knew him to be an excellent Officer. It was old home week in his office with a lot of hangar flying and recalling mutual friends we had both flown with in the Reserve. He was delighted to hear I would be assisting him with the C2 Program.

I am officially made the C2 Project Manager. My first pick was Stan Stone as my Logistics Manager. Stan was a young, ambitious logistician with a friendly disposition who immediately fit into the plans I had for improving the Operational Capability of the C2 in the Fleet. One of the first moves Dick Read made was to arrange for he and I to meet with the Force Material Officer of the Atlantic Fleet. The Operational Readiness of the C2 in the Fleet was substandard. They were having difficulty bringing the required material to the Fleet because of this low Operational Readiness. Dick arranged for a visit to the Fleet Base in Sigonella, Italy the home of VR 24 the C2 Squadron. We would be accompanied by a Lieutenant from the CNAL Staff and our Vice President from the E2/C2 operations, Jim Philbin would also visit the Squadron. It was arranged, a date set, the Squadron notified and we were on our way.

We arrived in Rome and were to take a shuttle flight to Sigonella however the Italian baggage handlers decided to go on strike at that exact moment. When Jim Philbin heard this he was furious and pounded his fist on the table in front of the baggage handlers. Jim stood 6 ft 7 inches and weighed about 250 lbs (he had played basketball for St John University) and looked very formidable with the angry expression on his face. There was some chatter among the handlers and the strike was called off and our baggage started to move on the conveyer belt once more. It was one of the few times I ever saw Jim get angry but I guess the handlers were impressed.

We arrived in Catania and our base manager met us and took us to our hotel. He provided us with information on the Base and the key personnel we would be meeting the next day. The Captain of the Base at Catania gave us a rundown of the history of the Base and what improvements were contemplated. We then went to the Squadron and met the Commanding Officer of VR 24. The Squadron was responsible for moving cargo between Bases in C130 Aircraft and then to the Carriers in C2 Aircraft. It was the C2 that we had come to examine and help identify the reason for the low operational readiness of this aircraft. The Maintenance Officer was at the meeting and I had a chance to talk with him. He seemed to think most of his problems were supply related. We all had a chance to see the Aircraft and meet with the Maintenance people. The general belief was that if the parts were available they could get the aircraft flying. That night, when we were back at the hotel I asked if I could stay for a while and work with the Squadron. Dick agreed and Jim Philbin said I should keep the Lieutenant from Air Lant here as well. We had a meeting with the Commanding Officer of the Squadron and my background was revealed to him. Jim also pointed out the interest the CEO ( George Skurla) had in this program and how he would ask for a complete debrief when I returned home. The CO was agreeable and said the Squadron would work with me in every way possible.

    The Navy Lieutenant and I checked into the BOQ on Base and prepared to take a hard look at the Squadron. I asked if I might examine the personnel records and was granted permission to do so. I explained to the young Lieutenant from Air Lant that I was anxious to check on the background of the various Maintenance Personnel. It was a slow tedious process but it revealed what I had suspected. The Squadron was a catch all for personnel from aircraft that had been eliminated from the fleet. There were people from P2Vs, A6s and other assorted aircraft that were no longer in the fleet. If these people came without their families they had a one year tour. If they came accompanied with their families they had a two year tour. In either case they had not worked on

C2 Aircraft before. This would be acceptable if there were experienced C2 personnel in numbers that could train them. This was not true and the trained C2 personnel were limited in numbers and spread too thin to be effective. There was no formal training for this aircraft and they were not considered a community. After a few weeks of studying the records we interviewed the maintenance personnel and discovered that while they were anxious to perform the tasks they lacked the knowledge and were ill equipped to perform the necessary maintenance. Those that had previous experience on the aircraft were overworked and had little time to instruct. To keep these aircraft flying they had to spend all their time performing maintenance. If they ran into a complicated task they would have to delay it to work on another aircraft that could meet the operational schedule. They needed hands on help as well as training for the personnel with no experience in C2s.

When I debriefed the CO and the Maintenance Officer I told them I would recommend that Grumman provide both CMS (hands on ) and CETS (training) personnel to assist the Squadron. I also recommended that we provide a LSR net work for the Squadron that would assist them in obtaining much needed parts in a more expeditious manner.

When I returned to Grumman I met with Dick Read and we worked out a program that we thought would fit the Squadrons needs.

We then took our proposal to Jim Philbin, Vice President, of the C2/E2 program. Jim scheduled a meeting with the CEO George Skurla and his executive assistant Bob Watkins. I explained in detail what I had discovered from reviewing the records and then explained the plan that Dick and I had devised to assist the Squadron. George Skurla amazed us all by saying Grumman would fund the program to get it started and if it was advantageous to the Squadron would expect the Navy to continue its funding.

Dick and I went to Navair first and had a meeting with LCDR Jack Wagoner the APML (Assistant Program Manager for Logistics) for the C2. Jack was a knowledgeable Naval Officer and gave his permission for the trial. Dick and I then went to AirLant and together with the young Lieutenant that had accompanied me on my visit to the Squadron presented Grumman's plan. After the Brief, AIRLANT agreed to allow the experiment. Now with AIRLANT and NAVAIR in agreement we set about forming the team. Grumman's Field Service went to work locating the required personnel. John Ryan and Mike Piluso interviewed candidates while Mike Lenzo and Ed Sachs provide a cost analysis. The team would consist of 3 CMS, an electrician/avionics rep, an engine rep and a metal smith. The CETs team would be the same but they would be in charge of training and would help in hands on maintenance if required. There would be an LSR (logistics support rep) at the Squadron level responsible for parts required for the C2. They would check supply, make sure the requisition was not cancelled and then inform Beth Page Supply Rep of the part number and requisition number of the part required by teletype, Another LSR would be stationed at ASO (aviation supply office) and another at Air Lant. The Beth Page Office had a technical Support Rep, my old friend Sal Vitale and a secretary reporting to a Project Manager. A team total of 12 people would be required. We felt that in a three month period the operational readiness of the C2 would dramatically improve. We had our training department at Grumman prepare training manuals for our reps to use in the initial phase of instruction. The program took about three months to get ready and we sent our people to Catania to begin. Housing was found for the families and schooling on Base for the children. This was a new concept for a Fleet Squadron and it took time for the Navy to get used to civilians working along side them. The supply end of the program worked like a champ. We had the information at Beth Page and copies were sent to ASO and Air Lant. The parts were located by ASO and shipped to Catania sometimes on the same day. Our men on the scene would know what airplane they would be arriving on and were there to meet them. The parts problem was solved early on but the maintenance problem took some time to work out. Each work center supervisor had to understand our men were there to assist but it took some time for the word to reach them. This was not an easy problem to overcome but gradually as the people became better known to the Navy they were accepted and used. Their expertise helped solve problems that had confused the crews in the Navy and they were sought out to help more frequently.

The Readiness improved and everyone saw the results. NavAir called us in and Dick Read and I helped prepare a contract that made our Reps sponsored and paid for by the Navy. Our next visit to AirLant allowed us to show positive results and the number of C2s operationally ready to fly to the Carriers justified the expense of our program. In fact the results were noticed by Air Pac (Commander Naval Air Pacific) and inquiries were made to Nav Air for a similar program for Cubi Point in the Philippines.

Dick and I visited Air Pac and outlined the program and then proceeded to Com Fair West Pac and Cubi Point to inform them. We repeated the procedure and hired the same number of people for Cubi Point that we had at Catania, Italy. We also hired an LSR for AirPac. The ASO Rep could handle the both Bases. We knew the problem now and when we sent our Reps to Cubi we accompanied them and thoroughly briefed the Squadron on how to integrate them and make maximum use of them. Small problems still arose but they were quickly solved. The :" can do" spirit of the Navy often interfered with the" I need help" and our men were often called after problem was compounded. It took less time for Cubi to become aware of the help our team provided and it took less time for operational readiness to improve. Because of the size of the Pacific a C2 would be assigned to a Carrier on occasion and one of our Reps would accompany the aircraft. The operational readiness of the C2 was so good that it would be used to fly flights as a ship spotter instead of another Carrier Aircraft. Now that the program was being used in both Fleets we could keep a handle on the readiness and our reporting system was used to keep all the Commands informed .

By increasing the readiness we provided three of four more C2s at each site that were able to deliver cargo and passengers to the Carriers. Previously the cargo had to be prioritized because there were not enough aircraft in a flyable condition to take all the cargo and passengers to the Carriers. Dick and I visited both Bases on a yearly basis to tweak the program and listen to our Rep's suggestions and gripes. We would meet with new Officers and enlisted personnel who could affect our program. It was important that they knew why the program had come into existence and how it functioned. Most importantly how they could use our reps to train and assist their personnel.

This became increasingly important as the program progressed because Grumman was preparing their Proposal for thirty nine new C2s to replace the ones we were flying. Some of the C2s were aircraft that had flown in Cubi during the war in Viet Nam and I was well aware of their age and the hard use they had endured during that war. Their airframes were rapidly approaching maximum time and even SLEP (service life extension program) couldn't help them much. Dick and I also frequently visited both Type Commanders, ASO and Nav Air to ascertain they were made aware of the improvement in the C2 Readiness.

We were fighting to keep the Program alive and funded as new Commanders always had pet projects they wanted to make sure were funded and looking for programs to cut to make money available. Nick DeJesu at ComFair Med and Chuck Zangas at NAS Sigonella our Area and Base Managers respectively helped by reminding their Senior Naval Officers of the progress the program had made. This support helped us keep our funding and the Program working. Our Reps at NAS Sigonella, Albrecht, Bornschein, Crane, LaRosa, Parrela, Romotnik, Schafer, Smith and Thomas all worked hard at their jobs and it was their efforts that sold the program in the beginning. The Reps that worked at NAS Cubi Point Benson, Duryea, Gilson, Jordon, Koerner, Mullen, Munsell. Norris, Norton and Soleo kept the program moving in the Pacific and both VRC50 at Cubi and VR24 at Sigonella fought to keep the program when funding was scarce.

I remember my first visit to NAS Cubi Point in 1979. I had told Dick Read all about the Catapult my men at The AIMD had designed and built and even showed him the pictures of it. When I arrived at the O'Club I was greeted by the Staff as an old friend. Most of the waiters were still there and it was a joy to greet them again after almost ten years. The joy turned to sadness when I discovered one of the Commanding Officers had turned the Catapult Room into a Teenage Club, The Cat was gone, the walls of Fame were not to be seen and nobody knew where they had been taken. The Pool was cemented over and the tracks on the inside as well. The new Club Manager when he heard from the waiters that I had been the one who built the Cat approached me and asked if Grumman would build them a new one. He said everyone was asking for it but he never volunteered who had removed it. I guess I could have discovered who it was but I really didn't want to know. It had become a tradition in the Fleet and every Naval Aviator was eager to test his skill on the Cat when he visited Cubi.

Later on when Cubi Point was decommissioned the Cubi O'Club was disassembled, the various plaques and signs carefully preserved for shipment to the Naval Museum in Pensacola. They were then meticulously reassembled and the spirit of that Club was preserved for posterity. The Cat was missing, someone with no feeling for tradition had removed it with no thought of preserving it. The Wall of Fame listing all the Naval Aviators who had caught the wire was destroyed, the Bronze Plaque, provided by Admiral Eiseman for the opening of the Catapult Room was never found. It wasn't anger that motivated me but sheer disappointment and I vowed to write the story of the Cat and the sheer joy and excitement it provided to the Naval Aviators who fought the war in Viet Nam. It was a place where they could relax and let off some steam. The "WINGS OF GOLD" became that vehicle and the winter edition of 1997 contains the Story of the Catapult. The next edition contains pictures proudly presented by my Skipper's wife Mrs. Rosalie Meyers. My pictures probably adorn some Iranians wall as I had to abandon them when I fled Iran in 1979.

In later years Mrs. Hilton in NAVAIR helped me bring the Cat back to the Cubi O"Club when she took my Story from "WINGS OF GOLD" and the pictures presented by Mrs. Myers and made up a presentation that I was able to present to the Curator of the Naval Aviation Museum at Pensacola. The Cat is now proudly, prominently displayed in the Cubi O"Club at that Museum. Incidentally I also made a similar presentation to the Museum at the Naval Test Center in Pax River where Admiral Guss Eggert has it on display. It continues to honor the memory of the hard working troops of the AIMD at Cubi whose ingenuity and dedication made it possible as well as the young warriors who manned those aircraft and fought the war from the decks of the Carriers that frequented Cubi Point. It is obvious that the disappearance of the Cat affected my first visit to Cubi but the subsequent actions have mitigated all that and I am able to speak of it now without rancor.

Dick and I had to make minor corrections to the program, some people changed jobs within the company and replacements were required. We also kept a complete history of the problems we encountered and the engineering assistance we required. Each team would receive from us a complete troubleshooting guide to supplement the maintenance manuals. We noticed problems that were affecting the Navy. NAS Sigonella was an important Base for the Mediterranean yet the supply facility was not adequate for the task. We had a short meeting scheduled with the Admiral in AIRLANT when I brought up this subject. I told him of the wonderful experience we had with supply at Subic during my tour as AIMD Officer in Cubi. He cited problems with the Med that might require evacuation in short notice. I volunteered these could be solved by putting trailers in where small cog items could be stored and quickly evacuated. He called Force Material and The Supply Officers to his Office and we talked on the subject for two hours. My experience at Subic with the Supply Department there proved invaluable and as none of them had been to Subic during the War they listened very attentively. It was really the beginning of the build up of the Supply Base at Siganella and it happened because of my experience with a master supply base at Subic.

The contract we had with the Navy called for Dick and I to visit both Cubi and Sigonella at least once each year. We arranged to visit COM FAR MED in Naples to make sure the Staff there was familiar with the program and was informed of its progress. Each cog in the Navy's chain of command was important to the program and it was important to us that they were kept current. Rumors could affect the course of the program and the best way to eliminate them was a well informed chain of command. We did the same thing in WEST PAC by visiting AIRPAC, COM FAIR WEST PAC in Japan and DEPUTY COM FAIR WEST PAC in the Philippines. We did this to preserve the program that each year was subject to review by the Navy. I said before that each new Commander brought with him some preconceived ideas and our program was expensive. The results of our program, being able to deliver all the required parts, mail and passengers was priceless but unless it was understood by the entire chain of command it could collapse and the C2s would revert back to their prior unsatisfactory performance. Our people had performed and the C2 was delivering the men and material to the Carriers. We had to keep it so. Dick Read deserves the credit. He fought for the program and kept the entire chain of Command informed visiting Bases whenever the Commanding officer was relieved.

He was his own man, bright and articulate. He was a master at putting proposals together. I can honestly say that we never had an argument in the years we worked together. We didn't agree on some items but we talked them through and each of us would compromise where it benefited the program. As I write this. Dick is dead and I have lost a good solid friend but I have benefited from my association with him and will always remember him with fond memories. On several occasions Dick and I had to visit the two Bases consecutively and this meant literally traveling around the world. It sounds romantic but believe me it was hard work. We needed visas as well as complicated airline routes. I'm sure the travel agents who worked for Grumman were kept busy providing us with a schedule that would fit our needs. It had to be flexible because we sometimes would get held up in extra meetings and would not be able to leave on the scheduled day. We could anticipate this and would leave room between scheduled meetings at the various sites. Any open time could and would be spent with the teams, debriefing them for their current knowledge of affairs at the base and briefing them on our progress with the program. We would always invite them to a dinner where we could enjoy their companionship. We could also hear from the wives how they were enjoying their stay and could assist in solving some of the problems they were encountering. All in all these visits helped keep the program working and I was able to inform my Boss at Field Operations how the people were faring. This was important because moral among the Field Operations people could effect our service to the Fleet.

We win the contract for 39 more C2s. It might not be readily admitted but Dick Read's Program that revitalized the C2 Operational Readiness and trained C2 operatives at both Fleet Bases was vital to our winning the contract. His visits to the Sites and his briefing of all members of the chain of command From OPNAV, NAVAIR, AIRLANT, AIRPAC, ' COMFAIR WEST PAC, COMFAIR MED and ASO helped keep the history of a C2 that was functioning properly in everyone's mind. He accomplished his goal and the Navy's discontent with the poor performance of the C2 in the previous years was replaced with the present excellent operational readiness.

We now had a new APML (assistant program manager for logistics) and a new program was forming. I was selected to be the Project Manager for the new C2. No problem that I could see as I had better knowledge of the C2 than anyone else but what about the old C2 that would continued to operate until replaced by the new C2s. The APML thought I should put all my man hours into the new one and it took weeks before I could convince him that I must divide my time between the two. Our teams were still functioning at both Bases and I would have to assist in having new manuals printed for the new C2s so they could familiarize themselves with the differences. There would be enough C2s to supply both Bases presently operating as well as shore Bases at

Norfolk and North Island. We could establish a community at last since the shore Bases could do the training for both their Base and the Overseas Base. We would have trained C2 personnel to fill the billets at both overseas bases and the need for contractor personnel would be reduced. Dave Seeman had been our test Pilot and had flown with both the pilots from VR 24 in Sig and VRC50 pilots in Cubi. Since the pilots, like the enlisted men had little experience in the C2 Dave gave them a complete check out in the aircraft. Dave and I had been in the Reserves together and I knew he was a damn fine pilot. He was of great assistance to the pilots of both Squadrons. Dave probably knows the C2s better than any pilot and passed on some of his expertise and I'm sure it was appreciated. He would be flying the new C2 soon and I was anxious to hear how it stacked up. The history of the problems we encountered with the old C2 was made available to the engineers of the new one and they tried, within budget constraints, to solve most of them. New material that was more resistant to corrosion, new and lighter curtains, weight control where possible, all of this was part of the program. We had great expectations but also realized this aircraft was very similar to the one that had preceded it. It would become the workhorse of the Fleet and would carry the parts and personnel to keep the Carriers operational. It didn't have to be pretty but it did have to be operational ready and the training we provided to the Squadrons would make this happen. If I can fast forward to the first war against Iraq I can say with some pride that Dick's and my fingerprints were all over the performance of those C2s even though we were long gone from the Company. I can also say that the 39 C2s are getting old and someone should be considering replacing them. The Fleet' fighters aircraft speak for themselves and have many champions but the Cargo Aircraft such as the C2s need to be heard as well. They need a champion.

The new C2s go to the Squadrons. A slow but constant movement of new and improved C2s made their way to VR24 and our Reps had a chance to work on them. The maintenance manuals had prepared them but there was a great deal of excitement from the pilots and enlisted men when the first aircraft arrived. Our group in Norfolk used the first aircraft that appeared there for training. That Squadron like the one at Sig was anxious to see the new aircraft.

I would soon be seeing my 62$^{nd}$ birthday and Joan was anxious to get back to our home in Town Creek, Lexington Park. I informed Jack Christianson, our Field Operations Director, of my intentions and told him I would stay long enough to give my replacement a complete brief on my work. Jack and I had been in the Navy together. He was a Carrier Skipper when I had the AIMD at Cubi and later he made Admiral. He had been picked up by Grumman when he retired and was made the Director of Field Service. He was a fine addition and greatly admired by the whole Field Service group. We had a confidential conversation and I revealed my desire to get back to Pax River as this was where my wife's heart was. He asked if I was unhappy with Grumman and I quickly dispelled that by saying outside of the Navy itself I couldn't think of a finer company to work for than Grumman. I told him I would stay with Grumman if I could be made Base Manager at Pax River. He thought that might be possible and he would think it over. In subsequent talks it looked like it would happen so I originated talks with the Director of Integrated Logistic and asked Harry Kline if he could have me briefed on the projects he had going at Pax River and what programs would be on the drawing board. He told me I was the first one to ask him for this kind of brief and if I was slated to go to Pax as Base Manager he would get me those briefs. We also agreed I would come up to Beth Page for future briefs as well. It looked good and I could imagine my using my contacts to bring future business to Grumman. I can say this without sounding commercial because in all the time I worked for Grumman I can't remember being in a position to influence the Navy where I didn't believe it was in the Navy's best interest to buy the program I was pushing. The Navy had given me an insight in the field of logistics that grew with each successive tour of duty culminating with tour as the AIMD Officer at Cubi Point during the Viet Nam war. CNO knew what he was doing

My first cousins and I visit Ireland and rent a castle in Limerick for the month of August 1983.

when he sent me there and the experience I gained there prepared me for my work at Grumman. Three tours as maintenance officer of squadrons and Three AIMDs (including the biggest and most important Cubi Point) educated me in a way few in the Navy have been. I was anxious to go to Pax when my hopes were dashed. The Area managers convinced Jack Christianson that it would hurt the moral of the Field Operations people if a Navy type (me) was promoted over Field Operations people who had been in the field for years. I could see the logic of their request but in my heart I knew I could have done a better job. I was a Navy pilot and a maintenance officer with great deal of experience. I also had worked with many of the people I would be meeting as Base Manager. It wasn't to be so I continued to

### CDR. Jack Sullivan USNR

plan for my retirement on my 62$^{nd}$ birthday. My replacement was on board and I did everything I could to bring him up to speed

In August I took leave and went to Ireland. My wife had rented an Irish Castle in Limerick and all my first cousins and their wives/husbands would be coming. We all arrived on the same plane, rented cars, and followed the truck, with our baggage, to Springfield Castle. We were assigned rooms and proceeded to make ourselves at home. The castle was owned by a British Lord, residing in South Africa. The castle was rented and supervised by his sister who lived on the farm. She was a lovely person and showed us around the grounds. It had been partially burned back in early 1900 s but the manor house was intact and provided plenty of room for all of us. The formal dinning room (we never used) had pictures of the Lords father one of which had a bullet hole in it. The shooting occurred the same time the Castle was burned. The kitchen was tremendous and had enough table space for all of us to eat together. The wives would each make breakfast but the rest of the meals we would eat out. Each day we would explore in a different direction. Driving our cars on those Irish roads was an adventure and there was always something to talk about when we arrived home at the castle. The scenery was magnificent as each section of Ireland is different. One morning Joan was not feeling well so we stayed home as the rest of the clan went on their expedition. She was napping and I was out on the lawn chipping golf balls when a car turned in and came up the long road leading to the castle. It was an American family that wanted to visit all the castles they could. It turned out to be a retired US Navy Admiral and his family and was delighted to find another Naval Officer at the castle. I Invited them for a tour of the castle and even woke Joan up to meet the Admiral and his family. They were delighted with the hospitality and we promised to meet again in the States. Later on when I returned to Pax and was again a member of the Rotary Club Admiral Gus Eggert approached me and excitingly described a meeting he had attended where an Admiral friend of his had described visiting a castle in Ireland. He further stated he was greeted by a retired Navy Commander who had taken him on a tour of the castle. He was sorry but he couldn't remember the Commanders name. When Gus suggested Jack Sullivan the Admiral excitedly proclaimed yes. Gus told him of our relationship and said sounds like something Sully would do.

If that sounds like a coincidence let me tell you another experience we had. The women wanted to make an Italian meal one evening. My cousin Tom and I were to go to the store and get the ingredients. We had everything but the Italian Cheese and asked a woman in the store for help. Her accent immediately revealed her to be an American, I asked her where she came from? She replied a little place you have never heard of, Rockaway Beach, Long Island. I told her I was born there and asked her what street? She was amazed but said 313 Beach 90$^{th}$ Street I said. You bought Roniger's house. I lived next door with my uncle Fred Hetzel. I thought she was going to faint." My God, my God wait till I tell my husband about this he won't believe it" she said.. We talked for some time and finally she said you won't buy the cheese here but you can get it in Limerick at the supermarket. We said goodbye as friends. The story was told at dinner and everyone was amazed prompting Joan to ask if our conduct in the store prior to our conversation with the woman was proper.

While we were at the castle I felt the urge to play golf. There was a course in the neighborhood and I asked Joan to drop me off there before the all the relatives went off on their daily trips. When I checked in at the pro shop I discovered there was a tournament scheduled for the day but the pro told me to stay because he thought one of the teams could use a man. He was correct and I played with three great Irishmen. We had so much fun that they invited me to play Bally Bunion (great Irish Golf Course) the next day with the caveat that I not say a word when we check in. It seem we Americans are notoriously slow on the golf course and we wouldn't be able to play before twelve o'clock if my true identity was revealed. They were kind enough to say that I wasn't slow but the starter wouldn't know that. It was a grand day and we agreed that if I returned we would tee it up again

Before we left we had a catered lunch for all our Irish relatives and they all came. We had over a hundred in attendance. One old gent over ninety years of age was looking at the Castle very carefully, studying it from every angle. Curious I approached him and engaged him in conversation. He had been a friend of my father and my uncles and told me stories of the early days in Ireland when they were all in grade school. I listened attentively as my father had passed on and these were stories I had never heard. After twenty minutes of these tales he told me that as a youth he had come over to the castle with a bunch of the boys and had burned it. My God here was the guy that had taken part in the raid that our hostess had told us about. When I told my cousins later that night they swore me to secrecy as our hostess was such a lovely lady and we might want to come back someday.

We were getting ready leave but we all made one last pilgrimage to the house our fathers were born in. It was located on the top of a hill and the view of the lake below must have fascinated them all when they were growing up. It was a small house and the walls were three feet thick. Later on my cousin would build a large house right around the old one and make the small house into a living room, and had a glass enclosed front porch that overlooked the lake down below. It was amazing, and each of my four visits showed me a different view of the house. My cousin being a stone setter was able to turn this old Irish house into what could almost be referred to as a mansion. I had seen the original house on my first visit and a tree my father had planted was now over a hundred feet tall. I guess everyone is nostalgic when they visit their fathers home, particularly when that home is in a foreign country and I was no exception. Saying goodbye to their cousins and relatives is hard particularly when you feel it might be the final goodbye. A few days later we were on the plane returning to the States. Joan was her usual nervous self although flying on a plane named St Patrick sort of got her out of it when we reached cruising altitude. She so enjoyed our visits to Ireland but never mastered the fear of flying.

Well it was back to work even though it would only be a matter of days before I retired. Maura came up for the retirement party and sang much to the enjoyment of my friends at Grumman. Words of praise, some gifts, and an airplane model of the C2, and I faded into history. I sold my condo, had a farewell golf tournament, said goodbye to my friends at Blue Ridge and we were on our way home to Pax River. Our house had been rented while we were gone and the tenant had left the month before we arrived so Joan took advantage of that fact and had new carpet put down and the interior of the house painted. Our furniture arrived and we were soon resting comfortably in our old home

# Chapter 21
# Back Home in Maryland

The Rotary Club asked me to speak about my stay in Iran and it was delightful to be back with my old club again. Carl Neidholt sponsored me and I was accepted back into the Rotary Club. The golfers out at the Base also welcomed me with open arms. Many of us had teed it up in the past and they were ready to test the old Dad. No mention of my winning the Club Championship at Blue Ridge was made but it wasn't long before they tagged me with a proper handicap. I met Wayne Putnam and Ed Forsman on the golf course and they would become two of my best friends. Both were still gainfully employed so I could only play golf with them on weekends and when they could squeeze it in during the week. Frank Mattingly was a retired Colonel in the Air Force and he became my number one golfing buddy. Our games were similar so we had some interesting matches. We didn't bet much but the money we did bet was used up when the winner bought the loser lunch. It was the bragging rights that were important.

I was settling in to a life as a country squire when I received a phone call from John Ryan at Grumman. The company was bidding on a new contract and he asked if they could use my resume in the bid. I answered they could. A few months later John called again and told me they had won the contract but the Navy was asking to see the man in the resume. They needed me and would I be willing to come back as a consultant for three months. The job would be on the West Coast at Point Mugu. They asked me to come to Beth Page and sit down with them to negotiate. I told them I was quite comfortable with my retirement income and I didn't expect to lose anything to taxes. It was agreed and I went to Beth Page. When I looked at the contract it was obvious they had an experienced Navy maintenance officer with overseas experience and a knowledge of contracting in mind. I fit the bill and they wanted to see me. We worked out a pay scale suitable to everyone and I soon left for Point Mugu. The contract consisted of maintaining a diverse fleet of air craft for missile work. The company that had the contract lost the bid to Grumman. Their employees were available and we would interview some of them for jobs with Grumman. We already had some Grumman people we would assign to the task that were ready to go but we needed more. We all interviewed people and picked a team. They were then screened for clearances and our Security People did the paper work. By knowing the aircraft and type of work required I could tell what type people were required and factoring in the flight time projected how many of each we should employ. When the people were hired we set up divisions. Grumman had hired two retired Maintenance Officers and I soon got to know each of them quite well. They were both knowledgeable and eager to begin work. One had the P3s and the other the carrier aircraft. Grumman was to perform all the maintenance on these aircraft and we had to maintain a certain operational readiness to meet the flight schedule. Glitches in the contract were soon worked out with the Navy. The contracting officer was a civilian but he had a young Lieutenant working for him. This young maintenance officer was harder to please than his boss. I believe he was finding it hard to work with a civilian contractor and thought the Navy should be performing the task. We had a couple of talks and I finally convinced him we were as anxious as he to do a good job for the Navy. As time passed he mellowed and I really believe he was as proud of our performance as we were.

I was living in a hotel at corporate expense and I convinced the finance people that it would be cheaper for me to have a small apartment. They agreed and I made the arrangements and signed a short term lease. They were also paying for the rental of a car. Since I had promised Joan I would buy her an RX7 I worked out a deal whereby they would pay me the price of the rental for the three months and I would buy my own car and pay for the cost of gasoline myself. This again proved satisfactory as the company saved some money on this deal as well. I contacted USAA and obtained the nearest Mazda Dealer and obtained the price of the vehicle I required. I think I bought the only RX7 with automatic transmission on the west coast but I knew Joan would be pleased The whole transaction took a little time but never interfered with the task at hand.

We were in place little over a month when we received an inspection from NAVAIR, They found certain discrepancies and would announce them at a formal meeting with the contracting officer. I knew what they were and before the meeting we had corrected them in writing. At the meeting the contracting officer was amazed when we answered that all discrepancies had been corrected prior to this meeting. It was a tactic I had successfully used before. The team from NAVAIR was impressed but stated they would check up on us in the near future. The work progressed smoothly and one day I was approached by an old Grumman buddy. He was in charge of the collateral equipment for a "Black Program" (super secret program) that was being discontinued. He was going to have to put all the furniture, typewriters and office equipment in storage. He asked me if I could use it since it would save the company money for a storage bill. I looked at it and compared it to the old Navy Furniture we had been given under the contract. I not only said yes but also requisitioned some paint from Public Works under the self help program, painted the entire work space we had been assigned, and bought some indoor /outdoor carpet. We brought in the new furniture and the moral of the office staff improved dramatically. We easily had the best looking office on the base. I very carefully had the furniture, typewriters and other collateral office equipment receipted for by serial number and returned to Supply. Other programs wondered where we had gotten the new furniture and I suppose this filtered back to the Contracting Lawyers at Long Beach. I received a phone call from a young lady one day who announced she was a lawyer at Long Beach and had reviewed the contract. The contract read that we were to be given furniture by the Navy and she interpreted that to mean we must use the Navy furniture. I explained how we obtained the furniture, that we had carefully returned each piece of Navy furniture to Supply and we would use the Grumman furniture and office equipment. She had even called the Grumman Office in Beth Page to report what she considered a discrepancy at least or at most a violation of the contract. When I received a call from John Ryan later I asked him if I could call him back in a few minutes. I then called Long Beach and asked to talk to the Naval Officer in Charge. The Captain I spoke to quickly understood what had happened and told me to forget it and said that if he had a chance to get new furniture in the same manner he would do the same thing. Problem solved when you talk to a man who can make decisions as a manager this kind nonsense disappears. John Ryan was glad to hear the results and agreed it was a tempest in a tea pot but the Company had to pay attention to any complaint from a Contracting source. Case Closed!!

At the end of three months I was supposed to turn over the job to one of the Maintenance Officers Grumman had hired but because we had employed many of the people from the previous company we suddenly faced a challenge from the union. They had been members of the union and the union wanted a vote as to whether Grumman would become a union employer. Grumman had never been a union company and the thought was to resist the union. The Company sent lawyers and we had lengthy discussions as to how to resist and obtain a majority vote to keep this from happening. The lawyers felt my presence was vital and my influence would be needed if we were to resist joining the union. They persuaded the company to have me remain on the scene until the vote was concluded. This meant an extra month on the job. I had planned to come back to Pax River when the three months were up and my wife was counting on it. A few phone calls to Joan persuaded her to agree to the postponement. Our plans would be deferred until I returned. There was only so much we could do. The labor law was written to protect the unions and it is tipped heavily in their favor. What we could do worked and when the vote was taken, Grumman won. The lead labor Lawyer representing the company had become a friend and before he departed he told me they would never have been able to do it without me and he would tell this to the company management. I was free to go so I turned the control over to Smitty and after a few parties departed for Pax River in my new RX7.

I made the trip from Mugu to Pax river in three days. I won't tell you the speed but I can say the RX7 will top 130 MPH on a deserted highway. I had to be back on time because the next day I had to be in Jacksonville for a Reunion of my old Fighter Squadron, "the Gladiators"

One story has to be told. When I returned home I told Joan the trip home from the Mazda Dealer took me through LA. And the new car had stirred some excitement. It was one of the first of the new line of RX7s and girls were blowing their horns and waving as they drove by me. Joan quickly deflated my ego by saying " yeah, because of the tinted windows they couldn't see the old fart behind the wheel". I drove to Jacksonville a much chastened man. It was great to see the old gang again and we really celebrated. Time has a way of disappearing when old friends get together. We quickly brought one another up to speed on our lives and it seemed like yesterday that we were flying from the carrier..

One more item has to be mentioned we had a golf tournament and I had a hole in one. This was made all the more remarkable since I was playing with what had been diagnosed as a sprained wrist but was actually a broken wrist. I had fallen and hurt my wrist. X rays, hastily read, revealed what was thought to be a badly sprained wrist. Joan heard from the Doctor while I was in Jacksonville that it was actually a fracture. When I returned to Pax River I wound up in a cast for three months. Now a hole in one with a broken wrist, how many people can brag about such a feat?

I made one more visit to Grumman Beth Page and went over all my accounts with the money people. I visited with friends and slowly went back to the country squire life in Maryland

# Chapter 22
# Retirement in Maryland

When you are a Rotarian its impossible to avoid becoming a responsible citizen. That's really a wrong way to describe it. You almost automatically become a volunteer, and I willing signed up to help drive cancer victims to hospitals. St Mary's County isn't unique in inspiring its citizens to help one another but the kindly attitude of it's citizens fosters this spirit. We noticed it immediately when we were first stationed at the Test Center and decided this is where we would live after I retired from the Navy. Now that I was back in the Rotary club I could see it in all our members. I believe at one time or another almost every charitable agency in the County and every government board of volunteers had members of my Rotary Club in positions of authority. With people like this you have to respond in kind. As the clubs historian I tasked myself with the job getting the clubs history written. I asked Bill Weiland, John Beaton and John Roemer to accept this responsibility and assist me in this endeavor. Bill had worked for the United Press and later on the US State Department in South America . John Roemer was a former teacher and John Beaton and myself would research the old files for pertinate information. We worked on this three days a week for over three months before it was finished. I was elected President of the club the following year and published the history. There were many undertakings of the club that required more time and effort. As an example the club sponsors the Oyster Shucking Championship of the United States. Oyster shuckers from all over the country compete for the title and the American Champion is taken on an all expense tour to Ireland to compete in the world championship. Various other clubs in the County that perform volunteer work are invited to participate in the gala, two day ,affair. The work necessary to make this possible involves the entire club and for days before the event we are busy making the fair- grounds ready. Some twenty to thirty thousand people come to the fair grounds for this event and many come from other States. It is the primary source of income for the Club and helps sponsor our various scholarships and charities. The coordinating authority for the event is King Oyster, the person who was last years' president of the Rotary Club. The ascendance is as follows: President one year, King Oyster the next year and official escort to the Oyster Shucking Champion to the

World Oyster Shucking Championship in Ireland the next year. The trip to Ireland is filled with wonderful memories of Irish Rotarians and the splendor of the event. It is to be remembered for the rest of your life, but the two years leading up to it are filled with hard work and devotion to detail. I know, I went through it and wouldn't change a thing and am proud of every one of my friends that followed that path.

There is so much energy in that club and even those of us that are now considered senior active in the twilight of our lives are happy to be chosen to help in some capacity. During my tenure as President I was chosen the outstanding President of the Rotary Clubs comprising the District 7620 covering Washington D.C. to Annapolis. I say this with modesty because I was nothing but a bow sprit (that figure on the front of an old sailing vessel) for an active club and their actions won this distinction for me. I can only be proud that it brought recognition to a club that had operated quietly and successfully for years. Two great presidents followed me, Paul Fletcher and George Bailey and both of them were judged the outstanding president of Rotary District 7620 for their terms. Both of them led the Club to further distinction and each new District Governor looks at our Club as a shining light in the District

Joan told me she would like to visit Ireland. Again so we called our relatives in Ireland Tom and Geraldine white to make our plans. Geraldine contacted her sisters Fiona and Maura and we

I turn 65 at Pax River, surrounded by my family Maura, John, and my wife Joan.

settled on a time and date. Joan wasn't a flyer but the plane had the name of a saint so she was a bit more comfortable. We arrived in Shannon and made our way to the automobile counter to pick up our reserved car. Checking my license they told me I could not rent a car as I was over 75 years of age. Joan at this time was sitting in a wheel chair with luggage piled up around her. Her legs bothered her and she could not walk great distances. She was a few days shy of her $75^{th}$ birthday so she rented the car. I drove! We laughed about that but I had the experience of driving in Ireland and England and driving on the other side of the road did not bother me. We visited the family in Ireland and discovered one of the husbands had a bar named" Jacks Bar. "We visited it one night only to discover all our relatives in Ireland were present to celebrate

Joan's birthday. What a surprise and Joan was delighted. We had a wonderful time and she brought it up so often in the time we had left together. To all our Irish relatives I will always remember your kindness and generosity.

Joan and I were getting older and Joan in particular was bothered by many of the infirmities that bother us in later life. She had had both knees replaced and suffered from diabetes and heart murmur. She took seventeen medications each day, yet she maintained her busy schedule of bridge events and did so with her usual happy disposition. We were married 55 years in October of 2002 and looking forward to 56 in October of 2003. She was planning my $80^{th}$ birthday party in August when she suffered a fall. She spent eight days in intensive care and then nine weeks in a nursing home for extensive rehabilitation. She would never walk stairs again, and I had to make plans to sell the house we owned in Town Creek and buy a house with no stairs.

*CDR. Jack Sullivan USNR*

1990 Rotary Meeting
After being the president of St. Mary's Rotary Club, I am now crowned as King Oyster and made chairman of our fundraiser, The Oyster Festival.

My daughter Maura,
my sister-in-law Judith Ruger,
my brother-in-law Joe Ruger,
St. Patrick's Day 2002.

St. Patrick's Day in 2002.
Guinness is being served.

My son John and his lovely wife Sue, who shared their house with me while I moved to Florida.

Here I must tell you of a story a young Jesuit priest told me when I was in prep school. We were talking about Crosses we must bear. He said there was a young man who was complaining to God about the cross he had to bear. One night, in a dream God came to him and brought him to a huge ware house filled with large crosses. God asked him to go through the warehouse and pick out a cross. He did so and finally found a cross about the size of a package of cigarettes. He brought this one back to God and said this is the one I choose. God smiled at him and said "this is the one I gave you" Why I remembered this at this time I don't know. but I must have felt somewhat overwhelmed at the time. My daughter Maura and I went looking at retirement homes in Wildwood and my good friend Jim Alvey, from Rotary showed me through one home that was available. It was expensive and had a large, at least by my standards, condo charge attached to it. The real estate agent who was representing the owner was called and I spoke to her. I didn't want the retirement village but I did need a house on one level. I explained my needs and she looked at me in wonder. She had just gotten a call from a woman whose mother had been an invalid. She had recently died and her father was going to Cedar Lane (retirement Community) and wanted to sell his house. I looked at it and gave Cooky Kennedy a thousand dollars and told her I wanted this single floor house. It had a two-car garage with a ramp leading to the dinning room that would accommodate Joan's wheelchair. It was a small house with three bedrooms, pretty and well built. Both of my children loved it and I hoped Joan would as well. They took pictures and we showed them to Joan and she appeared to like it. Now I had to paint the outside of my house and Cooky introduced me to Eric, a retired Navy Chief, who did this kind of work for her. Eric painted my house and I put it up for sale. The first person to look at it bought it and both closings were back to back the following month. I had fans installed in my new house and when Joan saw it for the first time she loved it. I remembered the story of the crosses and the fact the Good Lord never gives us more than we can bear. We were happy in our new home, happy with our neighbors, Tom Corbett on one side and Maria and Andy Rutherford on the other. Joan directed me and we established a new order for the pictures we hung. Our furniture fit the new surroundings although since we moved from a much bigger house to a smaller one we had excess of just about everything and the garage acted as a catch- all. We were slowly sorting though many of the items in the garage, holding onto some, because of sentiment, that we should have decided were excess to our needs. The girls were deferring to Joan's infirmity and most of the Bridge was played at our house.

One day Joan suddenly took sick. I was her helpmate and did all but the most simple of actions for her. If I had to leave the house I would take my phone with me and call her when arriving at a store and leaving it. She could always reach me. One day she called out for me in a voice I recognized as urgent. I rushed to her side and saw a look on her face that I had never seen before. It was a mixture of terror and pain. I held her in a sitting position and dialed 911 on the phone. Her face became calm when the 911 operator came on the line but soon became anxious again and I asked for help. In minutes the emergency team was there and Joan was taken to the emergency room. I followed as soon as I could but Joan was being given forced breathing and electric shock treatment to keep her heart beating. I held onto one nurse and begged her to call a priest. He too arrived in a matter of minutes and both of us prayed until they allowed us to see her. She couldn't talk with the pipe down her throat but I asked her if she could hear me to blink twice. She did so in response. I told her the priest was here and had given her extreme unction (last rites) and we were praying. I didn't want to leave her side although I knew all I could do for her was to talk to her and tell her I was there. I had to call the children. When the doctor told me she was stable I rushed out and called Maura on her cell phone. I asked if anyone was with her and when she said Laurel was I told her of her mother's condition. I asked Laurel to drive her to the hospital knowing Maura would have a tough time controlling her emotions. I then called my son and daughter in law and asked that they come as soon as possible. They both held responsible positions in the Florida schools system and would have to notify the proper authorities before leaving. Maura and Laurel arrived in less than two hours and were with Mom when she was moved from the emergency room to the intensive care unit upstairs. She was taken off the electric device that shocked her heart and her heart beat by itself. Our hopes were rising. She was bleeding internally and they had to give her blood but her color was good and I stared intensely at the monitoring devices and they were all indicating a normal range of the various functions.

On the second day John and Sue arrived and we spent some time talking to Mom. She appeared to be in a comma but we couldn't be sure she wasn't hearing us so we continued to talk to her. It made us feel better to hope she could understand her whole family was around her. Bev Putnam was with us and what a friend she was. None of us could do anything helpful to Mom at least nothing we could see, but I pray she heard and was peaceful knowing how much she was loved. She was in God's lap and we were in His ear with our prayers.

Later on March 2 Joan's vital signs deteriorated and she passed away peacefully with her family at her side praying. I had gone to Mass earlier that morning with the idea of praying for her recovery. That was all that was on my mind. Then the priest said something that made me think and I prayed that God would do what ever was best for my wife and I would live with it and try to understand. I came back to the hospital and waited to see what would happen and the Good Lord showed me His will now I must understand. The children were crying and I'm sure I did too but we all realized she was at peace and the Good Lord had a place for her. Maura picked out the dress ,she would have wanted, for the wake and her friends came to the wake and shared our grief. Father Mike had nice words to say and stood by as I said what I wanted to say. She had always said we should tell our friends we loved them and at her wake I did just that but it took my best effort to overcome my emotions and complete my words. I told our friends what my wife of fifty five years wanted them to know'" we loved them."

I promised myself I would not make any final decisions as to what I might do for six months .Bev Putnam and Jean Davis helped me sort through Joan's clothing and effects and give those items to charities that might distribute them to people who can use them, My daughter Maura and her friends Laurel, Sandy and Barbara took those items that they wanted and helped me organize the house. Maura and Cookie assisted me in selling the house. My son John and his lovely wife, Sue, have made me feel their home is my home and have been a great help in picking out my new home. Ed Forsman taught me to use the computer and has kept after me to finish this book. My friends Wayne and Bev Putnam have treated me as though I were a family member. Jean Davis and I have dined with them almost every night and their friendship and encouragement have kept me on an even keel. We are not sufficient unto ourselves we need love and friendship and people that care about us. I have had that and to my dying day I will be grateful to all my friends. To all of you who have invited me to play golf and join you in other pursuits. To my friends in the Lexington Park Rotary Club for your leadership and friendship. I thank you all. Now I'm going away to start a new life with people my age. I will never cease thinking about you and remembering your friendship in fact I will want you to join me in Florida when the winters become harsh and meet my new friends. I will return on occasion and we will remember old times and enjoy our reunions. I end this saga now not on a sad note but like the old naval officer that I am looking forward to my new assignment in life.

    We are all friends, forever!!

# About the Author

Cdr. John L. "Jack" Sullivan USNR will probably be remembered in the Navy as the Banshee Jet Fighter Pilot that led the last flight of the Korean War and made the last carrier landing. Since he was a recalled Police Detective from New York the headline read "New York City Cop Blows Whistle on Korean Police Action"

In 1969 he was the Officer that built the legendary Catapult in the Cubi Point Officers Club in the Philippines that was featured in the book The Flight of the Intruder by Stephen Coonts and the movie of the same name.

In later years as the Base Manager of Grumman Aerospace for the advanced Squadron of Iranian F14 Fighter Jets stationed at Shiraz, Iran he was the last one to leave that country after the Shah had abdicated and Kohmeini arrived and assumed control. This makes interesting reading because it tells a different side of this story than was depicted in our press at the time. The account of the patriotism demonstrated on the last Pan American 747 aircraft to take Americans home from Iran is emotional and heartwarming. This story of his life is filled with humorous anecdotes, many of which depict actions he would quickly state were "out of my job description," but lend to the balance of levity and patriotism that make up this book.